MW01139395

His Treasure

His Strength

His Princess

By

Kiru Taye

This is a work of fiction. Names, characters, places, and incidents are products of the author's imagination or are used fictitiously and are not to be construed as real. Any resemblance to actual events, locales, organizations, or persons, living or dead, is entirely coincidental.

Men of Valor, Books 1 – 3
Paperback Edition
ISBN: 978-1512006988
Copyright© 2015 Kiru Taye
Editor: Kristie L McKinley
Cover Artist: Love Bites and Silk

Kiru Taye

His Treasure

In a time when men ruled their households with firm hands, can a quiet man tame his rebellious wife with persevering love?

Angry at having to marry a man not of her choosing, Adaku stubbornly shuns her new husband on their wedding night. However, she soon discovers there are worse things than giving into a man whose touch awakens her deep desires. In a land where fruitfulness is celebrated, she could soon be labeled a barren woman.

Obinna knows there are several ways to tame a rebellious woman. Patience and perseverance are two of them. Adaku is his treasure and he will never let her go. When her fears push her into his arms, will he be able to convince her to stay with him forever by unleashing the passion within her?

Kiru Taye

South Eastern Nigeria, pre-colonization.

Stubborn pride was a foolish thing.

Adaku knew that now. It was a shame she hadn't realized it early enough; when it'd mattered. It would have saved her a lot of headache. Her current troubles wouldn't have existed. As it was, she was lost down this track of foolish pride she'd chosen. She couldn't go back and change things. Yet she moved forward with a heavy burden on her shoulders. It was her path. She would walk it with dignity, regardless.

Taking a deep breath, she let out the air slowly, loosening her clenched grip on the basket of farm produce under her arm. The early morning chill had not dissipated, though the sun had ascended. Yet she felt hot like she had a fever. If she didn't relax, her friend walking with her to the market square would start asking questions Adaku couldn't answer.

Today, she needed to barter the items in her basket for some game meat. While she raised her own poultry at home, she liked the variety of game meat occasionally. The earliness of the day would assure the variety. The extra bag of cowries in her basket would guarantee she acquired the best on offer.

"I have some news to share." Ifeoma had a full girly grin on her face when she leaned in to whisper to Adaku.

Ifeoma was her lifelong friend. The only one who still sought her company since Adaku's unfortunate fall from grace. It had been an eye-opener to find out how quickly one could lose friends when one was no longer favored. Still, she had enough to be grateful for. Things could be a lot worse.

However, her friend had a penchant for drama and gossip. Each time they met up, these days it was mostly during the *Oye* market day, Ifeoma filled her in on the latest news from the village. Oye was the busiest market day in the region. It attracted traders from afar. Occasionally, among them would be the nomadic Fulani tribesmen from the north. They brought with them varied ware including some of the most beautiful fabrics and leather. She was hoping to find a fabric for the New Yam festival to be held in a few weeks.

"Come on then. Let's hear it. Whose father is taking another wife? Or who was caught under the *udara* fruit tree with whom?" Adaku attempted a laugh, but it sounded hollow even to her ears. The truth was she was getting tired of hearing stories about other people's lives. She had problems of her own.

Ifeoma giggled merrily. "Oh, it's nothing like that this time. Look at me. Do you notice anything different about me?"

Adaku gave her a quick glance and shrugged. Although Ifeoma was a head shorter than her, she had the full bust and round hips that meant she never lacked the gazes of male admirers. Adaku sometimes felt inadequate in her tall, slender frame. She used to feel boyish when she was younger. Thankfully, her breasts and hips had finally flared out, albeit later than her age mates. She couldn't see any difference in her friend's appearance except the new fabric she was wearing. It was a pink-and-blue-print sarong, wrapped from her chest and stopping mid-calf. It skimmed her body, showing off her curves.

"Is the outfit new? I haven't seen it on you before."

"Yes it's new but that's not it. Come on, look closer," Ifeoma urged her, standing with her hands akimbo and a sheepish smile.

Adaku stopped walking and turned fully to face her friend. Ifeoma wasn't a classic beauty, but she had very good skin tone—the color of dark wood. Looking closer, Adaku noticed her skin seemed to glow and her eyes glittered. It seemed married life suited Ifeoma well. Though her husband was from a humbler background, she always seemed happy.

As she watched her friend's eyes sparkle with barely contained amusement, it hit her. "You are pregnant!" The statement slipped out and she had to lower her voice at the last word. She took a quick glance around to ensure she hadn't been overheard. Though the footpath was busy with people going or coming from the market, there was no one close enough to overhear their conversation.

"Yes!" Ifeoma squealed in laughter as she hugged her friend. "How did you know?"

"I just guessed it." She pulled back and stared at her friend's still-flat stomach. As much as she was happy for Ifeoma, she couldn't help feel the sliver of dread creeping down her back. "I'm so pleased for you. Afam must be overjoyed."

Afam was Ifeoma's husband. As the only son of his parents, it was his responsibility to raise heirs to keep the family line alive.

As it is your husband's duty.

Adaku fingers tightened on her basket again. She mentally shook her head to dismiss the taunting voice whispering in her mind.

"He's. He bought me this new fabric as a gift. He has promised plenty more gifts and a huge celebration when I deliver the baby."

Ifeoma danced around on the spot, showing off her new clothes. Adaku was pleased for her friend. Ifeoma deserved the good news after losing her parents as a young girl.

"Very soon, it'll be your turn, if you're not already." Ifeoma winked at her as they resumed walking. "Your husband is so virile. He's bound to give you twins."

Adaku nearly choked at her friends words as heat washed over her body. Her husband, Obinna, was virile all right. The best wrestler of the village, he had a body and agility crafted by gods for gods. Still, they were a long way from twins anytime soon.

She forced a bright smile on her face and kept walking.

"If the gods wish it." She chose to be philosophical rather than share the dark secrets of her married life.

Her marriage was not all it seemed. They had both been bound to their husbands in the same season many moons ago just after the last New Yam festival. Afam had wooed and courted Ifeoma before the marriage rites were finally performed. Adaku had several suitors at the time, but had refused all of them. She'd held out, waiting for the prince to formally propose as he'd promised.

When someone had discovered them together without chaperones, her father had insisted she had to get bound immediately. He'd practically given her away to the next suitor to ask for her hand. All her pleading and tears had fallen on her father's deaf ears. She would either marry Obinna, a man she barely knew, or be disowned. Her mother, the second of three wives, could not have borne the disgrace that would have brought to her. Adaku had no choice but to cave in to her parents. But she'd sworn she would never give herself willingly to her husband. Her heart and her body belonged to the prince.

That was almost a year ago. Now her friend, Ifeoma, was pregnant, as were most of the other maidens who had wed at the same time as them. A few had given birth already. Children were a sign of fertility and prosperity. Soon it'd be another New Yam festival; a festival to celebrate fertility and prosperity. And what did she have to celebrate?

Still she couldn't blame anyone else. She'd sealed her fate with her stubbornness. This was her life. Her pride wouldn't let her admit to anyone it was far from perfect.

Keeping her chin up, she walked into the already bustling market square.

***

Obinna approached his house, the footpath widening into a clearing at the front. Coming home filled him with mixed feelings. As the oblong, dried-clay structure with thatched roof came into view, his chest expanded with pride. He'd demolished the original structure built by his grandfather and erected this one when his father died. It was now a larger house with enough room for a large family. He'd also built a kitchen extension at the back and a separate bathroom. His intention had always been to marry and have children, as many as the gods saw fit to bless him with. The clearing in front of the house was surrounded by land covered in various trees: mango, palm nut, and coconut. He also had several acres of farmland with yam, cassava, and other staple crops. The vastness of the lands meant he had to employ laborers during the planting and harvesting seasons.

It was all his.

And so was the woman coming out of the bathroom as he walked into the backyard. He chose to stay hidden from her view. He liked to observe her without her knowing it.

She must have just bathed as there were droplets of water glistening on her skin in the late evening sunshine. Her dark skin glowed. Just before she covered it fully with her wrapper, he caught a glimpse of her breasts. Small. Perky. Succulent.

His body reacted the same way it always did since the first time he'd seen her. His heart rate picked up. Heat flooded his body, stirring his manhood, hardening it. She was the most beautiful woman he'd ever seen, tall, and slender; her flawless skin of darkest ebony, she had an oval face, dark-brown eyes fringed by long, black lashes, a small nose and a pair of juicy lips. Her hair was twisted in braids and adorned with beads. The decorative markings on her body identified her as the daughter of a titled man.

He ached for his wife. He longed to go to her as she stood drying her body. He wanted to taste her sweet lips, feel her softness against his skin, and sink into her warm depths again and again. Yet he didn't move, but stood there, watching her get dressed while he wanted to undress her.

This is madness.

If his friends saw him, they would laugh. What man ached for his wife and yet did nothing about it?

A crazy man. That's what I am.

Yes. It was madness but it was the safer path. He ached for his wife, yet he couldn't sate that ache. She didn't want him. She never had. He'd be damned if he would touch her while she rejected him. She had to come to him willingly. Totally. Without reserve. He would never compromise on that.

It seemed they were both condemned to a future together in misery. Because as much as she didn't want him, he would never let her go. Maybe he was paying for his sins in a previous life. This was his punishment. His torture. To have a woman and never fully claim her.

Pushing his heated body off the cool wall, he walked into the back garden and coughed.

Adaku swiveled round. "My husband, you're back. Welcome."

Joy filled his heart just as her sweet voice filled his ears. He put his tools down and waited for her to hug him as he'd hoped she would each time he returned home. He longed to feel her skin against his and inhale her fragrance. Instead, she curtsied formally like she always did, much to his annoyance.

She'd grown up at the royal court. Her father was the chief advisor to the King. So her ways were formal, he knew that. Yet he'd hoped she would have learned to be more casual with him by now.

He also knew she would never have chosen him as her husband. He'd known about her desire for the prince. When her father had accepted his proposal for her hand, no one had been more surprised than Obinna. But Ichie Omemma was a fair man. He hadn't made huge demands in terms of a bride price. Although Obinna would have sold his lands just to claim this woman. She was worth it all to him.

Each time he saw her, he watched for signs of unhappiness. In her father's house, she'd had servants catering to her needs. Obinna always tried to make sure her needs were catered for in his house. Yet he could never be sure if she was unhappy. As much as he wanted her, he wanted her to be happy even more.

If she was unhappy, she didn't show it. Her eyes sparkled with their usual defiance, and her chin was up, exposing her delicate throat. The urge to run his tongue along her neck took hold of him.

"Thank you." He'd already taken a step toward her when he stopped himself and turned away toward the bathroom. "I'm going to have a wash."

"I'll serve your dinner," Adaku said when he walked into the bathroom.

He longed for a vigorous swim in the river to cool his ardor but hoped the cool water of the bath would be as effective.

***

"My husband, you know the New Yam festival fast approaches," Adaku said. They were in the main chamber of the house, the sleeping rooms led off directly from it. Seated opposite Obinna at the table while he ate his dinner, she felt a little apprehensive about the topic she wanted to discuss with him and shifted nervously in her chair.

Obinna looked up at her, his eyes fringed by long, dark lashes, a black, expressionless pool she could drown in, always unnerved her. As she couldn't read his mood, gauging how to tell him what she wanted to say was difficult.

"Yes, say what's on your mind Adaku," he said in his usual deep voice, as he licked his long fingers.

Something stirred low within her belly. Her eyes hungrily followed his action, and she got distracted. For a brief moment she wished it was her fingers he was licking.

"That could be arranged."

Adaku looked up sharply and Obinna's brow was lifted with amusement. She realized she must have spoken her thought out loud. Embarrassment and heat washed over her as he took hold of her hand in his large one.

Somewhere within her mind something shifted. An awareness of Obinna at a primal level registered in her rapidly hazing brain.

The air suddenly felt warmer and her skin prickled. He took her fingers into his warm mouth in turn, twirling his moist tongue around each. Sensation flooded her body, and she forgot everything else she wanted to say. All she could feel was the stroke of his tongue on her fingers as he sucked and lapped each one.

His touch scorched her straight to her soul.

She gasped and his gaze came up, locking on to her and pinning her to the spot. His eyes were filled with a desire she couldn't explain. His tongue moved down her skin, searing a path to the spot at the center of her palm before licking it. Then he released her hand, and she realized she was trembling.

She felt a need pulsating in her core, leaving her confused. All he'd done was lick her fingers. Yet it seemed to turn her into a trembling mass, yearning for more of his touch. Prince Emeka's touch had never elicited such a response from her and she'd thought *he* was her life mate.

"What was it you wanted to ask me, or have I already fulfilled it?"

Obinna was still watching her intensely. His voice had a husky tinge that rumbled through her. She took awhile to catch her breath before she could speak. Willing her heart rate to return to normal, she stared at her hand, still tingling from his touch.

"I-I just wondered if I could buy some new fabrics in preparation for the festival," she said with a shaky voice that wasn't like her. She'd never been this affected before by his actions.

***

After she'd newly arrived at Obinna's home, she'd been so focused on her own misery at not being with the prince, her behavior had bordered on rude and childish. When Obinna had given her a trunk load of new fabrics, she'd turned it down. She'd known it was rude to reject her new husband's gift, but she didn't care. She hadn't wanted to marry him anyway. So she'd asked her mother to buy some fabrics for her. When they'd arrived, Obinna had discovered them. Incensed by her bad attitude and disobedience, he'd burned them all. He'd told her to stay naked if she wouldn't take the fabrics he'd bought.

She'd learned a quick lesson. Her husband was no pushover. She couldn't throw tantrums like she did in her father's house and get away with it. She was no longer the over-pampered, first daughter. She was now a wife.

***

"Of course. You can purchase what you need," he said before returning to his meal.

To be fair to him, he'd always provided whatever she asked for, whenever she'd asked it. The problem was she rarely did. She'd started off refusing to ask him for anything. These days she only asked out of necessity, but it was still difficult to acquiesce to a man she hadn't accepted as her husband.

Now she wanted him to be her husband in the full sense. However, she was stuck as to how to ask him without losing face.

***

Obinna stood beside the pallet watching his wife sleep. The sky was still dark and gray. The early cock had not crowed yet. He was simply an early riser. He loved to watch his wife sleep. It was the only time she was unguarded. Vulnerable. Open to him.

He watched her. Her chest rose and fell, her long, dark lashes fanned her cheeks. She was beautiful. Alluring. Captivating.

Sometimes he would sit up and watch her for hours while she slept.

Of course it didn't help that he wanted to do more than just watch her. He wanted to touch her, taste her, fill her, spill into her, and then do it all over again.

Gently he moved his hand, caressing her face. She turned her face into his hand and moaned softly in her sleep. His stare left her face and roamed the rest of her body. Her night cloth was loose, exposing one fleshy breast. He could see its brown nipple, stiff and pointing toward him. Sliding his hand down her neck, he left it hovering above her skin as he yearned to touch her breast.

Berating himself, he pulled the sheet up, covering her properly. He'd never taken to fondling his wife in her sleep, and he wouldn't start now. When he finally took her, she would be wide-awake and screaming out for him to possess her.

He marched over to the large, wooden trunk, which stored his belongings, opened it, and took out a roll of fabric. He also took out a bag of cowries and placed them on top of the fabric, laying them on the pallet beside his sleeping wife.

Walking to the door, then he opened it.

"My husband, are you leaving already?"

He turned around and his heart caught in his throat. She looked even more beautiful when she was awake, her eyes, with a befuddled look, still filled with the last fog of dreamland.

"Yes, in preparation for the festival, I have to supervise the completion of the tasks to store the harvested crops. Ezemmuo has already set a date, and we have to meet it."

Ezemmuo was the clan chief priest. Without his approval or performance of the required rituals, the new yams couldn't be eaten by the clan.

"Let me get you something to eat first." She started to get up, but he raised his hand.

"Don't worry. Go back to sleep. I will eat later. I have left you what you requested on the bed. It should be enough to purchase what you need."

He turned and walked out. If he stayed longer, he would be climbing into her bed.

***

The sun hung low in the sky, casting long shadows across the busy village square. A slight breeze was in the air. Still, the day hadn't cooled sufficiently for those seeking shelter to depart from the shades of the palm fronds, used as makeshift canopies, or the low-hanging branches of the trees.

It was a day of festivities; a day to thank *Ala,* the earth goddess, for the bountiful harvest and prosperity of the people of Umunri.

Adaku sat among the women folk who chatted about one thing or the other. However, she couldn't stop her gaze from straying. It settled across the square where the men of their clan were seated together, drinking palm wine and making merry just like their women folk. There were musicians playing drums, flutes, and other percussion instruments, while the male singer crooned. There had already been a wrestling match. Now the maidens were dancing. After these festivities, a few of them would receive formal proposals and be bound to their life partners once the required rites are performed.

Today, everyone was dressed in their finest regalia. Adaku was dressed in her best too; her final choice of fabric a surprise to even her.

She'd had an eye on a new fabric displayed in the market a few weeks back. Obinna had agreed she could make the purchase. However, when she'd awoken the other day to find the most beautiful fabric next to her in bed and the cowries to buy the one she'd seen in the market, she'd known there was only one she would wear today.

She'd fallen in love with the fabric from Obinna. It was woven with rich red and gold threads and felt soft to the touch. The intricate detailing of the design, and the quality of the fabric, had made her realize its high worth would rival those worn by royalty. She wondered how Obinna acquired it. He was a man of means. He owned vast lands. Though his wealth was not to the standards she'd been accustomed to in her father's house, she'd never seen a more intricate design of fabric before.

She'd immediately abandoned any ideas to buy fabric from the market and had chosen instead to wear this one. It had been the right choice. Though he didn't say anything, his dark eyes had softened.. For the first time since they were bound, pleasing him suddenly mattered to her.

As it happened, it seemed she was the envy of all the women in the square. Most of them had already complimented her on her outfit.

Yet as she watched her husband across the square from her, laughing and joking with the men, looking as virile as ever, she knew she would trade the adoration of the rest of the villagers to be with her husband. When their eyes met occasionally, his innate masculinity seemed to reach out to her core from across the square.

Since the day he'd licked her fingers, she hadn't been able to get him out of her head. When he wasn't around, she longed for his company. She'd started taking extra care with her appearance. After all this time living with him, she no longer looked on him as simply the man she'd been forced to wed. She looked on him as a man. Her man. Her husband.

She wanted him to look at her as a woman. His woman. His wife. She'd do just about anything to get him to look at her again with the same passion in his eyes as the night he'd sucked on her fingers.

Except things were not always so simple.

To all intents, they were husband and wife. They lived and were referred to as such. Yet there was a huge rift between them. One she wished she could bridge, yet wasn't sure how to do so.

At one point she thought he hated her, keeping her bound to him when she didn't want him. Yet he'd never been cruel or brutal toward her. His actions were always measured and considerate.

He was simply a proud man. And she'd disrespected him with her attitude on their wedding night.

"You will have to force me because I will never be yours, even if you were the last man on earth!"

She cringed as she remembered her hasty words. When she'd stiffened, her body expecting him to forcibly claim what was his right, she'd been shocked at his calm response. He'd watched her silently for a while before speaking, his cold voice sending an icy shiver down her spine.

"As you wish, Adaku. I'll not touch you, but you will remain my wife in every other sense."

That night and ever since, he'd slept on a separate pallet and had kept to his words, never touching her. Now she burned to have her husband the way it should be.

As she glanced over at Ifeoma, who was now blooming, the swell of her pregnancy just beginning to show, a sliver of desperation travelled down her spine. Soon people would start looking at her with pity in their eyes—as a woman who couldn't conceive or bear a child.

"Adaku, are you all right?" Ifeoma words drew her out of her reverie. She shook her head before replying.

"Why do you ask?"

"It's just that you had a frown on your face. You are not concerned about the rumors, are you?"

Dread traveled down her spine. She knew it wouldn't be a good thing. "What rumors?"

Ifeoma went pale. "Sorry. Don't mind me and my big mouth. It's nothing. Just hearsay."

She watched the way her friend's stare darted away briefly to where another group of women sat together. Something was up.

"Ifeoma, you have to tell me what you've heard. Right now," she persisted, keeping her voice low.

"If you're sure." Ifeoma was now fidgeting with her clothes, her eyes fixed on her restless hands.

"Go on. Tell me."

"I heard that Nneka, Ofonna's widow has been released by her in-laws after completing her mourning period. So she's free to remarry."

Adaku couldn't figure out how this affected her. Some widows, if they were still young enough and without children, were released by their in-laws to remarry another man of their choice. In most cases, they ended up as second or third wives to one of the dead man's brothers.

"And?" Adaku persisted. There had to be more to the story.

"And it is well known that she had a soft spot for Obinna before she was betrothed to Ofonna. It is rumored he may take her as a second wife."

It was Adaku's turn to feel faint as blood drained from her head. She gripped her seat to stop herself from toppling over. Taking a few deep breaths, she glanced over at Nneka, who looked happy chatting with her friends, oblivious to the thoughts churning in Adaku's head.

Was this true? Had Obinna been lovers with Nneka before he married me? Did he still have a fondness for the widow?

She glanced over to where Obinna was seated. He was chatting with his friend, Ikem, and they were both looking at the group where Nneka sat.

Her heart dropped into her stomach. Jealous rage washed over her, clouding her vision in red. It was true. Her husband still had feelings for Nneka. It was evident in the way he looked at the widow.

The realization was made worse by the fact he'd never touched her intimately except for the finger-licking incident. Now it seemed he was going to bring another woman into her home to compound her shame. She knew she shouldn't pay any heed to rumors. Yet she couldn't help the emotions coursing through her veins.

If her husband chose to take several wives, she could hardly prevent him. It was his right. In most cases, the first wife was consulted and played a role in choosing her husband's next wife. In her case, she couldn't blame Obinna if he didn't confer with her first. Especially, since she'd chosen to be antagonistic toward him at the start of their married life.

She needed to do something. She needed to regain her place. Being a first wife was null and void if she didn't have any children. If Nneka came into her home and bore a child before her, Adaku would be relegated to the place of a hand servant in her marital home. Nneka would take the position of first wife.

I can't let it happen.

So when the women started dancing, Adaku joined them. In her day she was the best dancer in her age group and could still charm with her moves. Like someone possessed, she danced and jiggled and moved and gyrated. The whole time, she made sure she was in full view of Obinna. Slowly a crowd of the other women gathered around her, cheering her on. She danced for as long as she thought Obinna was watching her. His expression was schooled, and she couldn't read his thoughts. Yet she danced, happy to have his attention regardless of how he felt.

When the music stopped, she glanced at Obinna and caught a brief glimpse of desire in his eyes before it quickly vanished. Feeling triumphant, she returned to her seat.

Adaku's mother, who had been sitting at the special table with other esteemed guests, came over to congratulate her and bid her farewell. She was preparing to return home.

"Does Obinna know you are leaving?" Adaku asked, glancing around to find her husband.

"Yes, I have already bid him farewell."

Adaku saw him, and her heart sank. The earlier feeling of elation fleeing her mind. Obinna was standing under a tree, talking to Nneka.

Not wanting to stay there any longer, she turned to her mother. "Let me walk a little with you."

They both left the square, her mother's attendants following behind. Adaku couldn't shake the despair that gripped her.

It is true. It is true.

The words echoed in her head, slowing her footsteps.

"My daughter, what is the matter?" Her mother gave her the knowing look, and Adaku couldn't restrain herself any longer. Her banked up tears escaped and flowed freely.

Her mother waved the attendants back, pulled Adaku to the shade of a tree, and made her sit on a felled tree trunk.

"Adaku, talk to me. I know all is not well."

Overtaken by grief and at a loss as to what to do about her marriage, she told her mother everything. That her husband had never touched her. That he may soon be taking another wife.

When she finished, her mother hugged her.

"You should have told me about this earlier. No woman should have to endure this in her husband's house." Her mother patted Adaku's hands, a frown on her face. "We have a saying. 'An adult does not sit back and watch while a she-goat delivers her kid when tied to the post'. I cannot sit back and watch disgrace befall you and our family. Wipe your tears, Adaku. I'll speak to your father immediately."

"But mother—"

"Do not worry about a thing. It will be well." Her mother shook her head. "Go home. I'll send word to you. Go."

Adaku couldn't do anything but return home. Now that she'd shared her troubles, she felt a little lighter. However she couldn't shake the niggling feeling she may have made things worse by telling her mother.

She prayed the gods would hear her prayers and save her from her troubles.

***

Obinna marched home, his blood bubbling with a mixture of rage at his wife's blatantly provocative display at the festival and the craving to mate with her and be done with it. Watching her dance had inflamed the desires already simmering in his blood. When he'd noticed other men watching her too, he'd wanted to drag her away. If it hadn't been for Ikem, who had distracted him at an opportune moment, he surely would have done so. As it happened, by the time he'd turned around to find his wife, she'd gone without even informing him.

What was she up to?

As he walked onto his grounds, he chided himself to calm down. She'd probably done it all on purpose just to rattle him so he would send her back to her parents. She had to learn she was his and he would not let her go.

He'd actually thought things were improving when she'd chosen to wear the fabric he'd specially commissioned the weaver to make for her. Seeing her looking resplendent in it had further thawed another layer of his restraint. He'd barely stopped himself from taking her into his arms. She'd made him happy.

Searching through the house, he realized she wasn't there. He wondered where she was until he heard a sound from the bathroom. He pushed open the door and was thunderstruck.

Adaku stood naked before him, her body slick from the bath she'd just taken. All the things he wanted to say to her vanished from his mind as his body froze where he stood.

Taking in everything in sight, his gaze roamed freely over her body. From her brown, almond-shaped eyes—molten with longing; small, pert nose; full sumptuous lips on a flawless oval face, to ripe breasts with their nipples tautening even as he watched. His eyes moved lower, past a narrow waist to hips that flared out. He could see the dark curls between her thighs hiding her feminine treasure from his sight. A treasure he wanted to explore right now as his manhood came alive. His gaze moved down still to her long legs that he'd dreamed of wrapping around his hips on several occasions.

"Get out!"

His gaze flew back up to her face. It seemed she'd recovered from the initial shock of seeing him and her eyes were now blazing with an odd mix of defiance and lust.

He laughed and took a step toward her. "Not before I've done this."

Pulling her into his arms, he lifted her chin and melded their lips together. She stiffened in his arms, her lips slightly open as she tried to speak. He took advantage of the opening and his tongue invaded her mouth. She was moist, juicy, better than he'd imagined. She tasted heavenly. Delicious. Sweeter than any *udara* fruit he'd ever tasted. His tongue plunged deeper, brooking no resistance, demanding a response.

He knew when she acquiesced. Her tongue darted out, delving into his mouth, his heart pounding sending a surge of warm blood through his body. She moved her arms up his back, clinging on to him. Moving her body closer to his, she crushed her soft breasts against his hard chest, his hardened manhood pulsating against her flat belly. He didn't care that the wetness from her body soaked his outfit.

Letting out a groan as he broke the kiss, his mouth travelled down, taking one taut tip into his mouth while his hand tweaked the other. A gasp escaped Adaku's lips as he sucked, bit and licked her breast. No mango had ever tasted this sweet. The way her body writhed beneath his touch drove him crazy, and he wanted to sink into her against the bathroom wall.

The tantalizing thought seemed to bring him back to his senses, and he released her, stepping back. She whimpered. A glance at her face told him she wanted him to continue. Her eyes were still clouded with lustful need. Maybe his stone princess was finally cracking. Maybe the jewel beneath would soon become visible. As much as he wanted to test that assumption right now, he had to be certain she was totally flaming hot for him before he finally claimed her.

"Get dressed. We need to talk," he said to Adaku, before walking out into the late evening air and breathing easier.

***

With her hands still trembling, Adaku dressed as quickly as she could, a jumble of emotions racing through her.

What just happened? Why did my legs seem to lack the strength to hold me up?

She self-consciously moved her hand to her lips, reliving the sensations evoked by Obinna's touch. She couldn't believe she'd completely lost all touch with reality and her anger when he'd taken her into his arms. Her annoyance with him had dissolved, replaced with pure longing. The ache still throbbed low in her belly, she yearned for his possession.

How could he set my senses ablaze so easily? If he hadn't stopped I would have surrendered totally to him right here in the bathroom. Without reservations. Where is my shame? My dignity?

He'd openly acknowledged Nneka at the festivities earlier. Now, with the widow being released from mourning, she was free to resume her liaisons with Obinna if he so wished. And here she was shamelessly surrendering to her husband's touch when another woman was poised to enter her home.

Was that what Obinna wanted to talk to me about? I can't sit back and keep quiet, can I?

She'd never been so confused before.

She finished dressing and went back into the house. Obinna was sitting outside on a chair. The sun had nearly sunk in the horizon, leaving an eerie golden glow in the sky. She hoped it wasn't a sign things were about to get worse in their marriage. Bringing out another chair, she sat beside him.

"You wanted to talk, my husband," she kept her voice even, not wanting to start a quarrel until she heard what he had to say.

When he turned to face her, he looked pensive for a brief moment. She wondered what had him so worried.

"Are you happy here?"

Puzzled, she frowned. This was the first time he'd asked her such a question. She opened her mouth to tell him she was unhappy and closed it again. It was the response she would have given when they had first wed. Now it wasn't so true. After the incidents of the past few weeks, she was no longer prepared to return to her father's house. Not without attempting to make a go of her marriage.

"My husband, I don't understand your question."

His shoulders rise as he let out a heavy sigh. The feeling of dread she'd felt earlier returned with full force. *What was going on?*

"My husband, is all well?"

"I should ask you that. It is nearly a full year since we were bound to each other. On that night you claimed I was the last man you wanted as your life mate. Since then, I have let you be, never forced you to fulfill your wifely duties in our bed. It is your choice, and I cannot change that."

He paused and looked away before continuing.

"However, I am the only son of my parents and my responsibility to produce an heir to keep the lineage—"

"So this is what you want to do? You want to bring that woman in here to take my place?"

He looked momentarily stunned and shook his head.

"What are you talking about, woman?"

"That husband snatcher, Nneka. I saw you talking to her at the festival. Don't even deny it."

"Mind your tongue, woman. Don't talk about another person like that. I expect more from you."

"There you go defending her already. Is this your plan, to humiliate me in my own home? What did I ever do to you to deserve this?"

"Do you really need to ask me that? Would I need another woman if you were fulfilling your wifely duties?" He stood up and walked off angrily.

"Oh, use that against me, will you." She stood up and ran into the house, feeling sickened. It was really going to happen. Her husband was going to take another wife. She had no one else to blame but herself. She hadn't realized how much it would hurt until it happened. Now she felt as if her heart was breaking.

She curled up on her pallet and cried. *When did I start caring about my husband or what he did?* She'd spent the last year resenting him and wanting to return home. It seemed the gods had finally answered her wish. Yet she didn't want it.

What do I want?

Before she had time to analyze her jumbled thoughts, she felt her body being lifted by strong, large arms. Obinna placed her on his lap. Confused, she hid her face in his chest, not wanting him to see her tears.

"Don't cry, *aku m*." My treasure.

But his tender words seemed to break down her walls of restraint. More tears erupted from her, streaming down her cheeks and wetting his chest. *Why is he being nice to me? Can't he see I just want to cry in peace, to wallow in the misery I've brought on myself?*

He pulled her even closer, rocking her back and forth while whispering soothing words in her ear. Gradually, her tears stopped. He lifted her chin and kissed the remaining tears away from her cheeks. The sensation of his lips on her skin left her with tingles spreading through her body.

"Forgive me for my harsh words. I shouldn't have said them."

Feeling even more miserable because of his kindness, she shook her head. "You were right. I am a bad wife. You have every right to replace me."

"Shhh...Don't say that. You're not a bad wife. I couldn't have wished for another. I have no wish to replace you."

Shocked at his words, she looked up at his face. Surely he couldn't mean what he said. He was just saying it to cheer her up. Still, his eyes had softened with a warm, sincere glint.

"You don't mean that." She sniffled.

"More than you could ever know. You are still my wife. We can both make things better if we so wish."

"But I've ruined things between us. I've pushed you into the arms of another woman. I should never have said the things I said on our wedding night. I wasn't being honest anyway."

She flicked her gaze downward but he held her chin up, making her look back into his face. His black eyes were smoldering, boring into her, melting her. She couldn't look away if she tried.

"What were you not honest about?"

His thumb caressed her cheek in a circular motion and, for a moment, she couldn't think properly. She tuned into the feel of his calloused palm against her soft face and hoped he would hold her like this forever.

"Tell me." His low voice rumbled through her. Her heart pounded in her chest.

"When I said I would never want you even if you were the last man on earth, it wasn't true," she muttered in a low voice, afraid of voicing her needs and making herself vulnerable. After months of being standoffish, it wasn't easy to shed it in a moment. "I was angry at my parents and took it out on you."

"And now? Are you still angry?"

"You have been good to me. I have no reason to be angry with you." She shook her head sadly. "Now I'm only angry at myself for being so foolish, for pushing my husband into another woman's arms. It's too late and I don't even know how to change things."

"Adaku, we are both here now so we can change things if we both want it. I still want to be your husband in all the ways it is possible to be your husband." His eyes were now shimmering with heat, the corners of his lips lifted in a teasing smile. "And I want you to be my wife in every sense of the word. What do you want, *aku m*?"

He'd used an endearment twice already, and her heart soared. Her name, Adaku, meant first daughter of treasure. By changing it to *my treasure*, Obinna was letting her know her status in his household, if not his heart.

Was it really so? Does my husband really place me that highly in his esteem?

He traced a path with his thumb on her lower lip, and her heart skipped several beats as the tingling sensation returned to her body. Transfixed, excitement and fear travel down her spine. After holding back from her husband, she was finally about to admit her secret yearning. She was still afraid it would backfire, and he would punish her by sending her away.

It was as if he sensed her fear. "Fear not. Speak your mind. The past is forgiven."

"I-I want to be your wife in every sense of the word."

His breath hitched, and he pulled her closer.

"You don't know how much I have longed to hear you say those words, *aku m*." He lightly brushed her lips with his.. She shivered, heat spreading through her. "I have craved you every day since the first time I saw you."

"My husband, if you've felt that way for so long, why did you not claim what was yours on our wedding night?"

"As much as I wanted you, I would never force myself on to you. I had thought that once we were married, you would submit to me. Yet I hadn't considered the strength of your will and the depth of your feelings for the prince. I could only pray for a day when you would come to me of your own volition."

His words shook her. For the first time, she realized Obinna truly cared for her. She knew of men who would have forced themselves on their rebellious wives and punished them too. A woman couldn't deny her husband. Obinna had chosen patience and kindness. In the end, he'd won her over because she knew he was a good man at heart.

"My husband, please forgive me." More tears stung her eyes as she tried to get off his lap so she could kneel and beg his forgiveness. Still he would not let her go.

"*Aku m*, I forgave you a long time ago. Tell me again how you long for me."

He didn't wait for her response. He kissed her like a hungry man. Ravenously, his tongue swept into her mouth. She dissolved into him, clinging on to his shoulders as if she were drowning.

A desire she'd never felt before sparked to life within her. Wherever his warm hands moved on her body, a trail of heat followed. By the time their lips parted, she was gasping for breath. Their bed chamber suddenly felt contracted. All she could feel were Obinna and the storm raging between them. Their heartbeats combined to rival the sounds of the drums at the festival earlier.

Before long he laid her back on the pallet as he leaned over her. His earthy scent filled her lungs. His eyes had such intensity, his gaze piercing through to her soul. She felt exposed, vulnerable, though she was still fully clothed. She wanted to reveal all to him. Wanted him to see straight into her heart and know what was in there.

No other man had made her feel this way. Not even the prince.

Lifting her hand, she touched his face. "My husband, I—"

"Shhh." He put his finger against her lips. "No more words."

He proceeded to kiss a path down her body as he slowly undressed her. The sensations built within her with each touch, the flames getting hotter. Yet she craved more. She held his head as he suckled her breasts, arching her body so she could feel more of him. When his lips moved lower to her stomach, she whimpered for him to complete what he'd started. Her body moved restlessly. He trailed his lips down to her thighs. She closed her eyes and her senses heightened, her body climbing to a peak of sensitivity.

When he touched her secret place, she gasped and her eyes flew open. Her body felt wound tight as he caressed her intimately. The pleasure overtook her in a feverish sensation. She floated in a cloud. When she became aware of her surroundings again, Obinna was kneeling between her legs, his hardened manhood pushing against her moist entrance.

He leaned down and melded their lips again, reigniting the fiery feeling in her body. She opened up and welcomed him into her body. He moved slowly. Her body gradually expanding as his thick hot flesh filled her. Then he paused and looked at her quizzically.

For a moment it looked like he would pull back and she panicked, thinking she'd done something wrong. "Please," her whisper desperate. She wrapped her legs around him to stop him from moving back.

He kissed her again, and with one push filled her completely. She gasped at the pain-pleasure sensation that flooded her before he started moving again. He set a slow, tender pace, gradually taking her back to her peak and robbing her of breaths. She explored the feel of his taut skin against her palm, moving her hands down his back. The sound of their lovemaking filled the bed chamber.

This time when her release came, it swept through from her toes to her head and finally exploded into a myriad of colors. She called out his name. After a few more thrusts, his release followed, and they both collapsed entwined in each other's arms.

***

Obinna lay beside his wife, watching her as she slept. She looked beautiful, as always. Yet this morning there was an extra glow to her skin.

She's mine. All mine. Finally!

He wanted to stand outside and shout it out so his neighbors could hear.

Smiling, he recalled the previous night. Their first joining had been the culmination of everything he'd ever dreamed it would be. Yet it had even surpassed his dreams. He'd been shocked to realize Adaku had been untouched by another man.

All the while he'd thought she and the prince were lovers. Especially considering the speculation in the village about her affair with the prince and the speed at which her parents had wanted her to marry. Though it had hurt his ego to think another man had touched her, his love for her had surpassed the pride. He'd wanted her regardless. To finally be rewarded by being the first man to fully claim her was the best gift he could have wished for. It sealed his assumption they had been destined to be together.

There was no other woman for him but Adaku.

He knew there were speculations about him and Nneka. The widow was a close, family friend and at one time he'd considered marrying her. Until he'd seen Adaku. It had been a festival and she'd been dancing with the other young maidens. As soon as he'd seen her, he knew she was the woman for him. Her grace and agility had surpassed that of the other maidens. He could see no one else but Adaku. But when he'd heard about her link with the prince, he'd been crestfallen, knowing he couldn't really compete with royalty. He was a quiet man and lived a humble life.

He'd spoken to his elder sister, who'd encouraged him to propose to her father. And here he was, more than a year later, and he'd finally claimed what he saw as his rightful woman.

Several times during the night they made love, exploring each other. He'd been amazed at the way she'd come alive, her usual stony attitude shed. In its place was a woman full of passion, who was willing to go wherever he led in their bed play. Their ardor had blazed all night. Though it was sated several times, it had taken just a little rest to be reignited again. It was as if all the pent up feelings of the last year had exploded during the night.

In the end, they had both drifted off to sleep just before dawn. Now he knew it was mid-morning by the brightness of the sunshine filtering through the cracks in the door. Luckily, since it was the day after the festival, no one was required to work. There was a break, and all the villagers would be having a rest for a few weeks before the start of the next planting season.

He thought about getting up to wash and get dressed as his stomach rumbled. But he didn't want to leave the warm softness and musky scent of Adaku. After being denied her delights for so long, he couldn't get enough.

"My husband, *ututu oma*." Good morning.

He glanced down at Adaku. She was awake and smiling at him shyly. He loved her smile. It left him feeling euphoric and reminded him that he'd indeed been her first lover. He smiled back at her, leaning in to brush his lips against hers.

"Did you sleep well, *aku m*?" He asked before he licked her chin. His smile widened when he heard her hitched breath. He loved the way she responded to his touch. It fueled his already simmering desire. He continued trailing light kisses down her neck, her pulse underneath his lips beating a frantic pace.

"I-I did," she stammered as she seemed to struggle with controlling her response to him. "I should get up and sort out your breakfast."

He lifted his head and gave her a wolfish grin. "Breakfast is right here. I think you should be more concerned about lunch." He laughed before claiming her lips again in a kiss filled with intent.

Breaking the kiss, the sound of their rapid breathing reverberated in the bed chamber. His heart pounded in his chest. He would never get enough of his wife. He wanted to devour her, hear her cry out his name in ecstasy as she'd done several times in the night. When their flesh joined again, he wanted her to be moist and ready for him.

Leaning over her, he moved his lips down her bare flesh, suckling her breasts, and nipping her flat belly before settling on the hooded jewel between her thighs. He inhaled her musky scent, and his manhood stirred, becoming harder. He looked up at her face. Her eyes were glazed in longing, her tongue darting out to lick her lips as she watched him with a silent plea.

When his tongue darted out and swirled around her swollen nub, she gasped out loud. He loved the taste and sound of her. She'd surrendered herself to him. Willingly. He could give her pleasure as he'd yearned to do for months. Totally.

Taking her hardened nub into his mouth, he suckled on it, lapping at her nectar as it flowed freely. She writhed beneath him, and he moved a hand onto her flat stomach holding her down. With the other he thrust his fingers into her, playing out what he yearned to do with his manhood.

Even after she'd screamed out his name in her climax, he continued licking her until her body went limp beneath his touch. It was only then he pushed his throbbing manhood into her warm depth. He kissed her again soundly. She came alive, responding promptly and clinging on to his shoulders, her legs wrapped around his hips.

Their joining was frenzied as they both demanded and surrendered to each other with equal vigor, reaffirming their passion for each other. As he drove her closer to her peak, he demanded she verbally declare her devotion. For some reason he wanted to hear it from her lips, though her body spoke it in volumes. The turmoil raging within him could only be soothed by her words.

"I am yours. Forever," she promised just before she floated off.

"And I'm yours, *aku m,*" he swore before he joined her in oblivion.

When he woke again, Adaku was not in bed with him. He got up, dressing quickly to go in search of her. He found her in the kitchen. The sumptuous smell of the food she was cooking directing his path there. He gave her a brief kiss before going to clean up in the bathroom. She had the meal ready when he came out. They normally ate separately. Today he set a new precedent. He sat her on his lap and fed her from his bowl.

Baffled, she queried the informality. He laughed, reminding her this was his house not the palace. He preferred to live very casually and intimately with his wife. They were still locked together when a visitor arrived. Adaku stood up to let the visitor in. It was her younger brother, Nnamdi.

Nnamdi greeted both of them. Adaku looked a little worried and Obinna couldn't shake the feeling something was wrong.

"Is all well at home?" Adaku asked her younger brother with a frown on her face.

"Yes, everyone is fine. I have a message from father. He wishes to see you immediately."

"He does? Are you sure nothing is wrong?" she asked again, moving closer to her brother.

"It's all right. You have to go and see why your father wishes to see you," Obinna said calmly, trying to soothe her concern. She turned to him immediately and he could tell she was worried about leaving him. He took her hand. "I'll be fine. There are things I need to do today anyway."

Turning to the boy he said, "Nnamdi, sit down. Your sister will get you something to eat before she gets ready to go with you."

He left the two of them and went into the bedchamber to get ready. Adaku came in shortly afterward.

"My husband, are you sure it is fine to leave you at such short notice? I can go see my father tomorrow or some other time."

He turned to her. She still looked worried. Though his instinct told him all was not well, he chose to ignore it. He didn't want suspicion spoiling the new love blooming between them. He pulled her into his arms and caressed her cheek.

"It is fine. I wanted to spend the whole day with you. But we have plenty of time, a whole future together." He brushed his lips against hers, inhaling her sweet scent and enjoying the way she molded into him. "I'm sure it's important if your father requests to see you. If it gets too late, spend the night there. You can return in the morning."

She looked up at him, her frown deepening as she shook her head. "I'll not stay long. I'll definitely be back before sunset."

"In any case, you have my permission to spend the night. It's a long walk from your parent's house. I don't want you walking home in the dark. Agreed?" He lifted her chin and looked into her eyes. Their warm depths sparkled as she broke into a smile, nodding her head.

"Good," he said before kissing her passionately. She wrapped her arms around him, pulling him closer. When he lifted his head, he was out of breath and wanted to take his wife back to bed. Stepping back, he opened the door. "Give my greetings to your parents when you get there. I'm off to see Mazi Ene."

"Go well," she said as he shut the door on his way out.
***

Obinna returned home later that evening. He'd spent most of the afternoon in discussions with his friend, Ikem, and in negotiations with Mazi Ene. He was happy things had concluded satisfactorily for all involved. In a few days, Nneka would be settled in her marital home and all the speculations would be laid to rest. His life with Adaku could begin in earnest, finally.

When Adaku didn't return before nightfall, he didn't worry. He wanted her to spend the night with her parents. Since they'd been wedded, she hadn't spent the night anywhere else but in his house.

Tonight, for the first time, he missed her physical presence. He lay on their now combined pallet, breathing in her scent clinging to the bedding. He thought about Adaku and their new found fondness for each other. He didn't want to dwell on the past they had missed out on, so he focused on the future. The future was the two of them together, hopefully with children.

He wondered how many the gods would bless them with. He was the only son in a family of three girls. His sisters were all married. He prayed the gods would bless him with plenty of sons and daughters. Mostly, he prayed they would all be healthy.

When he eventually slept, it was a dreamless sleep, and he woke up refreshed. He rose early as was usual and prepared for the day. He was looking forward to the return of his wife from her parents. Though she'd only been gone for less than a day, he missed her presence.

After he finished breakfast, he heard the sound of people arriving in his compound. Thinking it was Adaku, he rushed out to welcome her. However he came face to face with her unsmiling older brother, Ifeanyi. Accompanying Ifeanyi were some servants who were carrying several items.

"My in-law, welcome," he greeted the man. Before Ifeanyi spoke, Obinna knew all was not well, yet he kept his voice pleasant. "I hope all is well with this early morning visit. Please sit down."

"I would rather keep standing. This is not a social visit. I am here on behalf of my father. He's returning the bride price you paid for Adaku and claiming his daughter back."

As Ifeanyi spoke, the men with him deposited the items on the floor.

Sure enough they were items that matched what he'd given Adaku's family during their betrothal—the keg of palm wine, a bag of cowries, several tubers of yam, kegs of palm oil, bales of fabrics, even a live he-goat.

Though his heart sank and his blood boiled, Obinna maintained an outward appearance of calm. "Why are you doing this, Ifeanyi? I have no quarrel with my wife and I have no wish to send her back to her father's house."

"Your wife doesn't wish to remain yours any longer, and my father has granted her wish. If there is anything on the list outstanding, let us know and we will return it immediately. Goodbye."

Somehow Obinna wasn't shocked at the news. In the past year, he'd been expecting an event like this. He'd always been prepared for it and his stance had always been over-his-dead-body. Yet today, things had changed. He'd thought matters were resolved between him and his wife. Yet it seemed he was far from the truth. Even after she'd let him in, after she'd vowed to be his forever, Adaku didn't love him. She still loved the prince.

Ifeanyi turned around and stalked out with the servants. Obinna sat heavily on his chair, holding his head in his hand, his heart slowly breaking at Adaku's betrayal.

***

"Have you seen it? I told you it'd be the case."

Adaku paid little heed to her mother's words as she paced her bed chamber, folding her fingers in her hand. Worry twisted in her guts and she just couldn't settle down.

"Mother—"

"Don't *mother* me. It's been four days and still no word from the man you call your husband. Four days since your father returned your bride price to Obinna. Where is he? I told you he didn't want you for a wife. No man keeps a woman in the house with him and doesn't touch her. Never. It's not done."

"Mother, I told you it wasn't like that. It was my fault. I instigated his actions by rejecting him."

"Eh, you rejected him, and he stood there watching you. Is he not a man? Does he not have sexual desires? Just stop it now. You have to get prepared. The prince is visiting us today. He's finally going to do right by this family and honor the bond between our families. He's going to formally propose for your hand."

"But mother, I am already married. I can't marry the prince."

"Listen to me, girl. You will do as you are told. You are no longer married. In fact you were never married since your marriage was never consummated."

"I told you already, Obinna and I consummated the marriage the night of the festival," she said in a frustrated voice. She was tired of having to explain this over and over again to her mother.

"It may be so, but it was too late. Your marriage should have been consummated before the full moon prior to the New Yam festival for it to be binding. Since you didn't, you are not married. So the prince is free to marry you."

"I cannot marry the prince. I want to stay married to Obinna. Mother, help me here."

"You want to stay married to Obinna. The same man you rejected. The same man that didn't touch you for a year while you lived under the same roof. Are you well at all, my daughter?"

"Mother, please."

"I told you already, don't *mother* me. I'm not interested. I cannot sit back and watch you bring disgrace to this family. Moreover, marrying the prince is what you've wanted to do since you were a little girl. You spoke about him non-stop until you were betrothed to Obinna. Our family has a special relationship with the royal household. By marrying the prince, you will strengthen that relationship."

"But the prince could marry Ij'ego. Our family ties would still be maintained," she chimed in, hoping for a way out of the dilemma.

"Aside from the fact that Ij'ego is too young to marry at this stage, she's the daughter of my rival. This honor is due me, as you are the first daughter of this family. So the prince cannot bypass you and marry your half sister." Her mother paused and took her hands, pulling Adaku to sit down on the chair next to hers.

"My daughter, you have to do this for me, for our family. There is no other way. If you defy your father, he'll disown you, and I'll be unable to help you. Eh, my daughter, please. Think about me, and the shame this will bring to me if you annoy your father. I already have my hands full as it is."

Adaku watched her mother, confusion washing over her. She'd never been able to defy her parents. Certainly not her mother. She understood the woman's dilemma, her constant struggle to maintain her position in a household of multiple wives and children. Since Adaku's mother didn't give birth to the first son, a position every married woman wanted, being the mother of the first daughter was the next best thing.

Still, Adaku had her own life now. And it was with Obinna. She didn't want to marry the prince. Not anymore. Not after the last few days with Obinna. Still, what could she do? Her parents were her parents.

Sitting there watching her mother, she felt sickened. She wanted to do the right thing for her family. However Obinna was also part of her family now.

She tried several times to sneak out of her father's house to go to Obinna. She was constantly being watched. Even her attempt to bribe the night guard had failed. He was too loyal to her father and didn't wish to lose his job.

Where is Obinna? Why hasn't he come for me? Did he give up on me? Is he truly going to wed Nneka?

When she'd arrived at her father's house, he'd queried her about her married life. Her mother had already told him about her marital problems, so she couldn't hide anything from him. He had demanded to know how she'd lived with Obinna.

When she'd told him, he'd declared her marriage to Obinna was void because it wasn't consummated in time. Now she wished she hadn't told her mother anything.

How am I supposed to prepare myself for Prince Emeka when I yearn for Obinna? After all the years of pining for the prince, now that I'm going to get my wish, I don't want him.

She needed to convince her parents her heart lay with Obinna now. But neither of them was listening to her. The prince had been invited to their home to start the formalities of the betrothal.

Time was running out fast and she needed to find a solution.

***

Later that afternoon, Adaku was summoned to her father's quarters. Prince Emeka was there discussing the plans for their betrothal with her father.

Emeka stood when she walked in. He was a good-looking man, tall and fair skinned. As always, he looked regal in his rich, patterned clothes and jeweled, gold crown. She understood why she'd taken to him as a young girl. However, looking at him now, she felt no fondness toward him. Only saw him as a friend, not her life mate. She couldn't marry him.

"Adaku, you look well." He smiled at her fondly. In the past it would have made her excited to have his attention; now she felt nothing.

"My Prince, welcome." She curtsied, but made no move toward him as she would have done in the past.

The prince's smile faded slightly.

Her father stood up. "I need to speak to Adaku's mother briefly." He walked out, leaving them alone.

The prince moved toward her. She took a step back and blurted out her thoughts. "If you have come to ask for my hand in marriage, I'll have to inform you that you've wasted your time."

"Why is that, Adaku?" he asked, his brow lifting in puzzlement.

"Because I'll not marry you. My heart and body belongs to another."

Though her heart was pounding because she was going against her father's wish, she didn't care. She had to end this charade.

"But I thought your heart had always belonged to me. You said you would wait for me." Prince Emeka sat back down, frowning at her now.

"Well, you also said you would come for me, but you didn't. Instead, you took Nonye as your bride. You broke your promise first."

"You knew I had no choice in the matter. I had to marry Nonye to strengthen our clan ties with the people of Umulari. I never felt for her the fondness that I have for you. I would not be here if I didn't care for you."

"I know you care for me. I'm sorry I'll still have to say no to you. I want to stay married to Obinna. There was a time when I thought being a second wife in your home would be good for me as long as I was close to you. Now I know better. Obinna cares about me despite what I—"

Adaku stopped talking when she heard a loud noise coming from the courtyard. She ran outside, closely followed by the prince.

"I demand to see my wife!" Obinna roared. His expression was thunderous. His shoulders high, his muscles tensed up as if ready to fight. He towered over her father's guards, who flanked him. They looked ready to attack him if her father gave the order.

He looks so fierce, so masculine.

Her heart leaped with joy. He'd come for her. She wanted to run to him, yet her feet stayed rooted to the ground. A sliver of fear ran through her.

"You do not have a wife here," her father replied stonily, while her mother stood beside him looking worried.

"It would seem so, since she has chosen another," Obinna replied harshly as his cold angry eyes moved from the prince standing behind her to focus on her.

Adaku flinched as if he'd hit her. The pain searing through her would have been tamer if he'd done so. Her heart sank into her stomach. Tears stung her eyes but she blinked them back, determined not to cry. He had a right to be angry with her. She had brought this trouble on to herself. Yet she wasn't entirely to blame.

"How dare you accuse me of taking another when you have been speaking to Nneka's uncle about her betrothal?" she retorted sharply, glad her voice had not wavered as she physically trembled with annoyance.

This time it was his turn to flinch. A dark emotion she couldn't read flickered in his black eyes before they went cold again.

"Yes, I have been negotiating a betrothal for Nneka's hand," he said in matter-of-fact voice, and she gasped that he would admit it openly. "On behalf of my friend, Ikem. Their marital rites will be performed in a few days."

"Is this true?" Even as she asked it, she knew it was true. Obinna had no reason to lie to her. He'd never done so in the past. She turned to her mother, who just shrugged as if to say she didn't doubt him either.

"Yes," he answered quickly before turning to her father. "Ichie Omemma, I have always thought you to be a fair man. Yet you choose to give away my unborn child to another man. All I ask is that you wait the required time until he's born and returned to me. Then your daughter can marry whomever she chooses."

"What child?" her father replied puzzled, turning to look at her.

"You can ask your daughter about the child in her womb." Obinna turned and started walking out. Panicked, Adaku ignored her father. Propelled by a need she couldn't articulate immediately, she ran after Obinna and stopped behind him.

"You will just leave like that? Without even demanding my return?" Standing this close to him, she felt out of breath and not just from running.

He turned around before she realized he'd moved. Gripping her arms, he pulled her closer, fixing her with an intense stare that stopped her heart for a moment. His eyes were darkened by pain so severe, she would have fallen if he hadn't been holding her. He was deeply hurt, and she'd caused it. When he spoke, his voice was low and raw with emotion.

"Adaku, I kept you with me for a year. A whole year. I waited patiently, yearning for you. Despite your attitude, I told myself in time you would come around. I gave you all that I had, yet it wasn't enough for you. Even after you promised to be mine forever, you still returned to him."

He watched Emeka for a reaction to his words, as the prince continued to stand behind her in silence.

"Well, no more. I cannot keep you tied to me if your heart is elsewhere. You choose whom you belong to. All I ask is that you give me back what we created together. Our child."

Releasing her, he turned to leave again but she held on to him. She couldn't let him leave. Not now. Boldly, she fixed her stare on him, making sure he saw the need in her eyes.

"Is that all I am to you? The mother of your child? I thought I meant more to you."

His shoulders lifted and fell as he heaved a sigh. "Adaku, what do you want from me?" His voice was strained.

"I want you to take me home. I am yours."

His eyes widened with puzzlement, and he glanced behind her again. She turned around. Both her parents were nodding and smiling.

"She was never mine. Take your wife home," Prince Emeka said.

"It seems she has made her choice," her father said as he smiled kindly at both of them.

"Do you mean it?" Obinna turned back to her and asked in a gruff voice. His hands on her arms tightened.

"Forever," she said, almost choking with emotion, relieved her parents finally let her make her own choice of a husband. This time she was making the right choice.

He lifted her up, crushing her body to his and kissing her deeply. Not caring there were people watching. She didn't care either.

"And I'm yours, *aku m*." He breathed into her lips, sealing their future together.

THE END

Kiru Taye

His Strength

When a warrior seeks to claim a free-spirited woman, he soon discovers a tigress unwilling to be caged. Is the hunter about to be hunted?

As a young widow, Nneka yearns to be released from the obligations to her late husband's family and live as an independent woman. With a past colored by a brutal father, she'll never yield to another man willingly and will do just about anything to attain that freedom including flouting the laws of the land.

Ikem was unable to claim Nneka once because his lineage meant he wasn't good enough. Now fate has given him another chance. But he quickly discovers that claiming this unpredictable wildcat is easier said than done. Will he be able to convince her that succumbing to their passion is the key to her freedom?

Kiru Taye

Chapter One

Southeast Nigeria, pre-colonization

Ikem leaned against the cashew tree, waiting.

It was early evening; the sun had begun its slow descent into the horizon, creating long shadows against the heat-baked red soil underneath his feet. It hadn't rained for a few days, leaving a feeling in the air reminiscent of the Harmattan, the dry and dusty season, though the period was still a few full moons away. A gentle breeze swirled around him, lifting the dried leaves from the ground, turning them into a mini-vortex before sending them falling gently back down to earth.

This was now a daily routine. Recently he'd taken to standing by this tree, watching his quarry as she walked along the footpath on her way back from the stream. She always carried her *ite* full of water balanced confidently on her head. So far he'd been unobserved. At least he thought she hadn't noticed. He'd not made himself known or said anything to her.

As if on cue, he heard the sound of approaching footsteps. Pushing off the tree, he stood straight and waited. Anticipation thrummed in his blood. He flexed his shoulders, seeking to quell the adrenaline pumping through his veins.

Then she came into view, the vision that kept him awake several nights. His heart rammed into his rib cage with a heavy thud. Expectantly, he licked his dry lips. He was a grown man in his prime, one of the best wrestlers in the land, but the sight of this woman reduced his body to that of a boy who'd only recently discovered the pleasures of a maiden.

Nneka.

Petite, compared to his tall frame, her skin was dark and gleamed in the sunlight. The gentle lines of her face bore a hint of ethereal beauty. The rounded curves of her body were hidden beneath the loose, drab gray of her mourning clothes. Yet, this didn't diminish her beauty. It made him crave her even more, evidenced by his stirring manhood. He watched the gentle sway of her hips when she walked past. The need to touch her overtook him.

"Nneka," he called out from behind the tall, green grasses now covered in a layer of brown dust. He took a step forward so she could see him better.

With measured ease she turned around, looked left and right along the empty footpath before staring straight at him.

"Ikem, what are you doing here?"

The softness of her voice traveled through him, igniting his already sparking desire. His heart increased its pounding. The blood in his veins rushed downward, leaving him feeling light-headed. Such was her effect on him. Yet, he schooled his expression as he watched her.

Her hair was a mass of short, tight curls. As tradition dictated, her head had been shaved clean at the death of her husband. It drew his attention to her unadorned face, wide eyes, pert nose, and full lips. Her body didn't have any of the decorative *uli* marking other women wore; neither did she wear any beads or ornaments. Her appearance was designed to deter notice.

Except he noticed her. All of her.

He'd expected her to look puzzled, maybe even frightened, at seeing him standing there. She didn't. Instead she stared at him with boldness unbecoming a woman in a state of mourning. Her dark brown eyes held a brief twinkle of amusement. When he raised his brow in a silent query, she lowered her gaze to the ground.

"I want to talk to you. Come here." Though he spoke quietly, there was no mistaking the demand in his voice.

With haste, her gaze flicked back up to meet his. Her eyes had lost some of their sparkling amusement. Instead they held his stare with fiery defiance; she raised her chin a notch.

"I cannot be seen talking to you, Ikem. You know that." Her tone was self-assured as if she didn't care if she was found talking to him. Knowing the consequences of being seen with him in public, a woman in her position should have cowered and appeared appalled at his forwardness. Her confidence affected him at a most basic level. It challenged him and served to spur him on.

He wanted this woman regardless of the consequences.

Nneka was out of bounds to him. Tradition dictated it. Firstly because of who he was. He was a man with no known lineage. Though he was born and had lived in Umunri all of his life, he had the status of a guest. He was not *nw'ala,* a son of the soil. By virtue of his birth, he was a bastard, a man who couldn't trace his paternal lineage.

He'd had to stand aside and watch another man take her as his wife two years ago. His proposal had been rejected because of his heritage—or rather, the lack of one. It had nearly driven him insane. As a result, he'd sworn he wouldn't take another as his wife. Instead he'd let loose his previously tightly leashed decadent cravings. Since then he'd acquired a reputation in certain quarters of society.

He didn't care. If he was going to be scorned by people, he'd rather it was deserved and have pleasure in the process too.

As he watched the sunbeam filter through the trees onto her dark skin, illuminating it in a soft caress, he noted her attitude toward him held none of disdain he'd come to expect from polite society. While other women studied him surreptitiously when they thought he wasn't watching, her assessment of him was open. His flesh came alive under her scrutiny.

As a woman still covered in mourning gray, she remained out of bounds to him—to all men—until she completed the required mourning period.

"No one will see us. Come," he insisted, impatience slipping into his voice. He held her gaze without yielding. The gods had granted him a second chance to claim her. He wasn't going to waste it. Besides, the time to give respectful distance to a grieving widow was long past. He'd been counting down the moons. This was the time to act.

She stood still, neither making a move toward him nor walking away. One curved eyebrow arched up, as if waiting for something. Very few people failed to act when he instructed. He was the chief trainer and taught a company of young men in the art of warfare. None dared to defy his command. Certainly, no woman ever did.

Yet he realized he had to deploy other tactics to get this woman to comply. She reminded him of a tigress out in the wild. Fearless. Daring.

"Please," he added and smiled inwardly. He would enjoy taming this tigress.

It was the magic word. She walked toward him, her flowing movement ensuring his eyes were glued to her body as she came closer, her *ite* still on her head without the need for her to hold on to it. When she stopped in front of him within arm's reach, he leaned in to help her take the water vessel down. This close, her light, citrus scent mixed with another that he could only identify as her essence and invaded his nostrils. He tightened his grip on the *ite* when he lifted it off her head and put it on the ground. Instead of pulling her closer and inhaling more of her, he straightened and leaned back against the tree.

"I can't stay long. I'm expected back soon," she said softly.

Will I ever get used to the effect of her voice on me?

"I won't keep you long." He clenched and unclenched his fingers behind him to stop from reaching across and pulling her closer. "How are you?" He spoke calmly, though the fire in his blood raged.

"I'm well." For a brief moment it looked like she could read his thoughts and see the depth of his craving. Her pupils dilated, her brown eyes sparkled in fiery response before she glanced away, biting her lower lip. She was as affected by his presence as he was by hers. His smile widened.

"I want you to meet me tomorrow."

"Why should I meet you, Ikem?" she asked. Her brown eyes dared him openly once again, her chin boldly uplifted. He maintained eye contact for a while, not speaking. He loved the way the gold specks in her eyes blended with the brown. He watched as they turned molten. She was so different from any other woman he knew. They all acted timidly around him, always happy to defer to him while seeking his favor. Nneka was the exact opposite. She looked upon him as if she needed nothing from him. Yet he could tell she was interested.

He took her hand in his and felt its heat burn him like an open flame. The need to pull her closer thrummed in his veins. He caressed the back of her hand softly with his thumb. He heard her breath hitch in response.

"I just want to spend some time with you, Nneka. We'll talk and afterward you can leave."

"But you know I cannot be seen with you, or anybody else, for that matter."

He tugged her closer until he could feel the warmth of her breath against his skin. Lifting her face with one hand, he traced a slow path from her cheek to her neck with the other. The pulse at the base of her neck jumped when he touched it.

"I've waited for you for the past year and find I've run out of patience. Your mourning period is complete. I can no longer wait to do what has been my heart's desire for a long time."

She let out a soft gasp. Her eyes widened even further and darted away for a brief moment. When she looked back at him they'd acquired a calm determination.

"My mourning period might be complete, but my in-laws haven't yet released me. You know the consequences if I'm caught even talking to you like this. I have no wish to incur the wrath of my in-laws."

He knew the repercussions would be dire for both of them and had taken precautions to ensure it would never get to that. "I'll take care of your in-laws when the time is right, but I've every intention of making you mine. I let another man claim you once. I'll not do so again."

"What do you mean by that?" She pulled back from him, the frown on her face deepening. Needing some room to think clearly, he let her go.

"We'll talk about it tomorrow. Meet me by the *ube* tree in the clearing at the plot of land bordering the river. I noticed you're allowed out in the evenings. If you can make it a little earlier, that would be good too. If you do not show up, I'll come to your house."

It wasn't a threat, but he needed her to know how serious he was.

Her eyes widened. She folded her arms across her chest, watching him with increased interest. "I still insist on knowing why you want me to meet with you."

Pushing off the tree, he smiled as he walked back to her. He could count on his one hand, less than one hand— the number of people who would question him as Nneka did. She was bold and brave. Staring straight at him, she had the look of one who was certain of herself. Her confidence fueled his hunger for her.

"I intend to make you my wife."

For the first time, he saw something close to trepidation flicker in her eyes. Somewhere at the back of his mind he registered her response, but paid it little heed. The pulse at the base of her neck hopped rapidly. She lifted her chin.

"What if I have no wish to be your wife? I lost one husband. I may have no wish to acquire another."

Her gaze roamed his body with obvious appreciation, her action at odds with her words. His manhood stirred again. He was glad for the looseness of his loincloth.

"I have every intention of making it your wish to be mine."

She stared at him, her eyebrow lifted in obvious bemusement. "Do you want me that much?"

"You have no idea how much."

Reaching for her, he lowered his head. He lifted her into his arms and crushed her lips with his. Her body stiffened in his arms, though she didn't attempt to push him away. Her hand rested on his shoulders. He'd wanted to wait till after they'd talked properly to do this. Now he knew he couldn't wait. At such close proximity, he was unable to resist a taste of her.

Her impassivity simply encouraged him to get a response from her. He persisted, running his tongue along the rim of her soft lips, his hand on her nape massaging gently and the other hand around her waist ensuring her suppleness was crushed against his hard body.

"Open for me, Nneka."

Letting out a sigh, she wound her arms around his neck. Her lips opened to let him into her warm moist depths. His tongue flicked hers, delving in and reveling in her sweetness. She tasted heavenly—the pureness of ripened mango fruits fresh off the tree. A groan rumbled through him. He'd waited for what seemed like forever to taste her. She was beyond anything he'd ever imagined she would be. He wanted more of her. But it would have to wait. It was neither the right time nor the right place.

When he broke the kiss, they both panted, out of breath.

"Be here tomorrow," he said before letting her go. She didn't say anything in response; just watched him. He bent down and picked up her *ite*. Without any further words, he placed it back on her head.

"Take care." She turned and walked back down the footpath, her hips swaying seductively.

He watched her go, his heart slowly getting back to its normal beat. He was a step closer to capturing his quarry.

Chapter Two

How Nneka walked home on shaky legs, she wasn't sure. The encounter with Ikem had left her floating in a strange euphoric cloud. With knots of apprehension in her stomach, her heart fluttered in excitement.

Seated on a low stool in the kitchen she shared with her in-laws, she absentmindedly peeled cocoyam for the evening meal; her mind traveled back to that afternoon's event.

One day she'd been on her way home from the stream when she felt an odd sensation on her neck as if she was being watched. It occurred for several days each time she walked past the large cashew tree by Ikem's land. On the third day she decided to investigate. She'd allowed her sense of adventure to override her otherwise grief-subdued instincts.

So she put her *ite* down by the footpath and crept through the tall grasses as silently as she could muster. She spotted Ikem by the tree, his machete sheathed in its scabbard as he picked up his satchel and walked off. She had recognized him as Obinna's good friend whom she'd always admired. Ikem had never made any overt expression of his intent in the past. Yet she'd caught him a few times watching her silently.

From that day she'd continued to pretend she didn't know he was there, silently hoping he'd speak to her. She'd been excited that he noticed her, a woman in gray, designed to blend into the background and not be noticed. In the past twelve moons, no other man had paid her any attention. Except her brother-in-law, Edozie. But then again, Edozie made her uneasy, even when her husband Ofonna was alive. She shuddered at the thought and pushed Edozie out of her mind.

However, Ikem was a different story.

He was a man accustomed to feminine attention. She'd heard things about him that well-brought-up girls should never know. He certainly could have any woman he chose; and he did, if rumors were to be believed.

So knowing he'd been watching her appealed to her baser self. From the moment he'd spoken her name, she'd come alive, all her senses honed to respond to him. His mere presence commanded attention. He occupied any space as if he owned it.

Even now, she remembered how fast her heart had battered her chest when she stood close enough to him. His eyes were the color of the sun. Looking into them, she'd felt as if she were sinking into their golden glory. They'd been the most mesmerizing thing about him, keeping her rooted to the spot, unable to get away from him if she'd wished to.

She hadn't wished it.

Then he'd kissed her. *Oh, what a kiss!* There was nothing to compare it to. No one else had kissed her with such thoroughness, such forcefulness, such passion.

The kisses from her late husband had always been too gentle and sloppy to ignite any great passions within her. She'd lived with it because Ofonna was her husband, though the marriage had been arranged between his father and her uncle.

Still, within her she'd yearned for him to be more potent, more masculine, and more fiery in their lovemaking. It had never happened. She'd resigned herself to their time of intimacy being little more than a quick fumble and Ofonna spilling his seed within her. The only real fulfillment she'd achieved had been at her own hands while she dreamed of a more masculine husband to take her and brand her with his strength.

Finally, today she'd had a taste of such a man.

Ikem had the outward appearance of the kind of lover she yearned for. He was a giant, the top of her head barely reaching his shoulders. His body had the dangerous strength of someone who worked hard; his calloused hands on her sensitive skin had been a testament to that. Each time he moved, his muscles moved with sinuous quality and grace unexpected for a man his size. Though their homeland, Umunri, was at peace with its neighbors, Ikem was a natural warrior. His features seemed molded by the gods out of fiery rocks. Tales about his physical prowess in combat were already woven into folklore by the village bard.

Thinking about him now, her heart beat fast and loud, enough to rival the pounding feet of an antelope as it raced for its life. Ikem certainly made her feel alive again simply by his presence.

He was also the kind of man instinct told her to avoid. His commanding strength should have instilled fear. His request, or rather demand, to meet with him infuriated her. She had no wish to accede to him. No wish to allow another man to control her life. No wish to allow a man to destroy her life like her mother's life was destroyed. No matter how much her body yearned to be fulfilled in a marital bed.

She'd only agreed to marry Ofonna because his personality had been the opposite of her father's. Her spouse had been a weak man. It had suited her well. She'd decided it was better to marry a weak man than to be wed to a bully. However, with her husband's passing, she could now pursue her lifelong dream of living a single, independent life with no man telling her what to do and when to do it.

Being a widow brought with it some privileges. It meant that most men avoided her. There were also some intrinsic dangers associated with the status. It left her vulnerable to those who would choose to take advantage. She had to tread carefully.

"Nneka, you're back. What took you so long?"

She looked up to find Mgbeke, her sister-in-law, standing over her, looking as belligerent as ever. She'd been so lost in her thoughts, she hadn't heard the other woman approach. The irritation in Mgbeke's voice was augmented by hands on her hips and flashing eyes.

"I didn't know there was a limit to how long I could spend at the stream." Nneka couldn't keep the sarcasm from her voice as she turned back to the cocoyam meal she was preparing in her kitchen.

"Do you not know you are a woman in mourning? Do you want to start a scandal? Moreover, you cannot be out there gallivanting when there are chores to be done in this compound."

Nneka let out a sigh and bit her tongue. It was one of the disadvantages of living in the large communal compound that she shared with her in-laws.

She'd complained about it to Ofonna when they had been newlywed. Though there were three separate huts for the different families, they all shared the same kitchen and bathroom space.

After living with her uncle's immediate family where she could have her privacy, moving to a house where everything was shared jarred her nerves. It wouldn't have been too bad if her in-laws were nice people, but they weren't. With the exception of her father-in-law, who had taken her in like she was of his blood.

Mgbeke was spiteful and bossy. Edozie was downright sinister. The way he looked at her sometimes was like he was undressing her with his eyes. It was also evident he'd been jealous of his younger brother Ofonna.

Ofonna had been the favored son and the better-looking one. She couldn't help being suspicious that Edozie had had a hand in Ofonna's death. His death had been mysterious enough, going to sleep at night and not waking the next morning. The last person to see him had been Edozie. Anyway, she couldn't go around accusing him. She didn't have any proof. If he had had a hand in Ofonna's death, she prayed the gods would punish him in their time.

When Nneka didn't reply to her taunt, Mgbeke huffed, "You better hurry up. You know it's your turn to cook dinner for everyone tonight."

Nneka looked up with a knowing smile at the woman. "Are you sure you want me to cook for your husband?"

Mgbeke blanched at Nneka's insinuation, harrumphed, and walked off, muttering angrily to herself. Nneka couldn't help smiling. The sly retort should keep the woman off her back for a little while.

When the dubious image of Edozie came into her head, she lost her smile and a sickening feeling twisted in her belly. Maybe it wasn't a good idea to tease Mgbeke. She had no intentions of making a pass at Edozie anyway.

***

The next day Nneka didn't go to the rendezvous as Ikem commanded. Instead she went to the stream first thing in the morning to avoid encountering him on the footpath that evening. Later that afternoon, she went to see her father-in-law. She'd seen him return from an outing and decided to seek an audience with him.

He sat under the palm tree. It was his favorite seating spot, especially on a hot day like today. It also provided a vantage position to see the activities going on in the courtyard.

"Our father, there is something I wish to discuss with you," she started tentatively when she'd pulled up the low table he usually ate from and placed his food on it. She stood there uneasily. She was a confident girl, but she knew she had to broach the subject softly so as not to cause offense.

"My daughter, sit down and tell me what's on your mind. I hope nothing is wrong," the old man replied as he dipped into the earthenware bowl of beans and maize casserole. It was one of his favorite meals and she'd prepared it with lots of smoked fish fillets and spices.

She pulled out a low stool from the hut and sat next to him.

"I was just wondering when I'd be released to return to my people now that I've completed my mourning. I'm currently in limbo, as I've heard nothing from you about your plan for me."

He paused from his meal briefly before looking at her. In his eyes, she could see his sorrow. Her heart went out to him *He has lost a beloved son and has grieved deeply for that loss.*

"Are you in such a hurry to rid yourself of us?"

"No. No. No. That's not what I meant, our father. I'm sorry. I did not mean to offend you." She cowered. The old man was like a father to her. More of a father than her biological father ever was. He had always been nice to her. Nice was not a trait she could use to describe her own father.

"Fear not. I understand your restlessness to move on with your life. I've only been reluctant to make a decision as I'm in no hurry to lose a daughter as well as a son. Let me think on it for a few days. I'll let you know soon."

Nneka felt remorseful. She'd been so engrossed in her own quest for freedom, she hadn't considered the impact on Ofonna's father. He'd lost his son. She was happy that he considered her a daughter, truly, and didn't want to lose her as well. She would have to be patient and think of his needs. Moreover, when she moved on, he would be left with a malevolent son and a vicious daughter-in-law. It wasn't a good thing.

When she stood to go back to her hut, he told her to stay and keep him company. She did, obliging him.

Chapter Three

When Nneka didn't show up at the agreed time and place, Ikem was neither angry nor happy. In his life, very few things amazed him. He'd learned to deal with whatever life threw at him as it came. As a young boy trying to find his way among peers who considered him less than their equal, adapting quickly to situations had become a survival method. He'd fought to be respected and had eventually gained that respect during intense training sessions. It was an area he excelled in and had no equal.

So while Nneka's behavior caught him unawares, he wasn't totally astonished. He'd simply underestimated her. Beneath the deceptive gray cloak of grief-induced demureness was an obstinate and courageous woman. He knew about her past, the tragedy that meant at the age of twelve, she'd lost not just one parent but two in the space of a few days. Unable to have any close contact with her, he'd watched her grow into a beautiful young maiden. The only interactions he'd had with her had been vicariously through Obinna, his close friend, whose family was also close to Nneka's.

As he finished up his work at the farm that day, he considered that Nneka's childish impetuousness had developed into outright fearlessness. Despite her initial show of aloofness, he'd experienced her fiery nature in their kiss. So he'd expected her to acquiesce to him. No other woman had ever disobeyed his command before. Instead of discouraging him, it fed his determination to have her. While his patience was quickly running out, he wasn't averse to teaching his fiery quarry the pleasure of submission. In disobeying him, she'd also underestimated him.

He returned home and waited for the sun to start its descent. Then he went to Nneka's hut. While he wanted her to understand he kept his word, he would not put her in danger by blatantly displaying his attention toward her.

Not yet. That time would come soon enough. Certain rules and traditions prevailed in their society. He still had to be seen to play by them for her sake. He didn't want her being punished on his account.

When he arrived at her compound he stayed hidden until activity quieted and the residents retired for the night. Then he went to her hut, knocking softly. He heard rustling inside before the door opened.

Nneka stood before him, her smooth brown skin glowing in the lamplight in her hands, her dark eyes and mouth wide open, shocked. Dressed in light nightwear, she looked ready for sleep. His gaze was drawn to the way her dress was wrapped around her body, accentuating her curves. It drew his attention to the swell of her breasts in the dimness of the light.

"W-what are you doing here?" He noticed the slight quake in her subdued voice. Its tremulous tone resonated in the pit of his stomach. His body's response was primal. To stop himself from reaching for her, he folded his arms across his chest. His body filled her doorway.

"I told you I'd come here if you didn't meet me today. I keep my word."

With a dismissive shrug, she lifted an eyebrow. The self-assured gleam back in her eyes. "Well, I never said I was going to meet you. You assumed. Your mistake."

He'd give her that. She hadn't verbally agreed to meet him. He'd assumed she'd agreed after she succumbed to his kiss. "A mistake I won't be making again." He frowned to show his displeasure.

"You shouldn't be here. Go home. Someone might see you."

She moved to close the door, but he put his foot out to stop her. "You'd better let me in then, unless you want your in-laws to know I'm here. I don't mind, either way." Flexing his fingers, he kept his arms folded. He yearned to run his hands down her smooth, pliant skin.

Her eyes held a furious glare for a while, but she opened the door wider, moving out of the way. Stooping to avoid hitting his head on the low door frame, he walked in. She shut the door behind him and placed the lamp in the wall sconce.

"You need to be quick about your visit. It's been a long day, and I need my sleep."

She remained standing near the door as he surveyed the room. It was of modest size with a long table and bench. In the corner, she stored her cooking wares. A door led off the room to what he assumed was the sleeping chamber. The air was scented with orange zest. He'd smelled it on her the other day. Realizing it was Nneka's scent, he turned to find her with her arms folded across her chest. It lifted her breasts into prominence. The twin peaks of her nipples pouted in his direction. The smoldering embers of his desire crackled to life again. His manhood swelled.

"The night is still young, Nneka. There'll be plenty of time to sleep yet."

Advancing in her direction, he smiled at her the way a hungry lion smiles at its prey. In response to his insinuation, her eyes widened in astonishment, and her small nose flared. She backed up to the wall, and he followed her there. He leaned one hand against the wall beside her head, the other touching her face. His finger traced a line down to her neck. She gasped softly. The pulse at the base of her neck beat a fast rhythm. He leaned forward and inhaled deeply, her scent of arousal overtaking the zesty fragrance.

"Why did you not come to see me when you want me so?" He cocked his eyebrow cynically.

Her mouth formed an O. "I-I don't want you," she replied in a petulant fashion, shaking her head vigorously. But her eyes told him another story. They were a warm brown and stared at his lips as if expecting him to kiss her.

Maybe I should oblige her.

He chuckled. "Liar," he whispered before he lowered his lips to her. But he didn't claim her lips immediately. Instead he feathered her face and neck with kisses, alternating between nipping and licking her sweet-salty skin. Her breathing increased rapidly. When he looked up, he noticed that her eyes were closed. He licked the pulse at her neck before he trailed his lips back up and hovered above her lips. She opened her eyes and moaned softly.

"Say it, Nneka. You want me to kiss you."

"Never!" Her voice, as well as her body, trembled as she spoke.

"Why do you have a tough time admitting what you want? Your eyes and body betray you easily." He laughed as he pushed his thigh between her legs, parting them. He felt the heat and dampness of her hooded pearl against his bare skin.

"You are such a boastful man. Do you think every woman in this land clamors for your attention? I have no wish for you or any other man." Nneka said, her voice sounding breathless.

How could she admit that the mere presence of this man caused her body to behave outrageously? That all he had to do was look at her, and her pulse rate increased. That each time he touched her, he branded her skin like a torch. Still, she fought that feeling because she didn't want to acquiesce to another man. She didn't want to get married again. Not so soon after Ofonna. It was what Ikem wanted, and what she wasn't ready for. Another man in charge of her life. Telling her what to do.

No!

"The women come to me because they are guaranteed to receive pleasure. You simply tell me you want the same, and I'll happily oblige you."

She stiffened at his mocking words. How she wanted to wipe the smirk off his face. When his teeth grazed her earlobe, sending waves of heat straight to her core, her body melted. She could feel her wetness seeping through her nightdress down her thighs. Her tight restraint was gradually being worn down. He continued his assault on her earlobe, the pain-pleasure bouncing though her body with need until she could no longer control her body's tremors.

"On the other hand, I have no problem telling you what I'd like to do to this delightful body of yours." As he spoke, he slid his hand down her neck in a slow, lazy motion as if he had all the time in the world. Her skin came alive. As much as she hated to admit her lack of restraint for him, her body leaned into his touch.

He caressed her breasts gently through her clothes, holding them delicately like they were prized possessions.

"I intend to suckle your ripe breasts until you beg me for more," he whispered softly against her ear, his voice coated with a husky tinge. "I'll touch and taste every part of your body till I stamp my brand on you. You'll crave no other man but me."

She held her breath in anticipation as his hand traveled down her body, stopping just above the apex between her legs.

"And when I get to your honey pot, I'll dip my tongue as well as my fingers in there and drive you crazy until you scream for me to take you any which way I choose. Shall I show you?"

"No," she protested, but it came out as a needy whimper. Her body was already wound tight, aching for him to do all he'd promised.

"You're already hot and dripping wet, and I've barely touched you." He shifted his thigh, rubbing her already throbbing nub. She rode him involuntarily, seeking some relief. Moving his thigh out, he pushed off the wall. She moaned in protest at the loss of his touch. He laughed softly and went down on his knees.

"I can smell your sweet essence. Stop protesting, and let me show you what you've been denying yourself." His voice had an entrancing quality, soft and filled with desire. When he looked up at her, his golden gaze was heated and filled with intoxicating promise.

What harm could his touch do, except fulfill my deep-seated fantasy? It is just one night, not a lifelong betrothal.

She couldn't afford to give up the independence she craved much more than the gratifying touch of a man. She could succumb for tonight. Experience what it felt like to be satisfied by a man for once. Ikem's touch promised a bountiful reward.

Gasping, she nodded, unsure she could use her voice as her body coiled with lust. She watched him with trembling anticipation as he lifted her loose nightdress, bunching it at her waist with one hand. With the other, he parted her hooded flesh and smiled before looking back up at her face.

Then he leaned into her and licked her, swirling his tongue around her.

Oh gods!

"Sweet and beautiful."

Panting hard, she trembled as sensation thrilled through her body. His tongue on her flesh was a pure wicked delight. She'd heard about such an act. Her friend had whispered conspiratorially about how her husband loved to eat her up. But she'd never experienced it.

His tongue tunneled into her, then came out tracing every inch of her sensitive flesh. He nipped, sucked, lapped, and nibbled until she trembled and her knees gave way. She gripped his shoulders, and in the process, let go of her already loose wrap, which went falling to the floor.

Ikem stood up. In one movement, he scooped her up and laid her on the long table.

"Place your hands on the edge and keep them there," he instructed as he pulled up a stool and sat between her legs dangling off the edge of the table.

Excited, she did as he directed, unsure of his intention. When his fingers slid into her wet heat and his mouth descended on her flesh once more, all sane thought ran away from her.

She was simply aware of the pure rippling sensations that built within her in tidal waves. As she came close to her zenith, he would withdraw, only to start building her up again. He repeated this ritual until she was mindless and whimpering for him to give her some release. In all of her life, never had she been this stupefied with lust.

"Remember, all you have to do is tell me what you want and it's yours," he murmured against her flesh, his voice vibrating through her. She lifted her hips, trying to get more of his tongue into her core, but it didn't help. She needed release now or she would surely die from the pent-up tension. She no longer cared what he did to her as long as he gave her some relief.

"I want—I want release. Please."

His large fingers resumed their motion within her. There must have been three of them, for they filled her as they pumped into her. As he continued, the sensation built to such an extent that when he blew against her and growled, "Let go," she exploded into pieces in a fever of ecstasy. The intensity put her in a daze. When she opened her eyes she was no longer on the table but in Ikem's arms. He took her into her sleeping chamber, placing her on the pallet.

He kissed her lips briefly. She tasted her own essence on his tongue. "Next time I'll be inside you and the pleasure will be so much more intense. Sleep well, Nneka."

She didn't have time to respond because he turned and walked out. Still in a daze, her legs barely keeping her up, she stood, walked to the door, and hooked the latch. She managed to get back to her bedchamber before collapsing back on her pallet. When sleep claimed her, the only image in her mind was of Ikem kneeling before her, devouring her.

Chapter Four

The next few days passed in a haze of frustration and anticipation. Nneka woke the morning after Ikem was in her hut with a smile permanently on her face. Not even the bossiness of her sister-in-law could spoil her mood. As she did her chores around the house, the images and sensations from the previous night remained in her mind.

She'd had her first taste of ecstasy. Nothing in the past had prepared her for the intensity. Any relief she'd had from her hands paled in comparison.

It left her with a deep craving to be joined with Ikem. She was now certain it would be nothing like the awkward fumbling she'd been accustomed to with her late husband. Ikem's touches had been masterful and purposeful. He was a man sure of his abilities and not afraid to use them.

She wanted him.

Yes, but as a man whose company she could enjoy, not as a potential husband. Her encounter with him still hadn't convinced her to give up her quest for independence. She'd already planned out what she would do once her father-in-law released her. She didn't need another husband in her life, and she would resist it for as long as possible.

That evening she went to the stream at her usual time, but she didn't see Ikem by the cashew tree. She assumed he would show up at her hut later. So she waited up. But he didn't show that night. When she eventually slept, her dreams were of him, looming over her, touching her. She woke early before dawn, hot and slick with sweat. Her body wound so tight, even touching herself brought her no relief.

She wanted Ikem deep between her legs, pleasuring her like he'd promised. Throughout the day, a restless energy flowed through her. The elation was still there, but her body was coiled tight with need and anticipation. She hoped he would come to her that night and complete what he'd started.

The irony was that when her husband was still alive, she'd spent each night wishing he'd be more passionate and spark a desire in her. After he passed away, she accepted she was never going to get that wish. Now that she'd prepared herself for a life without a man in it, Ikem had awakened those desires within her.

Later that night, when she heard footsteps approaching her door, she was already trembling with anticipation to see Ikem again. Even when the knock on the door sounded heavier—unlike during Ikem's visit—she paid it no heed. Taking deep breaths to calm herself, she walked to the door and opened it.

Disappointed, her heart sank into her belly. It was not Ikem blocking her doorway. It was Edozie.

"What are you doing here?" She couldn't hide the annoyance in her voice.

"Is that any way to address your brother-in-law and soon-to-be husband," he replied as he pushed past her and walked into her hut. He walked over to the long bench and sat down.

Nneka's annoyance grew along with her increasing heartbeat. Bile rose in her throat.

Is that what my father-in-law has in store for me? For me to marry this oaf of a man? I cannot allow it.

Wasn't it bad enough that Ikem had gotten her so wound up, yearning for his touch? Now she had to put up with the vile Edozie, whom she couldn't stand. How dare he claim he would be her husband soon? She would rather pluck out her own eyes than be married to him.

While she wanted to yell and tell Edozie to get out of her hut, she bit her tongue and took a deep breath before responding. It would be to her disadvantage to rile him at this stage, no matter how much he irritated her.

"Edozie, I'm not out of my mourning clothes yet and you talk about becoming my husband. Do you have a wish to annoy Ofonna's spirit or worse, the gods?"

She stood close to the door with her eyes lowered when she wanted to glare at him. But she had to bide her time. Her future was at stake here. Diplomacy was the tactic of the day.

He grunted before patting the space on the bench next to him. "A dead man can do me no harm. Come and sit next to me." He leered at her. His gaze stripped her naked. His tongue darted out of his mouth, licking his lips, reminding her of a lizard.

The thought of Edozie touching her body caused an itching sensation, like ants crawling on her skin. She wrapped her dress more tightly around her chest.

She shook her head. "Ofonna's ghost may not frighten you, but I wish to sleep peacefully at night. Our father has not decided my fate yet. When he does, I'm sure you'll be one of the first to know. Until then, I cannot allow you in here. Moreover, I don't want Mgbeke at my throat for seducing her husband."

She gave him a demure smile. Though she wasn't agreeing with him, she knew that mentioning his wife's name would put him on the defensive. It was all a game and she'd learned to play it well in her years of marriage.

He laughed. "You know better than to worry about Mgbeke. I'll take care of her. She has to go along with whatever I want. When I take you as my wife, as I'm entitled to, she cannot object."

She bit her tongue.

And you want me to marry you? A man who has no care for anyone but himself? A man who would use any means necessary, including force, to get what he wants?

It isn't in my destiny.

He stood up and walked toward her. She stood her ground. She couldn't let him see any fear in her. He would only take advantage. He stood so close that his warm breath blew against her face and she could hear his heavy breathing. The sick feeling returned to her stomach. His hand moved over her arm. She had to stop herself from jerking away.

"I have waited this long to have you. A few more days will make no difference. Make no mistake. I'll have you in my bed, and you will discover that I'm more of a man than Ofonna ever was."

He turned and walked out of her hut. Nneka's body trembled as she suppressed the scream building up inside her. Instead, she walked to the table and gripped it so hard her nails broke.

Enough was enough. She needed her freedom now more than ever. There was only one person she trusted enough to help her out of her problem. She would seek him out in the morning.

***

Nneka arrived at Obinna's farm the next day. Tentatively, she approached where he stood directing his team of five male laborers. They were harvesting tubers of yams, a task that needed to be completed before the New Yam festival in a few weeks.

She knew she was taking a risk coming out here in the middle of the day. She was still in mourning clothes and speculation was bound to be rife if people saw her with Obinna. But she was desperate. She had to seek his help now.

The bustle calmed, and the workers stopped their tasks as she approached. Obinna turned around. His eyes narrowed in a squint. She couldn't be sure if it was the effect of the noonday sun or her presence.

"You can take your break now," he told his workers before walking over to her. "Nneka, is everything well?" His frown deepened, creasing his normally handsome face. She realized he was concerned for her.

"I urgently need to talk to you." She spoke as calmly as she could to settle his disquiet.

"Couldn't it wait? Did you have to come here?"

"I had no other choice. Please, I need your help."

"Okay, come with me." He pointed to a clearing shaded by some trees and led her to it. He indicated a felled tree trunk. "Please sit down and tell me what's bothering you."

When she was seated, he sat down next to her.

"Obinna, you have known me for most of my life. You know my past—how it was living with a brutal man like my father, being a child and watching my mother die at his hands, knowing he was banished from our lands forever, and that I'd never see him again. I have carried that stigma all my life."

She looked up at him, determined not to cry, not to let her past overwhelm her. She'd never discussed her past with anyone, not even her late husband. Tragedies like that were rarely discussed, anyway, for fear of bringing a curse on the person talking about them. She'd carried on with her life. However, her father's cruelty shaded her life decisions—her choice of Ofonna as a husband and now her choice to live as an independent woman.

Obinna's expression remained sober. He took her hand in his. "Yes, I know of your past and you've coped incredibly well, turning into a beautiful young woman."

She nodded, her smile tinged with sadness. "You also know that when my uncle chose Ofonna as my suitor, I accepted him because he was not a violent man. In fact, he was the opposite of the kind of man my father was. He was a gentle man."

You mean insipid and boring, don't you?

She ignored the taunting voice in her head and carried on. "I also agreed even though we were close friends and I'd thought you would propose to me. But your eyes were on Adaku."

Darkness crossed his eyes and his lips tightened at the corners. "Yes, but what has it got to do with your problem now?" he asked impatiently.

"I say this because now Ofonna is dead, and my mourning period is completed. I await my father-in-law to grant my release. But I have since found out that Edozie wants to take me as his wife. I can tell you now that I'd rather die than let that happen. That man is revolting, and I personally think he had a hand in Ofonna's death. Though I cannot prove it."

Obinna frowned again. "That may be so, but without proof nothing can be done about it." He lifted his water gourd to his lips, taking a sip.

"I know, which is why I need your help. I cannot marry Edozie. The truth is, I'd rather have my freedom. I have been saving and have enough to start a trade. I want to be independent of any man. But I know my uncle would never allow that. So I want to ask you to marry me."

"What?" Obinna spat out the water in his mouth and coughed.

"I know how it sounds, but hear me out. I know you don't want a second wife. Neither will I be one in the real sense. It will be purely a pretend marriage. I'll live under your protection so no other man seeks my hand, but I'll live independently. You will not take me to your bed, and so I pose no threat to Adaku."

"You've got this all worked out." Obinna's laughter reverberated through the clearing. Some of his workmen who sat a distance away in a group turned to look at them before continuing with their lunch break. "So you will be my wife and yet not in my bed. What's in it for me?"

He carried on laughing and the tension in her body eased. She started laughing too. She knew it sounded ridiculous for her to propose to a man. But these were desperate times. She also knew Obinna well enough to know that he could understand her position. It was the reason she was asking him something she couldn't ask any other man.

Not even Ikem? What do you think he will do when he finds out you've asked his friend to marry you?

The taunting voice was back in her head. She stopped laughing and physically shook her head to push back the voice asking questions she dared not answer right now.

"Obinna, please, you have to help me. I really don't know what else to do here."

He stopped laughing and turned to her again, speaking quietly. "If you have no wish to marry Edozie, why not marry Ikem? I know he has proposed to you personally."

Her face heated up in embarrassment. How much had Ikem told Obinna? From the way Obinna was looking at her, she couldn't tell how much he knew about her liaison with Ikem.

"Ikem is just another man like my father. He—he is so powerful and thinks he can dominate and control everything around him. I cannot marry such a man."

Yet Ikem's strength is his appeal to you.

Mentally shaking her head again, she clenched her hands together, her blunt nails digging into her skin. She was having trouble keeping her inner voice quiet. She'd never known it to be this outspoken before. She couldn't afford to let the words get to her. She needed to focus on her goal. Freedom from men's dominance.

"Ikem is nothing like your father. Your father was cruel and had no regard for anyone but himself. Your father abused his strength against the weak. Ikem is never cruel. He is a man in control of himself and has never abused his power. While he is fierce in battle, he is never violent toward an innocent. You're not being fair to him by making him out to be like your father."

Guilt coursed through her body. She knew she was being harsh by comparing Ikem to her father. However, she really didn't want to have a man controlling her life, regardless of how he made her feel. She was simply fortifying her defenses against Ikem. Whether she liked to admit it or not, he affected her deeply. Could she really trust that he wouldn't turn out to be like her father?

"I'm sorry, but I don't want to marry Ikem. Please, Obinna, help me. You are the only one who can help me now. Please."

He sighed calmly. "All right. I'll think about it. Do you know when your father-in-law will decide?"

"He said soon, but I don't know when."

"It would have to be before the New Yam festival coming up in a few weeks. I'll let you know what I decide. But be certain, I'll not leave you to Edozie. I'd not wish him on my enemy." He grinned at her. "Go home before tongues start wagging."

Relieved, she hugged him briefly. "Thank you. Please give my regards to Adaku."

Feeling slightly elated, Nneka stood up and walked home. Her mission had been accomplished. Obinna would not leave her to Edozie's mercy.

Chapter Five

When Ikem arrived at Nneka's hut that night, his fury was under control. At least he thought it was until he found himself continuously knocking on the wooden door frame when she didn't respond immediately. Earlier that evening, his friend Obinna had come to see him and told him about Nneka's outrageous request. To say he'd been overtaken by rage would be an understatement. Not only had she recklessly defied several societal rules by going to see Obinna in broad daylight, she'd also shown her contempt for Ikem by asking his best friend to marry her. She had put herself in danger, at the very least, of speculation, and at the very worst, of punishment.

Ha!

At first he'd laughed when Obinna had told him, thinking his friend was making a joke. Who ever heard of a woman proposing to a man? It was never done. However, Obinna had confirmed that it wasn't a joke.

Nneka had really asked him to marry her!

He'd nearly kicked Obinna out of his house in anger at that point. His friend had explained to him about Edozie's threat and Nneka's desperation. He'd then understood her need to be protected. It didn't stop the sickening sensation he felt in his stomach or the feeling that she'd ripped his heart out.

Why didn't she come to me? Does she really regard me with such disdain? Does she think I'm not good enough for her? Does she deem me a bastard as everyone else does?

The questions had battered his mind all evening, nearly driving him insane. Even as he stood at her door now, his knocks on the door even more insistent, he still didn't have sensible answers. He needed to see her to get the response he needed. Her eyes would tell him the bare truth, even if her lips didn't.

The door swung open. "I thought I told you—" Nneka stopped talking when she saw him standing there. "Ikem!"

Radiant. She looked even more so tonight. Her dark skin a tempting contrast to the cream-colored night attire she had on. In the pale light, she looked wraithlike, a river goddess who had come to tantalize and lure him to danger. His heartbeat became erratic, pounding against his ribcage as he held his breath.

When had he ceded control of his person to this siren...this tigress of a woman?

He should be angry for her rebellious actions earlier today. As he stood there staring into her stunning, unembellished face, his craving for her overtook all other emotions. His blood bubbled with his need to touch her supple smoothness, taste her honeyed saltiness, and inhale her intoxicating zest.

For sure, he would do all those things in good time. But first he had to wrest some of his control back. He had to tame his tigress.

By the gods, she is mine...mine alone.

Mentally shaking his head, he let out the breath he was holding and folded his arms across his chest. "Who were you expecting?" He was surprised his voice sounded unruffled, a sensation he was struggling to maintain.

"Oh, nobody." Her voice sounded breathless as she replied quickly, her gaze darting downward.

Tilting his head and cocking his eyebrow, he studied her composure. The pulse on her neck jumped and her skin tone darkened. "I've told you to stop lying to me. I can see through you easily."

Her gaze flashed up to meet his. Her emotions raced across their dark depths—surprise, guilt, determination. There was no scorn in her eyes. A sensation close to relief washed over him as his heart raced again. She might not hold him in high esteem—her actions had proven that. But she wasn't disdainful of him either. He hadn't realized how important it was to him until now. Never before had his lineage mattered to him. He'd learned to live with the derision in people's eyes. Now he knew it would have crushed him to see that in her eyes too. Her opinion of him mattered. She mattered to him. She'd crept under his skin and become a source of strength to him.

She remained silent, as if immobilized by his presence.

"Are you going to let me in?"

"Come in."

He saw her shoulders lift in a resigned shrug before she moved out of the doorway. It was as if she knew what was coming and had accepted there would be a consequence for her actions.

He strode into her hut, took a pace away from her, and stood still, not turning to face her. To soothe his erratic heartbeat, he inhaled gulps of air. The scent of orange blossoms assaulted his nostrils, inflaming his already fizzing blood. A groan rumbled in his belly. He gritted his teeth to stop himself from letting it out.

Turning around, he faced her. Her gaze still avoided his. Instead she focused at a spot just off his right shoulder.

What else was she guilty of aside from proposing to my friend in broad daylight?

"I'll ask you again. Who were you expecting?" He allowed the steel back into his voice.

Flinching, she still refused to look at him. "I wasn't expecting anyone. It's just that..."

She frowned, biting her lower lip. Wishing he was the one biting into its juicy plumpness, his felt his manhood pulse in response.

"Just that what?" he persisted, his voice acquiring the rumble of a million grains of sand crashing against a boulder in a sandstorm.

"It's just that Edozie was here the other night and I told him not to come back. I thought you were him at the door."

The anger in his blood flared again. The thought that her brother-in-law had been in her hut grated on his nerves. It reminded him of the precarious nature of their relationship. The moment she was released from her marital bonds to Ofonna's family, she'd be seen as fair game to any man who chose to lay claim to her. He needed to act fast to forestall any potential suitors, including Edozie. If he got his hands on Edozie, he would break the man's neck for daring to threaten her.

"I've only been gone for two nights, Nneka. Have you taken to entertaining other men in my absence?"

"Certainly not!" she replied, her gaze finally connecting with his. It flashed with indignation. "Moreover, it's none of your business anyway. You're not my husband."

She remained standing by the door, just like the other night, as if she expected him to leave soon. He smiled inwardly. *With her obvious guilt, she still thought she could manipulate the situation. She was in for a shock.* In the dim lamplight, her dark skin had the luster of burnished wood. The effect of the flickering light on her delicate neck called him to run his tongue along its smoothness. Even in her indignation, she was stunning.

Ikem had been away from their clan the past two days on a mission for the king. Knowing he would come back to her had quickened his pace and fed his need to return expediently. He'd come home to claim her, to make her his. Finally. Tonight.

"Yes, I'm well aware of that fact, Nneka." He took a step toward her. He could no longer keep his distance. He needed to connect with her. He had to touch her. "I'll soon rectify it." He took another step. "What else have you been up to today?"

"Nothing," she answered very quickly, her eyes darting away just as quickly.

"What did I just say about telling lies to me? You'd better start telling me the truth otherwise your punishment will be even more severe."

At his words, he saw a flicker of fear in her brown eyes. Still, her chin rose in a challenge. "You don't control my life, and I'm not a child you can punish at whim."

"You had your chance."

Crossing the space between them, he picked her up around the waist, slinging her over his shoulder.

She yelped. "What are you doing? Set me down right now."

Her clenched fists bounced off his back as she pounded him in protest. He ignored her and walked to the long bench. He sat on it, placing her facing downward across his lap. She wriggled and tried to get up. He held her down with one hand. The other caressed her bottom cheeks through her nightdress. They were warm and soft, pointing upward, enticing him to explore their roundness.

"Are you going to answer my question or should I carry on?"

"You wouldn't dare." Her voice sounded more breathy than indignant. He raised his hand and brought it down on her bum. A loud smack echoed throughout the hut.

She yelped, squirming on his lap. "Okay. I'll tell you."

Lifting her nightdress, he licked the spot on her bum where he'd spanked. Her soft gasp sent lightning through him. His erection swelled, jerking upward against her belly.

"Let's hear it." His voice sounded gruff to his ears.

He caressed her bottom and dipped his finger into her core. She was wet and hot. His tigress liked being spanked. He suppressed a grin.

"I—I went to see Obinna earlier today."

Knowing how breathless she sounded, Nneka bit back the soft moan bubbling in her throat as Ikem's cool hand caressed her hot bottom. She couldn't believe her body's response to his spanking. She should be infuriated, afraid, and disgusted at him. She should feel degraded. She'd promised she'd never let a man raise his hands to her. Instead, here she was, spread across his lap, actually aroused.

Aroused!

The sting of his hand had vibrated through her, melting her body. Her core pulsed with need, her juices threatened to overflow down her thighs.

What kind of person am I?

When Ikem had walked into her hut looking menacingly cool, a sliver of fear had traveled down her spine. He hadn't looked too pleased with her. At that moment, she'd known he knew about her visit to Obinna. She'd gotten annoyed and cursed Obinna silently for betraying her confidence—a typical male behavior of not considering the woman's interest.

"Yes, continue." Ikem dipped his finger into her wet heat again. Her inner walls contracted around it. The moan she'd been suppressing escaped. Her mind melted along with her body.

He withdrew his finger but his hand continued its luxurious caress of her bottom. "I'm waiting." There was a brisk tinge to his husky tone.

She felt his hand leave her body and expected another sting soon. A thrill of anticipation coursed through her. What was wrong with her? She was about to be spanked again and she was *excited*?

"I went to ask for his help."

"What kind of help could Obinna provide that I couldn't?" His voice was stern and demanding.

Annoyed at his autocratic tone, she pushed up and turned her head to look at him. He still held her down. "Look, Obinna is my friend and..." She did not wish to complete her statement. She didn't even know how to classify their relationship.

"And I'm not?" His eyebrow rose as he mocked her. "Do you allow every man who is not your friend to put you across his lap and touch you the way I am right now?"

"Of course not. You took me forcibly and put me across your lap. I didn't ask you to." She bristled at his taunting tone.

"So why aren't you shouting out for someone to save you from me? Perhaps you want Edozie to come and rescue you," he spoke evenly.

His words were like cold water on her fiery anger. She lost the impetus to argue with him. Questions bombarded her mind.

Why hadn't she called out for help? Why was she allowing this man such power over her body? Instead of being repulsed, why did she yearn for his touch? Why did she long to hear his commanding voice tell her what to do?

"I don't know," she whispered softly at last.

"Perhaps it's because you recognize that I'm more than a friend to you." She lifted her head to protest, but he continued, "Even if you won't admit it."

She chose to remain silent, not willing to accept his words openly. She didn't want to give him more power over her than he already possessed. He was bound to abuse it at some point, even if not now. He was a man like all others. He would disappoint her eventually.

"So what was the help you asked of Obinna?"

She sighed in resignation, her body going limp. Did he have to persist in hearing her say it when he already knew the answer?

Whack! She yelped again, jolted out of her reverie. "I asked him to marry me," she hissed, her breath caught in her throat, as her backside stung.

"Do you want to marry Obinna?" His voice was low and tense. She had to strain to catch the tail end of his words.

"No! Marrying Obinna was never my intention. Being an independent woman is what I want most of all."

"So you only asked him to marry you because you thought you had no other choice?"

"Yes." She was relieved that he seemed to understand her motives. She hoped he didn't take it as a personal affront.

"Do you realize the awkward position you placed Obinna in by going to him when you knew we have been lifelong friends? Have you forgotten that he looks on you as his younger sibling?"

Really? What have I done? Guilt and embarrassment rose in her mind, playing havoc with her sensibilities. Obinna was the one constant friend she'd had all her life. To have his opinion of her diminish because of her actions appalled her. Her quest for freedom had blinded her. She'd already annoyed Ikem; now it seemed she'd alienated Obinna as well.

The gods forgive me!

She let her head fall dejectedly, her sense of shame overtaking her. "I'm sorry."

"You should be. If Obinna wasn't a man I knew well and respected, I'd have taken his head off with a machete when he told me what you'd said."

Gasping, her head jerked upward as she considered his words.

Does he really feel that strongly about me? Still, why should I take all the blame?

"Well, it was your fault. If you hadn't left me hanging and disappeared for two nights, I wouldn't have felt pushed to seek out Obinna." She turned to glare at Ikem. He looked nonplussed. A smile curled her lips. She turned away. *That should teach him.*

"It would seem you still haven't learned anything." She felt his hand caress her buttocks. Whack. Her body jerked in response. She hadn't been expecting it. "These lovely buttocks of yours that were designed to drive a man crazy are mine." Whack. "Do you agree?"

"Yes!" she whispered hoarsely.

"No other man is allowed to touch them." Whack. "Do you agree?"

"Yes!" She squirmed. Her overheated core melted as her body vibrated.

"The same goes for the rest of you. From the hair on your head to the nails on your toes. They all belong to me." Whack. "Agreed?"

"Yes!" She held her breath in anticipation of each sting and rush of cool air on her bottom.

"I, and I alone, am responsible for providing for your needs both in bed and out of it." Whack. "Agreed?"

Her face heated at the implication that Obinna would have bedded her if he'd wed her. "Yes. I'm really sorry. I'll apologize to Obinna."

"You are forgiven. But you'd best leave him alone for the near future. He has his hands full with his own matters."

He lifted her up, carried her into the bedchamber and placed her on the bed face down. Her buttocks felt so sore she thought she'd probably have difficulty sitting down for a while. Gently he caressed her sore area with his tongue. The sensation of his cool tongue soothed her stung flesh. A soft moan escaped her lips.

"Stay there." His voice was husky as he stepped away. She turned to see him walk into the main room and come back with his satchel. From it he withdrew a small earthenware jar and removed the cover. He knelt beside her. Dipping his fingers into it, he rubbed the oil on her sensitized skin. When she inhaled the fragrance, she realized it was coconut oil.

Slowly he worked the oil into her skin. Starting from her legs, he massaged her body working upward. It was almost unbelievable that a man as large as Ikem could be so gentle, his touch so relaxing she felt like she was floating in a cloud. Especially since only a few moments ago, she'd been on the receiving end of his stinging palm. However, her whole body bore witness to the firm strokes of his hands gently kneading her muscles.

The effect of his fingers on her body transformed from soothing to arousing as his hands moved up her back. She closed her eyes, relishing the sensation that slowly built up within her body. His strokes were masterful. He knew how to handle her body. Even as she tried to regulate her breathing, it increased along with her heart rate. Her fingers clutched the bedclothes as his hands moved back down her body.

He replaced his fingers with his lips. They feathered kisses all over her back, setting her body off with tingles. Sensations flashed through her core weeping with overflowing juices. As if he sensed it, his fingers breached her lower lips, dipping in and out as his other hand played with her nub.

"You are so warm, so slippery."

He withdrew his fingers. She whimpered in protest at the loss of his touch. Looking up, she saw him kneeling by the bed. He parted her legs and delved in with his mouth. His tongue stroked her in a long sweep before tunneling into her wet folds. Mindless sensations overtook her body. She writhed, unable to control her body's response as he took her higher and higher toward her peak. As she coasted the wave, he pulled back.

"Please," she whimpered. She didn't mind begging for release. If she didn't crest soon, she didn't know what she'd do. His effect on her was strong, stimulating and addictive. She'd missed it the last two nights. She needed it now.

"Please what?" He stood up and flipped her over so she lay on her back.

"Please...let me have my release." She licked her lips as she watched him, her hunger for him clouding her eyes.

"Not until I'm deep inside you."

He took off his clothes a piece at a time. She stared at his body in awe. She already knew he was a powerfully built man. His well-toned upper torso was always in view, wide shoulders and chest that tapered at the waist. His chest, back, and right arm had markings that identified him as a Clan Warrior. His muscles rippled with each movement like the undulating flow of a river. He had strong leg muscles and she quivered when she remembered the firmness of his thighs against her body. There was a long scar running down the side of one thigh. She wondered how he'd received it.

With all his clothing on the floor, he stood bare before her, his manhood jutting magnificently upward. Excitement coursed through her. She couldn't believe that this man wanted to claim her. Young maidens and married women alike fought for his attention. She was a widow, seen by most as a cast-off. Yet he was here, looming over her. Tremors traveled through her as he knelt between her legs.

Leaning over her, his lips swooped down on hers, reigniting the shameless desire within her. His tongue invaded her mouth. She tasted her tangy sweetness on his lips. His earthy spiciness assaulted her nostrils with each breath she struggled to take. Her body keened with inflamed feelings. He roamed her body with his hands, tweaking and rubbing her breasts, which grew heavier, and nipples that got tighter. They moved lower to caress her stomach and waist. Overcome by rippling sensations, she couldn't tell where she ended and where Ikem began. When he lifted his head, she was gasping for breath.

"I want you inside me. Please."

She looked into his eyes, pleading. The emotion she saw in their golden depths knocked out her breath. In that moment, his soul was laid bare to her. This wasn't just a nonchalant affair to him. He was serious about claiming her permanently. A faint warning went off in her mind. She should be concerned. She didn't want permanent. She should stop this now. But her mind was already a desire-filled fog. The warning died before she could take action. All she wanted now was fulfillment, in Ikem's arms.

"As you wish."

The huskiness in his voice wrapped around her already heated body. The blunt head of his manhood nudged at her moist entrance. With one push he filled her till he could go no farther. Her pulsating core clenched around him. She couldn't hold herself back any longer. Overwhelmed by feverish heat, she shouted his name and shattered into a thousand pieces. He muffled it by kissing her again.

When he lifted his head, he had a boyish grin on his face. "Shout like that again and we'll certainly have an audience." His teasing words reminded her that they were making love in her hut, surrounded by other huts with her in-laws in them.

Still, instead of being frightened and stopping their act, she got more excited by its illicit nature and encouraged him. As he withdrew slowly and drove into her, she couldn't help the soft moans that escaped her lips. He continued the excruciatingly slow pace for a while, building her up until she started panting for release again.

Moving her legs around his waist, she held on to his shoulders and tried to increase the pace. But he gripped her hips and continued his slow motion. She couldn't even begin to compare Ikem with her late husband. Ikem's lovemaking was set apart. When he said that women were guaranteed to receive pleasure from him, he did not tell a lie. Every touch, every movement of his body against hers drove her to the peak of her pleasure.

Soon he was setting a fast tempo, pounding into her. The sound of their joining bodies resounding in the small room. Having learned the new rhythm, she held on to him and kept up with his pace, enjoying every smack of his body against hers. She felt the heat of her release rising on her body. His lips melded with hers, his tongue matching his body's actions. He moved his hand between them and touched her hooded flesh and she exploded, screaming his name into his mouth.

After several more strokes, he let out a groan and spilled his seed inside her. Collapsing on top, he rolled to the side, pulling her with him. He held her close. She placed her head on his chest. She could hear the disjointed pounding of his heart.

"I'll commence the negotiations for our betrothal tomorrow." His voice was low and deep, and she detected some emotion in there too.

When she lifted her head to look at him, his eyes still shone with intensity, but there was tenderness there too.

"There are plenty of beautiful untouched young maidens who would be more amenable to you. Why do you want me? I'm a widow and not that beautiful."

He shrugged. "A hundred young maidens will never equal you. You are the most beautiful woman I know, and I want no other." His words warmed her heart. His fingers caressed her face. "Moreover, your rebelliousness is part of your appeal." He winked at her.

Feigning anger, she frowned and swatted his chest. "Are you saying that I'm headstrong?"

"That, among other more appealing qualities." His laughter reverberated through her. She suppressed a smile.

"Oh well, if you're going to laugh at me, maybe I should find myself another husband who will be more malleable."

"You will never be happy with him." He pushed her back on the bed and pinned her with his body. "Moreover, I may just kill the man first."

He kissed her until she was out of breath. "No other man will ever make you feel this way."

She hadn't realized he was fully aroused until he pushed into her again. He stayed inside her rocking while he sucked on her breasts, alternating from one to the other, nipping and lapping. His manhood stroked her womb walls, stretching and filling her. She tried to touch him, but he held her hands together with one hand above her head. With the other hand he teased her already swollen flesh, making her crazy with sensation. She writhed beneath him, her body arching toward him with each stroke. She wanted more and he gave her more. The tighter her body coiled, the more her senses heightened. Her body blazed with feverish heat. She wasn't sure she could take much more without coming apart. He increased the pace. His features got more intense. She could see his eyes getting darker. His jaw clenched as he controlled his own release. He drove into her a few more times, and then pinched her nub. She came apart, her body jerking upward with the force of the release. He rocked into her once more, then groaned out her name before falling back on the bed.

"You are mine," he whispered huskily against her face before she drifted off to sleep.

Chapter Six

Nneka woke up and stretched languorously. A kind of delicious heaviness draped her body, making her want to stay in bed longer. The gray light of early dawn filtered in through the small, shuttered window. She turned to her side and caught an earthy masculine scent—Ikem's scent. Sighing, she inhaled deeply, wishing he was still there. It hit her then. It wasn't enough for her to fall asleep in his arms. She wanted to wake with him next to her too. What was she going to do about him?

He'd visited her hut every night for the past week—arriving when everyone else was settled in their huts and departing in the early hours of the morning. In the first few days she'd been worried that someone would discover their liaison, but as the days had gone on she'd come to look forward to his visits and their time together. She'd gradually grown a fondness for him as they discovered much about each other.

Contrary to her initial fear about the kind of man he was, she'd come to discover the man beneath the tough, fearsome exterior was tender, passionate, and veracious. He cared deeply about and took care of all her needs both in bed and out of it.

Last night, she'd tentatively raised the topic of her wish to weave and sell raffia baskets. When Ofonna was alive, he hadn't been happy and had complained that it appeared he couldn't provide for her. Part of the reason she wanted to be self-reliant was so she wouldn't have to seek permission from a man to use her talent.

Ikem appeared so stereotypically masculine, she'd worried that he wanted a lifemate whose main purpose was to attend to his needs only. So his response of, "If it's truly your heart's desire, then do it. But make sure it doesn't interfere with fulfilling your responsibilities as my wife," had caught her off guard. She'd leaped at him with utter elation. His laughter had rumbled through her as she'd proceeded to kiss him and show her gratitude in the most pleasurable way she could think of at the time.

Letting out a sigh, she recalled their incredibly fiery lovemaking last night. Her attempt to return some of the delights he'd shown her had been well-received, going by his unrestrained explosive reaction.

She got out of bed and dressed, her lethargic legs slowly coming to life. Their long nights together were finally taking their toll on her body.

When she walked outside, ready to start her morning chores, she discovered a pile of firewood stacked in front of her hut. Puzzled, she stood there staring at the god-sent bundle, wondering how it got there.

"I see you have a new admirer."

Confused, she turned around. Mgbeke stood behind her. "Good morning, Mgbeke. What do you mean?" she asked calmly, unsure of the woman's intentions.

"Was it not Ikem, Obinna's friend, I saw earlier this morning depositing *this* by your door?" Her sister-in-law pointed at the stack.

Oh?

She'd complained to Ikem that she hated the tedious task of gathering firewood, especially since Mgbeke always left it all for her to do. *And he's done the chore for me!* He was fulfilling his declaration to take care of her needs. She couldn't remember the last time anyone had done something like that for her. A warm feeling wrapped her heart. Ikem cared greatly for her.

But Mgbeke had seen him!

Alarmed, heat flooded Nneka's face. The last thing she wanted was Mgbeke discovering her affair with Ikem. She dreaded to think of what the woman would do with that kind of information.

"You must be mistaken." She shook her head more to hide her alarm than to deny Mgbeke's words.

"Are you calling me a liar? Of course I'm sure of whom I saw. It was Ikem." Mgbeke glowered at her. "Come to think of it, I've been hearing strange noises late at night. They seemed to come from your hut. I'm sure you've been entertaining Ikem. I wonder what our father would say when he finds out you've been flouting your obligations."

Nneka's heart felt as though it sank into her stomach. If Mgbeke told her father-in-law any of what she'd just said, then to be sure, Nneka would wave good-bye to her freedom. She panicked. "That's not true. I could never have anything to do with him or any other man. You know that. All I want is my freedom. I'm not going to jeopardize it for someone who's not even *nw'ala*. Think about it."

Even as she said the words, she felt sickened. She was openly denying Ikem, the man she'd spent several blissful nights with. She wasn't proud of herself.

Still, what other choice did she have? If she admitted it and her father-in-law found out, everything she'd worked for in the past year would vanish. She'd be publicly humiliated and made to repeat the full year of mourning incarcerated. She would never be released. Worse, she'd probably be given to Edozie. A cold shiver of dread ran down her spine.

Also, Ikem's punishment would be even worse. He would be banished from their land permanently. His mother had no one else. The old woman would never see her son again. She couldn't be responsible for the woman's loss.

As much as she was disgusted with herself for her cowardice, it was better this way.

"So how do you explain the firewood?" Mgbeke scrutinized her with her usual malice. She didn't look convinced by Nneka's profuse denial.

"Yesterday I wasn't feeling too well. I was on my way back from gathering some firewood when I saw him with Obinna. Obinna asked about my well-being and I told him I wasn't feeling well. Maybe Ikem took it upon himself to bring some today in case I wasn't feeling better." She shrugged with a nonchalance she didn't feel. "You can't hold it against him for showing some kindness to a sick widow. We should be showing gratitude."

"Hmmm," Mgbeke frowned at her. "You could be right. You do look sickly. Anyway, that doesn't exclude you from doing the rest of your chores today. By the way, our father wants to see you this morning." The other woman gave her another disapproving look before walking away.

Relieved, Nneka nearly smiled. She let out a deep breath she hadn't realized she was holding. It seemed that Mgbeke had accepted her explanation about Ikem's gesture. Though the summons to see her father-in-law this early kept her stomach tight with apprehension. She wasn't out of trouble. Not until she found out why she was needed.

Deciding to confront whatever it was head-on, she steeled her body and walked over to his quarters. She knocked at his door.

"Come in," he called out to her from inside.

When she walked in, she saw him sitting, having his breakfast.

"Our father, good morning." She curtsied and stood by the door, waiting to be summoned forward. She hoped her apprehension didn't show.

"Good morning, my daughter. Have a seat." He waved his hand, indicating the seat next to his. When she sat down next to him, he took her hand in his frail hands.

"I hope all is well, father. I was worried when Mgbeke said you wanted to see me."

"All is well. I have given a great deal of thought to your request to be released from our family." He let out a soft sigh. She held her breath in anticipation. This was the moment that would determine her future. "As much as I have loved having you here as a member of my family, I understand that you are still young and wish to live your life bountifully. Though it will pain me to see you go, I know it is best to let you move on."

He paused to cough before continuing, "Your uncle, Mazi Ene, informs me that there have been a few suitors interested in your hand in marriage. This gives me great relief, as I do not wish to see you spend the rest of your life alone. You are a free-spirited young woman and I know with the right husband you will fully blossom and be fruitful. Unfortunately, it wasn't to be with Ofonna. My only regret is that he did not fill your womb with his children."

When he looked at her, she could see his sorrow in his rheumy eyes. "Regardless, I grant your wish. From henceforth you should discard your mourning clothes and adorn yourself like the vibrant young woman you are. Tomorrow you shall attend the New Yam festival as a free woman."

"Thank you, father." Nneka leaped from her chair to kneel in front of the old man. She was overjoyed, torn between shouting her joy and showing restraint in front of an elder. Tears stung her eyes.

At last, I'm free!

He placed his hands on her shoulders. "May our ancestor guide your path and may *Ala* fill you with fruitfulness. Help Mgbeke with the preparations for the festival. You can return to your people after the festival when everything is much settled here."

"I don't mind, father. Thank you." She stood up. She didn't care what she had to do for Mgbeke. She was a free woman and that was all that mattered. She could now move freely like any other woman of their clan. She could shed the drab grays of mourning and replace them with the unused colorful fabrics in her trunk.

"Can I go?" she asked, as her feet itched to run outside in exhilaration.

"You can go."

"Thank you." Closing the door behind her, she ran into her hut and finally released the shout of joy that had been bubbling in her throat.

"Yes!"

***

Ikem sat with the men under the palm-frond canopies drinking palm wine and talking loudly. It was the day of the New Yam festival. Ezemmuo, the clan chief priest, had already performed the ritual that meant the clan could now consume the yams and other crops recently harvested. In the middle of the village square, the location of the ceremony, the young men were now in a wrestling contest. In his time, Ikem was the best wrestler within his age group. The only other person who occasionally bested him was Obinna. However, he had the upper hand, as he'd won more wrestling matches than his friend. These days, he didn't compete anymore, but he was still the lead trainer in wrestling and warfare to the young men of the Umunri.

His gaze didn't stay with the young men for long, though he was supposed to watch them so he could advise the participants on what they'd done wrong later. His attention moved across to the women seated in the busy arena, laughing and chatting. His gaze focused on one particular woman.

Nneka.

She sat with a group of her friends, giggling, and her movement vivacious. She looked different out of her mourning clothes. So happy, so animated, so effervescent. Her life force radiated outward to him. Today, for the first time in months, she was adorned. There were coral trinkets around her fine neck and beads hanging on her slim waist, Her body and face were decorated with the beautifying *uli* markings. Her smooth skin gleamed like polished wood. Her wrap skirt was black and gold patterned, and clung to her rounded bottom. She looked like an unwed maiden. When she looked across and their eyes met, everything else faded for a moment.

Even with the physical distance, he connected with her on every level. She could have been sitting next to him. She was his life. His mate. Soon they would be joined formally. He couldn't wait to stop all the hiding and publicly declare she was his woman. When she gave him a teasing smile before turning back to her friends, his heart contracted.

"Ikem, did you hear anything I just said?"

The sound of his name roused him from his thoughts. "Sorry, what were you saying?"

Obinna laughed. "It seems your body is here, but your mind is across the square with the women. With one particular woman, I'm sure."

Ikem laughed. His friend knew him too well. "You've got me there. I cannot wait to formalize our betrothal now that she's been released from Ofonna's family."

"Yes, we have to see her uncle soon to finalize the negotiations. I hear Edozie has been making inquiries too."

At the mention of Nneka's brother-in-law's name, Ikem's fury rose. He clenched and unclenched his hands to calm himself.

"It will cost him his head, if he touches her," he snapped angrily, keeping his voice low so no-one around them would hear him except Obinna.

"You cannot say such things, my friend. Surely Nneka is not worth all that trouble."

Ikem turned and glared at his friend. Obinna's eyebrows were raised, but his expression was serious.

"How can you say such a thing to me? Would you give up Adaku for anybody?" He kept his voice low. He knew how much Adaku meant to Obinna. Even before his friend responded, he knew what the answer would be.

"Of course not." Obinna shook his head.

"So why should I give up Nneka? She is my lifeblood."

"It is great you feel that strongly for her." Obinna smiled and put his hand on Ikem's back. "You know she is like a younger sister to me. I knew you were keen on her but I wanted to be sure as to the depth of your feelings. I have your back on this and will make sure Mazi Ene agrees with your proposal. We'll go and see him tomorrow."

"Good." Ikem lifted his gourd of palm wine and drank from it. "Let's drink to that."

When he glanced across at Nneka again, she was walking away from her friends. His eyes followed her until she disappeared behind a hut. Wondering what she was up to, he stood and went in search of her. When he walked past the corner, he found her walking back toward him out of the woods. Smiling, her eyes rounded seductively when she saw him.

Unable to resist her allure at this proximity, he pulled her farther into the woods, pushed her against a tree trunk and kissed her lips. Tasting the honeyed sweetness of her lips, he ground his hardened body into her yielding flesh. With each breath, her arousing scent filled his lungs, inflaming his desire for her. The rumbling groan in his belly jarred him out of his temporary insanity. Panting, he lifted his head.

"Someone might see us." She was out of breath as she reminded him of their location. It was risky for both of them being out here with the celebrations going on only a little distance away. That didn't seem to be a deterrent.

Her warm, molten-brown eyes told him of her arousal. She wanted him as much as he wanted her.

"In a day or so, you will formally be mine and it won't matter."

He blew gentle kisses over her face. Something he'd wanted to do all day. Tracing a soft line to her neck, he kissed it before blowing into her ear. She moaned softly, and he struggled to control himself. He wanted to sink into her against the tree.

"But still, there are people everywhere. I have to get back to my friends." She tried to slip out from beneath him, but he thrust his body into hers, his hardened manhood pressing against her flat belly.

He ran his hand down her body. "Relax, nobody's here. Just you and me." He whispered into her ear as he lifted her skirt, his hand slipping between her legs to find her core hot and dripping. He slipped his fingers into wet heat.

She gasped, inhaling sharply. He moved his lips down, past the trinkets on her neck to gain access to her soft breasts, their nipples already taut, seeking his attention. He took one into his mouth, sucking and laving it. With his thumb he parted her hooded flesh and caressed it while pumping his fingers into her. She moved her hips against his hand's actions and soon she was gyrating at a quicker pace as he stroked her intimately. Her inner walls clenched around his fingers and he knew she was close to her climax. Tweaking her nub with his thumb, he kissed her lips again just as she splintered in his arms. Very few things gave him as much pleasure as watching her come apart.

"Nneka!"

She opened her eyes at the sound of someone calling her name. He released her body and straightened her clothes.

"I think someone's looking for you." He grinned at her.

Her soft lips widened in a blissful smile and her dark eyes sparkled. "I told you I'd be missed." She brushed her skirt down and tightened the wrap.

"Not as much as I already miss you." He grazed her lips lightly with his, holding onto her one last time before she had to go. As much as he wanted her, he would have to wait a little longer for that pleasure.

"Nneka!"

"I really have to go before they find us together."

"And you think I care about that? Anyway, you should go. I won't be at your hut tonight. But I'll come to help you move the day after tomorrow. Don't go to your uncle's until I'm there. Understood?"

"Yes." He kissed her again and let her go.

She took a few steps away from him and ran back to him, giving him a hug that surprised him. She stood on her tiptoes and kissed him. He leaned into her embrace, his heart pounding.

"I miss you already," she whispered before running back toward the village square. Pure exhilaration rushed through his veins. His tigress was no longer fighting him.

Chapter Seven

Two days after the festival, Nneka packed her things into the wooden trunk she would be taking home. She didn't have too many belongings to take with her, just her personal items. Everything else, she would leave behind—including all the house ware gifts she'd received when she got betrothed to Ofonna.

As she folded her clothes into the trunk, her thoughts went to Ikem and their future together. She found she thought about him a lot these days. She had a glimpse of the kind of relationship she would have with him. He was nothing like her father. Though she knew she was headstrong and difficult at times, he'd never been violent toward her. He never did anything to her she didn't want. She looked forward to finally having a man she could trust in her life, who would remain in charge but still listen to her opinions and let her be herself.

Engrossed in her thoughts, she didn't notice someone had entered her hut until he spoke.

"So you think you can escape me, you deceitful woman!"

She jumped up to find Edozie standing in the doorway of her bedchamber. His expression was hard and angry like a crazed man. In his hands was a long, twisted raffia rope.

Though terrified, she stood her ground and asked him as boldly as she could muster, "What are you doing here?"

"You dare to ask me that question?" He stomped toward her and slapped her hard on the face. Momentarily stunned, she fell backward onto her sleeping pallet. "All this while I held back from taking you because I thought you were honoring Ofonna's memory. Meanwhile, you've been at it with Ikem."

Shocked, her eyes widened and her breath caught in her throat. *How did he find out?*

"Yes, I know. I've been suspicious since Mgbeke told me he delivered some firewood for you. So I monitored your movements. I saw you two at the festival. He followed you. I followed him and witnessed what he was doing to you in the forest. You let him do all those things to you and you enjoyed it. And all the while I thought you were just being chaste."

He advanced toward her. Trying not to panic, she scrambled backward on the pallet until her back hit the wall. There was nowhere else to run. The only route to escape was past Edozie.

"Edozie, don't do this." She tried to keep her voice calm so he couldn't see her fear. On her cracked lips, she tasted blood. Her head and lips throbbed with pain. Edozie packed a mean slap.

He sneered at her as he continued rambling, ignoring her plea. "You should have told me you liked rough sex. I'd have obliged you gladly. Do you know he likes to bind his women? I bet he's tied you up a few times while he fucks you. And I bet you liked it too." He laughed at her like a demented hyena.

For the first time since the death of her mother, fear iced her blood. The loud pounding of her heartbeat overtook all other sounds.

"Edozie, stop this!" she shouted as he lunged at her and delivered another blow to her face. Adrenaline pumped through her veins. She fought back, kicking and clawing at him. She lost count of how often he hit her when her vision blurred with the pain. He tore her clothes. Then he bound her mouth with a piece of cloth. She tried to fight back, but he hit her again. Overwhelmed by the pain, her body went limp and tears clogged her eyes.

He bound her hands behind her with the rope. Her shoulders hurt as he pushed her face down. As she lay there, she realized he was going to rape her and kill her. Just like her father had raped and killed her mother. Strangely, the terror that had flooded her body departed. In its stead, she was blanketed by a depressive feeling. Her tears flowed down her face. She was never going to see Ikem again. She would never have the opportunity to tell him how she felt about him. She loved him heart, body, and soul.

As Edozie knelt between her legs and fumbled with his clothes, she prayed to the gods for one thing above all else. A chance to have a life with Ikem.

Edozie fell forward, limp over her. She shouted, nearly gagging from the cloth tied over her mouth. Someone she couldn't see dragged Edozie off her body onto the floor. With teary eyes, she twisted her head to look. Ikem stood over Edozie's prone body. The way the veins on Ikem's body appeared ready to burst indicated his present murderous intent toward Edozie. When he looked at her, his eyes were clouded with his barely restrained rage.

Ikem sat heavily on the pallet, lifting her onto his lap. He remained silent as he gently unbound her hands and removed the gag from her mouth. She sobbed with relief and hugged him tightly. He'd arrived in time. She still had a chance at a life with him. She said a silent prayer of gratitude to the gods.

"I'm sorry," he whispered gruffly to her as he rubbed her sore wrists.

Frowning, she leaned back and looked up at his still angry face. "Why are you sorry? It wasn't your fault that Edozie attacked me."

"I'm sorry I wasn't here to protect you from him."

"You saved me before he could do any serious damage. That's what matters."

"Now I have to prevent him from doing any more damage to anyone else." With his thumb he gently touched her aching lips. She winced in pain. "I'll get you a salve for this. For now you stay here."

He put her back on the pallet and stood up. Picking up the rope, he tied the unconscious Edozie's hands with it before dragging him out of her bedchamber. The look on Ikem's face told her he was going to do something really bad to Edozie. While she hated Edozie right now and wanted him punished, she didn't want Ikem to get into trouble for taking the matter into his own hands. Especially if he killed the man.

"Ikem, wait. What are you going to do with him?"

"It is nothing for you to worry about, Nneka. And for once you will obey my instructions. Otherwise you know the punishment will be severe. Don't push me." He glared at her. Though she could see his anger, she knew it wasn't directed at her.

"Ikem, I can't let you kill Edozie."

He ignored her and dragged the man outside. She tried to follow him, but he looked fiercely at her dress and shut the door. Angrily she looked down and realized she couldn't go outside dressed like she was. Her clothes were torn to shreds. She ran back to her room and changed into a new dress before running outside. Mgbeke and her children sobbed as Edozie was dragged away.

Unsure of what to do, Nneka ran to Obinna's house. He was the only person she knew who could talk to Ikem. As much as she disliked Mgbeke, she didn't want the woman to become a widow on her account. Plus, her father-in-law would lose a second son. She couldn't let that happen.

When she got to Obinna's house, she was out of breath from all the running. Luckily, the man in question was sitting outside but there was no Adaku in sight.

"Obinna, please come. Quickly."

He stood up as she approached. "Nneka, why are you out of breath? What is the matter?"

"Please, you have to come with me quickly. Ikem is about to commit murder."

"What? Why?" He stood still, frowning. She grew frustrated.

"Please let's go. I'll tell you on the way."

"Right." He followed her and on the way she told him what had happened. Looking worried, he stopped and looked her over before asking if she was all right. She told him she was fine, apart from the sore lip and headache.

"Edozie is a menace that needs to be stopped. It seems he has finally met his comeuppance," he said angrily as he resumed walking. "But still it is not for Ikem to deliver justice by his own hands. The matter needs to be referred to the elders for their decision."

"That's what I thought, too. You have to convince Ikem to stop this madness before it costs us all a lot more than one life."

It seemed Obinna understood her meaning. He quickened his pace. If Ikem killed Edozie in cold blood then his life would be forfeit. They arrived at the village square, where Ikem had tied a now-awake Edozie to a tree trunk. There was a gathering of people who seemed to be cheering Ikem on.

"You will confess your atrocities for all to hear, or by the gods you will meet your ancestors today," Ikem shouted as he paced up and down, his machete in his hand.

Nneka stood to the side as Obinna walked up to his friend, his hands raised in a placating manner. "Ikem, please calm down. You have to leave Edozie for the council. You cannot take matters into your own hands."

Ikem shook his head. "No. Edozie crossed the line this time. He attacked someone personal to me, someone dear to me. I'll not let him go until he confesses publicly. Enough is enough. He has touched the tiger's tail and he has to bear the consequences."

Edozie remain reticent until he saw Nneka. He stared straight at her, his evil intent visible in his eyes. "Is it that slut you're protecting?" Edozie nodded in her direction. "Do you think you're the only one who's had her?"

Ikem turned to look at her and stopped pacing. She sucked in breath quickly, a sickening feeling twirling in her stomach as Ikem's eyes narrowed in a frown.

"Why do you think I was in her hut today? We have been rutting like wild pigs for weeks. She promised she would be mine. I was only angry she'd reneged on her promise. I bet she plans to renege on her promise to you, too. She would rather be single so she can take her lovers whenever she wants. Moreover, she says you are not a son-of-the-soil so she would never stay true to you. You know I speak the truth. Ask her for yourself."

"Shut up!" Ikem growled menacingly, punching Edozie across the face. His blood ran cold with fury. So much of what the man said niggled at his normally tightly controlled insecurities. Most of his life he'd never allowed the fact that his father was not a citizen of Umunri to rile him. In fact, he'd worn it as a badge growing up. He'd gotten into many fights about it and won. In his adulthood, nobody dared mention it to him directly. Although he knew people spoke about it behind his back.

However, with Nneka, he'd never felt it was an issue. She'd never mentioned it to him before or shown any contempt about it. So they'd never really discussed it. Also he knew her ambition had been to stay single once released from her in-laws. He'd thought she'd finally seen sense and agreed to be his wife. Although she'd never given a verbal consent.

Fates!

She had him again. Just like she'd done that first time he'd asked her to meet him. And she'd said she'd never agreed to it. She'd never agreed verbally to marry him either.

And here I'm about to kill another man for her sake.

His chest tightened with excruciating pain. For a moment, he couldn't breathe well and had to force air into his body through his mouth. All strength departed from his body. He felt hollow. The pain of rejection he'd felt as a child when he'd realized he wasn't *nw'ala* did not match the pain he felt now. He'd made assumptions about Nneka that were never his to make. She needed her freedom more than she'd ever need him.

Stepping away from the tree, he lowered his machete. Behind him he could hear Obinna order some young men to untie Edozie and take him to the palace security holding cell. Sheathing his machete, Ikem turned and walked off without looking back. He'd only taken a few steps when Nneka blocked his path.

"You don't believe any of what Edozie just said, do you?" She looked angry, her brown eyes flashing fire, her arms akimbo. Flummoxed, he wondered what she had to be angry about. She'd gotten what she'd wanted above all else. Freedom.

"It doesn't matter what I think." Shaking his head, he tried to sidestep her, but she blocked him again.

"It matters to me, Ikem," she replied, peering at him with those blazing eyes he knew he was going to miss.

Letting out a resigned sign, he folded his arms across his chest. He would surely touch her if he didn't keep his hands out of the way. "Did you tell him you were never going to marry me because of my bastard status?"

"I didn't tell him anything. I was only trying to deflect Mgbeke's suspicions. She saw you delivering the firewood bundle and she started prying into our affair. It was the only thing I could think of to shut her up. I didn't mean it. She must have told Edozie."

A glimmer of hope flickered within his heart. He could see how his well-intentioned gesture would have caused suspicion. But still.

"Did you agree to be Edozie's wife?"

"I never agreed to be his wife. He had been pestering me for weeks. I was simply being diplomatic to avoid getting him upset until I secured my release. You know I'd never give myself to a man like that."

He watched her eyes as she spoke, knowing she couldn't hide the truth from him in their dark depths. They appeared sincere enough.

"I remember you saying the same thing to me, Nneka."

"But that was different," she replied, sounding exasperated. He knew what was in her heart, but he wanted her to say it out loud for a change. It was no longer enough for him to make assumptions. He needed her to say how she felt.

"How is it different? You've never agreed to marry me. I've been the one relentlessly seeking your attention. While all you've ever wanted was your freedom. Well, you've got it now. You can live your life as a free, independent woman. I won't stand in your way."

"I won't be living very independently if my uncle marries me off to the next suitor that comes along." Her apparent frustration almost made him laugh.

"Well, you don't have to worry about that any longer. I paid your bride price yesterday, so technically you're my wife. But I release you. You are free of any obligations toward me."

She looked at him, her mouth opened, stunned into silence. When she didn't say anything for a while, he broke the silence.

"You are free to go, Nneka. Go and let me be." He turned away.

"Don't you see I don't want that freedom if it means a life without you?" He felt her cool hand on his arm, stopping him from walking away. "I'm willing to do whatever you want. I'll even turn into a meek little wife, if that's what you want."

He turned and faced her, keeping his expression schooled. Did he really want to cage this tigress? She was a free spirit by nature. He didn't want her to change.

"You lie, Nneka. I bet you will disobey my commands and argue with me nonstop."

"No, I won't," she insisted as she pleaded with him.

He shook his head and laughed. He definitely didn't want her to change. It would take the fun out of their relationship. "You just did."

"Please." She knelt in front of him and lowered her eyes. "You did promise that you and you alone would provide for my needs. Who will you have doing the job in your absence?" She looked at him seductively through her long, dark lashes, the tempting tigress. She knew exactly how to get under his skin. She was throwing him a challenge. There was no way he would allow another man to touch her the way he did. And she knew it too.

"I only have one question for you and I need the truth. I need you to say it out loud so everyone here will hear."

"Yes, I'll be totally honest." She nodded vigorously.

"Nneka, will you be my wife?" he spoke loudly so those around them could hear him.

Her eyes widened and her breath hitched. "Yes!" she shouted for all to hear too.

He understood what it took for her to make such a public declaration. She hadn't said it lightly. Drawing her up, he pulled her into a hug and whispered in her ear so that no one else would hear. "In that case, you have to be punished for disobeying my instructions earlier."

The sound of her rapidly increased breathing filled his ears. "Whatever you say, my husband."

He smiled widely. At last, he'd caught his quarry.

THE END

His Princess

*With the weight of a kingdom on his shoulders
and his honour at stake, can a Prince truly love
a slave?*

Ezinne is dismayed when her mistress presents
her to Prince Emeka as a concubine to cater for
his every need for a few weeks. She's a slave
whose previous encounters with men make her
fear their brutality.

Yet the more she gets to know the powerful yet
honourable prince, the easier he breaks down the
walls around her heart. She soon comes to want
him more than she wants anything else, even
freedom.

But Emeka is the heir to the throne and Ezinne is
a woman with secrets that threaten not just their
budding relationship but a kingdom.

Kiru Taye

Chapter One

Southeast Nigeria, pre-colonization

"You stupid girl!" Princess Nonye's loud, irate voice rang out in the sitting chamber of the prince's quarters.

Ezinne gritted her teeth and bit back the rising annoyance of her own clumsiness. With haste, she withdrew the cotton napkin she kept attached to her waist beads for accidents such as this. She dabbed the water pooled on the wooden dining table, her movements controlled.

Any moment now, she expected the hot, stinging slap from her belligerent mistress whose hand was quick to connect with the face of any offending servant following similar outbursts. Stiffening her back, Ezinne kept her line of sight lowered as she should have done in the first place.

"Can you not even complete a simple task without messing it up? What would be next? The platter of food on the floor? What kind of servants do we have in this palace? None of them ever get things done correctly," her mistress ranted, raising one hand midair in a haughty manner. Then she rose from her hand-carved ornate lounging chair next to the prince's, and walked toward the dinner table.

Ezinne drew her lips tight in a grimace. She wasn't in the habit of making mistakes. With a mistress such as Princess Nonye, she couldn't afford to get into trouble.

This time though, she had no one else to blame but herself for getting distracted. Since the royal couple's wedding, it was Ezinne's duty to serve their evening meal. They always ate together in the main chamber, a room filled with opulent grandeur and decorated with bronze sculptures and leopard fur.

Ezinne was to set the intimate table with her gaze lowered as was customary for common servants. It was smaller than the grand ornate elephant table in the King's receiving chamber. So she should have completed the task in a speedy fashion as she always did. However, the table was carved out of iroko wood; the image of a black panther formed its base.

She'd remembered one of the palace servant's whispered words earlier. "The table contains the spirit of the beast Prince Emeka slayed in his coming of age hunting ritual."

Fixated by the intricacy of the beast's features, she stared at it as she attended to her tasks before curiosity made her raise her gaze in the direction of her new master and future king of Umunri.

His aura was unlike any other she'd encountered in a man of his position.

She usually avoided men and paid little attention to them. Since her arrival in the palace, she had taken to catching glimpses of Prince Emeka when she thought no one was looking, masking her gaze with the veil of her long lashes.

Today, her bedeviled eyes didn't stay lowered for long.

Prompted by her ever-probing spirit, she had raised her stare, spying Prince Emeka as he discussed some matter with Princess Nonye.

As always he looked regal in his bejeweled crown of elaborate gems and beads, his attire of richly woven gold and black threads.

It wasn't his clothes that drew her gaze.

It was his face: the raised angular cheekbones, curved bushy brows, strong square jaw, wide sensual lips, and most of all, the piercing midnight eyes because they caught her attention, keeping her transfixed.

In a brief moment of insanity, she had wondered what it would feel like to have those captivating eyes really notice her or to feel the firmness of his lips against her skin.

It was pure madness to have such a fantasy in her mind. She had never dreamed of a man in such a manner before.

Until Prince Emeka had turned, his onyx gaze pinning her to the spot, the sound of her heartbeat rivaling the hooves of a racing antelope pounding into the hard earth.

She should have taken the hint, her instincts warning her of danger.

In the moment of connection, she had forgotten where she was and her place in it. His stare raked her ample frame, spreading tingling warmth along its path on her skin. It was as if he had actually seen her; the real her—a woman worthy of desire—not the lowly servant.

A new and unintelligible longing awakened within her. It was something so outside of her grasp that she dismissed it immediately. She had told herself the warmth in his eyes had been her imagination. Princes didn't notice servants. Men in his position only trampled those beneath them.

From the way his eyes had sparkled briefly with amusement, she could have sworn he had read her errant thoughts. With her mouth feeling parched, her face flushed in mortification. Chiding herself, she had quickly lowered her gaze only to discover the water she had been pouring into the bronze chalices had overflowed onto the table, eliciting the twisted expression and tirade from the princess.

From the corners of her eyesight, Ezinne saw Princess Nonye lift her hand to strike. Steeling her body, she closed her eyes momentarily. However, the expected blow never connected with her face.

"No." It was the gritty, sonorous voice of the prince.

Ezinne opened her eyes to find him providing a barrier between her and Princess Nonye. Prince Emeka stood adjacent. Tall and strong, he radiated authority and heat. The temperature of the air rose, swirling his masculine scent around her body. His near presence overwhelmed her mind, pulling her into a dizzy spell.

Shaking her head to clear the fuzziness, she took a quick glance at the prince. His hand held onto the princess's raised arm. Stunned, a frown creased Ezinne's face. Still, she resisted the temptation to look up at him.

Prince Emeka had come to her rescue.

But...why?

It made no sense to her. She was a mere servant and of no importance. Yet the prince's next words confirmed his baffling actions.

"Leave her be. She has cleaned it up, and there is no harm done. Come and sit. Let's eat." His voice remained calm though it had an edge of steel as he reprimanded his wife, steering her bodily to her chair.

At the unexpected but delightful reprieve, Ezinne moved backward to the corner of the room. Relief washed over her as she almost blended into the darkness. Though she would have withstood the slap, she didn't want to have to suffer the humiliation in front of the prince.

Does it really matter? Have you forgotten your position in his household, in the palace?

Pushing back the quiet voice in her head, she straightened, ignoring its cautious note. Instead, her eyes scanned the large chamber. The only light in the room was from the wicker lamp flickering on the dinner table, throwing the rest of the space into early evening shadows.

Ezinne liked the semidarkness. She felt comfortable in it. It seemed the darkness was the only time she could let her imagination loose. It also seemed the prince preferred the darkness. It was his idea to blow out the flames from the wall sconces leaving just the table lamp. Ezinne thought it gave the room a rather cozy, intimate setting.

She stood in the shadows without moving or making a noise. If she was required she would be available to attend to their needs without delay.

Watching the royal couple, her gaze stayed mainly on the prince who appeared unruffled, though she could feel the malicious glare coming from the princess.

Gooseflesh rose on Ezinne's skin. Her stomach tightened as if she'd eaten food that had soured.

No person seeing the princess's expression would believe they had once been playmates, friends even, albeit for a short while. It amazed her to think how things changed in a short period of time.

In truth, the princess had grown into a person Ezinne hardly recognized. There was no longer any trace of the child she played with years ago. The little, pleasant girl had turned into a pampered, vindictive woman.

"My prince, you spoil these servants too much. Little wonder they all make mistakes," Princess Nonye said in a sweet voice. Batting her eyelashes, she spooned some of the food onto Prince Emeka's plate.

The feeling of revulsion in Ezinne's stomach increased. She gritted her teeth to stop herself from throwing up, her earlier anger rising, this time directed at the princess.

Who was she to talk about mistakes?

"Nonye, everyone makes blunders. It is no reason to raise your hands to the servants." His tone was sober. However, she detected a note of grief in its depth.

Squinting, her frown deepened as queries disturbed her mind. She wanted to understand the prince – this man – who would come to her rescue when others would have added to her suffering.

What is his purpose? Does he expect favors in return for defending me from the princess?

Her past encounters with men in positions of power had taught her not to let her guard down. No favor was ever given freely. Shrugging, she dismissed the prince's rueful words as the princess's shrill voice jarred her back to the reality.

"How else am I supposed to make them learn from their errors? In my father's palace in Umulari, any slaves or servants who misbehaved were whipped as an example to others. They all soon learned to behave properly."

Prince Emeka's lips twisted and he shook his head in a slow motion. Could it be he was disappointed by Nonye's words? He certainly appeared unhappy as he poured some wine from the gourd, a crease appearing on his usually relaxed forehead.

More astonishment speared through Ezinne's body causing her heart to jolt in her chest.

"Here in Umunri, we do things differently," he replied. "Whipping is only reserved for those who actually commit a crime after being judged guilty. Every member of our community is a free person as we do not have slaves."

He paused, chewing on a piece of roasted goat meat.

Nonye turned and glared in Ezinne's direction. It was as if she was telling Ezinne with her eyes not to get any ideas about becoming a free person.

Now that the prince had said it, it made sense to Ezinne. She had wondered why the servants in this palace appeared happier than the ones in Umulari.

In the short time she'd been here—only two cycles of the moon—she'd not witnessed anyone being whipped in the palace. The only time there was any physical punishment was when the princess reprimanded her handmaidens. She gathered was that Prince Emeka was a firm but fair master.

For the first time in years, Ezinne felt she was treated as a human not as her master's property.

"All servants are compensated for their service. As such, those in my household and in the palace are treated with the same respect we expect as masters. My father has never raised his hands to anyone. Neither have I. I expect you to be as equitable as the princess and future queen," he concluded before returning to his meal.

"Freed slaves? Paying servants for their service? That's the height of decadence. Why would you want to waste the palace resources on paying servants? They should feel privileged for serving the royal family—a household provided to govern them by the gods. Don't say I did not warn you if they all get out of control. I'll certainly not take the blame," the princess grumbled, shooting Ezinne one final glare before turning back to her meal.

Prince Emeka remained stoic, patting his wife's hand on the table. "Do not worry. If the servants in my house should revolt, then the responsibility will be mine to bear."

Glancing in Ezinne's direction, the lamp flame caught the sparkle in the prince's eyes, and his lips lifted at the corners in what she could only guess was a smile.

"You may leave us now."

Distracted by his reassuring smile, it took Ezinne a few moments before she realized he had dismissed her. Stunned, she remained immobile. She had never been dismissed during their dinner service before.

"My prince, what if I need her?" Princess Nonye's mouth thinned in a straight line, showing her renewed annoyance.

The prince's wide muscular shoulders lifted in a dismissive shrug. "Let the poor girl go and have her own meal. If nothing else, let her sit down. She stands at attention all day."

"She can relax when she's asleep. Her place is by my side serving me."

"In that case, she can sit down with us at the table. She will be closer at hand when you need her."

A loud, outraged gasp escaped the princess's lips, and her eyes narrowed as she pinned her gaze on Ezinne. "You are dismissed but don't go too far. This table will need to be cleared soon." She lifted her hand in a dismissive gesture.

Without further delay, Ezinne retreated toward the door. She wasn't allowed to turn her back to the royal couple so she had to walk through the door facing them. Before she stepped through it, she stole one more surreptitious glance at the prince.

His gaze caught hers. His lips trembled with suppressed amusement, laughter lines wrinkling his eyes. It was as if he'd just shared a silent joke with her.

And he winked at her.

Then she understood. He had turned the table on the princess by threatening to invite Ezinne to sit down with them when he knew the princess would never allow it. He'd known she'd have to relent and dismiss Ezinne.

Suppressing the smile that tugged at her lips, she reversed out of the room. With her heart thumping against her chest, she walked to the servants' quarters, still baffled though.

Why would a man like Prince Emeka help me?

She still couldn't understand it. No one in his position was that nice. Not in her experience. He'd noticed her. She wasn't so sure it was a good thing. A part of her wanted to go back to the anonymity of being just another servant. Despite its downside, there was some comfort in blending into the shadows and being faceless.

Now it seemed she couldn't merge into the shade any longer. Like everything else in life, there had to be a price to pay. Would she be willing to pay it?

Finally sitting down on her pallet in the quarters she shared with the other handmaidens, the fluttering sensation returned to her stomach. This time it was a mixture of apprehension and anticipation.

Several things seemed certain in her mind. She wanted a life away from service. She wanted a life as a free person. She could attain it here in Umunri.

And Prince Emeka held the key to her freedom.

Chapter Two

"I'll be gone for four market weeks," Princess Nonye said, her sing-song voice lowered so no one outside the room could hear her.

For the first time in the two months since they arrived in Umunri, she appeared excited. Ezinne would go as far as saying the princess was happy. Nonye's eyes had none of the restless hardness that had confronted Ezinne last night in the prince's quarters. As she spoke, Nonye's lips rose in the corner but didn't break into a full smile. It was as if she was smiling because of some teasing mystery.

This was a side of her mistress only Ezinne, and perhaps Prince Emeka, was privy to. In the princess's quarters when they were alone, it was as if they were as close as they used to be as children. She was glad to be Nonye's confidant even if they were no longer best friends.

"Maybe even longer if I can get away with it. You will have to stay here and cover for me," Nonye continued, her fingertips brushing her lips in a light motion, her stare focused at a point on the wall as if studying the details of the landscape mural. She appeared lost in thought.

Dread crept down Ezinne's spine. Stiffening her back, she froze where she knelt, her nails digging into the wooden traveling case she was packing for the princess's journey. She could guess at the source of Nonye's fledgling happiness.

In her mind, she didn't even want to contemplate idea. Or its alarming consequences.

Creasing her brows in a frown, Ezinne turned to face her mistress, still on her knees. Nonye sat on a high-back hand-carved chair, one of two located near her bed.

Her private chamber was one of the most lavishly decorated in the palace. Only recently, an artist had been commissioned to paint a mural on the wall facing the large, raised straw-padded pallet. Peculiarly, it was the painting of the palace in Umulari.

Ezinne had no wish to be reminded of the place. Her memories of her hometown were not pleasant. However, she understood Nonye's reluctance to let go of her former home.

"That long? Why can I not come with you?" Ezinne asked. Unable to hide her unease, her voice quivered with her agitation. "I'm supposed to stay with you at all times. Remember?"

"Oh, don't be childish, Ezinne. You know very well the festival of light is only for a week, but I've told the prince I need to be in Umulari for longer to spend time with my father." Nonye adjusted her sitting position, uncrossing her legs.

"In any case, I'll be in my father's palace. There are plenty of servants, and no harm will befall me there. I'll explain to him that I needed you to stay here. Don't worry." She flicked her hand in the air in her usual flippant manner.

Despite Nonye's reassurance, Ezinne couldn't stop the nausea that twirled in her stomach. Something still didn't feel right.

She had lived with the princess since they were children. At one point they had played with each other daily. Ezinne's mother had served the queen, Nonye's mother, just as Ezinne now served Nonye.

The two girls had spent enough times together for her to know when all was not right with Nonye.

In this instance, the niggling feeling spread from the pit of Ezinne's stomach covering her arms with goose bumps.

"My princess."

Ezinne cleared the lump in her throat, taking an immense breath before continuing. She needed to address this issue with fastidiousness and care. Nonye was nothing if not volatile.

"May I ask if you will be seeing Dike while you are in Umulari?"

Ezinne held her breath and watched Nonye flick her gaze back at her.

"Of course, I will. He'll visit the palace as always. It'll be good to see him again."

"But is that wise, my princess? I thought you decided to leave all that behind before you married the prince."

"Oh, you worry too much. I haven't said anything will happen. I just want to see him again, that's all. These past months, I've felt adrift...lost. I know my marriage is important, but so is my happiness. Surely you can see that."

"Surely, Prince Emeka makes you happy. You are the wife of the future king of Umunri. You are revered with practically everyone at your beck and call. Surely all this pleases you."

"You would not understand. You have never desired a man more than anything else. Neither has a man desired you in such a way."

Ezinne flinched, her grip tightening on the clothes in her arms. She frowned, surprised that Nonye's words hurt. She didn't want any man desiring her. Neither did she desire any man.

Still, she couldn't shake the sting of the other woman's words, and it reflected in her voice when she spoke.

"It may be so. But surely no man can be worth risking all this, not one like Dike." Ezinne voice was harsh, surprising even her.

Most times, she hid her annoyance. This time, she couldn't keep her feelings under restraint. Nonye's behavior last night had contributed to it.

"Don't take that tone with me, Ezinne." Nonye's kept her voice low, her annoyance creasing her otherwise flawless egg-shaped face.

"Dike is more man than most men I know. I won't have you speak of him in that manner. You know very well my marriage to the prince is purely a political move for both kingdoms. Prince Emeka cares no more for me than I do for him."

Ezinne knew she'd hit a sore point about Dike. But she couldn't recant her words. The consequences of Nonye's actions would be disastrous. She had taken a vow to watch out for Nonye. It was her responsibility. Despite the apparent danger to herself if Nonye got angry with her and decided to punish her, she had to make her opinion known.

"I can't believe that. I see the way the prince is with you. He pays attention to you. I have never seen him offended or be aggressive toward you. He must care about you," she said, hoping Nonye would appreciate her reasoning.

Nonye shrugged. "So what?" she said. "This palace bores me. Being stuck here with no excitement." She paused, shaking her head before turning to Ezinne.

"I have to go to Umulari. I have to see Dike again. All I need is to see him, and I feel alive. The thought that I can't have him, that I shouldn't have him drives me wild with insanity."

"But surely the prince is a good and considerate lover."

"Pah. What do you know about sexual affairs? You who have refused to take a lover. The kind of decadent pleasures you would have been introduced to are beyond your childish imagination. Sure the prince is a great lover, but I crave a lot more than he is able to give me. Do you know that...?"

Nonye came closer and whispered into Ezinne's ear.

The words Nonye breathed into Ezinne's ears painted pictures in her mind she couldn't decipher, and her face flushed. Mouth agape she stared at Nonye unbelieving of her words.

The tinkle of Nonye laughter resounded in the chamber. "And you could have not just one but two at the same time."

"The gods forbid!"

"The gods have nothing to do with it. It is purely human pleasure, but I'm sure even the gods look upon it and feel jealous."

"Don't say such things. I really worry about you. Don't do this. What if the prince finds out?"

"He will not find out. Who will tell him? I know you will never do such a thing to me."

The princess's golden eyes hardened as she touched her cheek in a gentle caress. "Remember what we once were. We are tied to each other. You cannot allow my downfall."

She broke the contact and moved away. "Even if he found out, he will be unable to do anything about it. A break in our marriage means war. Prince Emeka is a dutiful prince. He will not risk the future of Umunri for his personal pride."

Desperate, Ezinne tried a different approach. "Do you not even care that he will miss you when you are gone for all that time?"

"That's why you are staying behind. You will take care of his needs and make sure he has little time to wonder at my absence."

"How am I supposed to do that? I'm just a servant in the palace."

"You will be his companion," Nonye said, in her usual instructive tone. "You will carry out the activities that I usually perform for him. Stay with him while he eats, massage him after his evening bath, and let him take his pleasure with you when he needs to."

Gasping with horror, Ezinne grasped her neck. A burning sensation twirled low in her stomach. "Surely you do not expect me to bed the prince."

"You will see that his needs are met if he requires. You are a beautiful woman, and I'm sure with a little inducement he'll have no problem taking you to bed."

Nonye glided back to her lounging chair but didn't recline. She stood erect, her fingers tapping her arm in a gesture Ezinne recognized as mild irritation.

"I would rather it was you than some other social climber trying to get a foot into the palace. I know with you it would come to naught because you can never betray me. But there are others, especially Adaku, Ichie Omemma's daughter. I want her nowhere near the prince."

Ezinne frowned thinking her mistress irrational. "But isn't she already married? What would she want with the prince?"

Nonye' curved brows lifted, her expression mocking. "What has marriage got to do with it?" she asked. "Just keep close to the prince and make sure she doesn't come anywhere near the palace. If she does, you have to let me know. Do you understand me?"

Ezinne's chest rose in a defeated sigh and nodded in ascent. Like attempting to capture rain drops with a basket, she'd lost this line of reasoning. She would have to do as Nonye bid her. She had sworn to do whatever it took to safeguard Nonye. If covering for the petulant princess for a few weeks ensured her wellbeing, then there was no other option.

Nonye's downfall was surely hers too. They were bound together. Their link was irreversible.

"Good. I'm going to request the women prepare you and beautify you. I'll present you to the prince myself," Nonye said. A smile lifted her lips as the corners. She appeared content with Ezinne's compliance.

Ezinne rose from her kneeling position and stood still awaiting further instruction. Oddly, the thought of the prince touching her did not instigate icy sweat to spread over her skin as expected.

Her pulse did not pound with fear.

For years she had avoided men after the trauma she'd endured. The thought of a man touching her body usually churned her stomach with fear and outrage.

With the prince she experienced different sensations—a strange smoldering of excitement and apprehension washed over her body. Why was that?

She clenched her hands at her sides. She had to stop this madness before it progressed any further. Ezinne couldn't take the place of the princess while she took an indulgent break from her role as wife to the future king.

Acting as the prince's concubine was wrong.

Yet as she saw Princess Nonye summon other servants to begin Ezinne's transformation, she knew she was fighting a losing battle.

Nonye's life-force was like a tropical storm. It drenches everything in its path and sweeps them along until its fury is done. Her mistress would not abandon her scheme until she has completed it.

All Ezinne could do was to heed her wish and pray to the gods that Nonye came to her right mind soon.

Chapter Three

"The young men appreciate your efforts in safeguarding their interests and the future stability of Umunri, my prince." Mazi Amobi nodded his head as he spoke.

Though their relationship was driven by their roles in the kingdom—Emeka as prince and Amobi as special adviser, they had a relatively easygoing friendship and strong bond.

However, Emeka cringed each time Amobi referred to him as "my prince" whenever there were other people present. He'd conveyed his wish to be addressed by his given name. However, Amobi always insisted on protocol, especially when there was an audience.

It was one issue they didn't always see eye to eye on: his casual approach to the standard formalities of palace life. Despite some of their disagreements, he trusted Amobi with his life. The man had never given him reason to doubt his words. He was also a man of integrity; his advice always precise.

"It is the least I could do as the prince. The requirements of the peace deal are easy for me to meet," Emeka replied. He raised his hand dismissing his adviser's praising words.

Today, he had received a delegation of young people from their community led by Amobi. The group had now departed, leaving just the two of them and Emeka's personal guards who stood at attention behind him. One of the guards waved the large multi-colored fan made of peacock feathers dissipating cool air around the prince and his guest.

They both sat in his obi, the receiving chamber as part of his quarters in the palace. It was a large, formal room. The stone floor was covered in a tiger fur rug in the middle. Rows of hand-carved chairs lined both sides of the room. The prince's chair backed the main wall under which a lion skin and head hung.

Emeka sat on the high-back chair hand-carved for him by the carpenter commissioned by the palace. It wasn't as elaborate or ornate as the throne in his father's obi, but it was unique enough to identify his status as the crown prince. However he had insisted that his chair not be raised on a dais like his father's. He'd never liked the idea of being on a higher level than other citizens of this land. He wasn't the king yet.

"This is not a matter to be dismissed with ease," Amobi said. "Considering the upheaval of the past, our alliance with Umulari and the negotiated peace deal provides security for all our futures after the wars of the past. The gifts are to show their appreciation."

Emeka lips curved in a smile at his friend's tenacity.

"Amobi, all I've done is my duty to our community. The people need not bring me gifts. It is of importance that I support my father's efforts to carve out peace with our neighbors for generations to come."

Emeka understood the man's point but he didn't feel as if he'd done anything more than was required of him.

"With peace," he continued. "Our communities can be stable and prosper. I have no wish to be the king that dragged Umunri back to war. It is much better this way."

"Regardless, my prince, the people still appreciate your efforts." Amobi lips curved in the corners in a rare smile. His confidant was a sober and intense man by nature.

"We know of other princes in other kingdoms who are not as benevolent to their citizens. Truly, there aren't many who will sacrifice their own personal choices for the service of a kingdom. Especially since we know that you had your eyes on another much closer to home."

Emeka's deep laughter resounded in the chamber. "I accept my plans were changed. But I consider it as fate. The gods have chosen it this way. I've no complaints being wedded to a princess as beautiful as Nonye. Adaku is now married herself. So everyone involved is happy."

He wasn't a man who dwelt on things when they didn't go his way. He had strong faith in there being a purpose to everything one encountered in life.

Adaku had been his childhood sweetheart. Her father, Ichie Omemma, was the Onoowu, the king's right-hand man and special adviser, and a revered member of the council of elders. Due to the intimate relationship between their families, Emeka and Adaku had been expected to wed.

As they had both grown up, he realized he didn't have the same strength of fondness as when they were children. When his father negotiated a peace deal with the king of Umulari that involved marrying Princess Nonye, he hadn't felt the need to disagree with it with any vigor.

Duty to Umunri was a higher calling. He valued it above any personal considerations.

His father had made it his mission to bring peace to Umunri after several years of war with its neighbors. Emeka understood this drive for peace. Unfortunately, his fondness for Adaku couldn't compete with his sense of responsibility to his citizens.

It hadn't stopped his self-reproach for disappointing the girl he'd grown up with and made unspoken promises to. Her distress when he'd given her the news that he would wed Nonye had been heartrending. He'd come to view her as a close friend if not a sister.

When he'd heard that she'd wed another, he'd been glad. Relieved.

She'd moved on with her life and didn't spend too much time missing him. There would've been little point in her waiting for him. The best he could have done for her was to make her his second wife.

Still, he didn't feel such an arrangement suited docile Adaku. Also, he doubted the fiery Nonye would be eager to accommodate a second wife, though he was entitled to it.

As if he'd conjured her up by thinking about her, Nonye walked into his obi at that moment. A smile creased his lips as he watched her glide across the room.

Nonye was a consummate princess—born and bred as one. There was no doubt as to her status and sophistication when she was in attendance. All eyes gravitated toward her.

Except, today it wasn't entirely accurate. There was another girl following behind Nonye.

The moment, he glimpsed the new arrival entering his obi, his gaze focused on her. Senses alerted, his heart stumbled in his chest. Awareness spiked through is body hardening it.

Strikingly beautiful, the girl's visage took his breath away. Compelled, he stared unable to look away. His physical response undeniable; the girl roused him as only one other person had been able to.

It couldn't possibly be her, could it?

There was something familiar about her—something just out of reach. He scrolled his memories seeking to place the unknown female visitor.

He'd seen her somewhere but wasn't sure where. Was she one of the Ichie's daughters? Perhaps a princess from another kingdom?

From the corners of his eyes, he notices Amobi staring at the girl with appreciation. A vice tightened Emeka's gut, jealousy speared through him.

The violent strength of his emotional reaction stunned him.

Nonye curtsied in front of him. He indicated for her to rise up.

His stomach churned, guilt washing over him like the splashing of cool water from the waterfall. Cold wisdom returned banishing the steam of lust from his mind.

Why was he ogling another woman? He was married and had no intentions of taking a second wife. Also, he had made a promise to work at keeping a good relationship with his wife.

Here he was, admiring another woman in her presence—with unconcealed delight. If he sought to sow seeds of respect and companionship with his bride, this wasn't the avenue to explore it.

His disgust for his actions left a bitter taste of bile on his tongue.

Forcing himself to, he turned toward Nonye and smiled, taking her hand to guide her to her chair next to his. When her pretty lips lifted in a sweet smile, his guilt eased a little.

Yes, his marriage wasn't perfect, but he was committed to it. Nonye was a beautiful woman, though there were certain behaviors of hers he didn't like. He had already made a vow to himself that they would work through whatever issues they had together.

Though every pore of his body remained aware of the other woman still standing in front of him, he turned to his side, giving Nonye more of this attention. He needed the woman gone as soon as possible and wondered why Nonye would bring her to his chamber.

"Nonye, I was in a meeting with Amobi. Is there something you need from me?" his irritated nerves reflected in his voice and abrupt question.

"Please forgive me, my prince, but I need a private audience with you." Nonye batted her doe eyes at him, her face screwed up in a frown.

His guilt rose again. His grip tightened on the chair's armrest. He'd never raised his voice to Nonye, yet because of another woman's presence, he was so riled that he lost his temper. That wasn't good. He needed to take back control of his person. Loosening his grip, he extended his arm and took Nonye's hand in his.

Amobi said, "My prince, I think we have concluded our discussion. If it pleases you, I'll come back another time."

Emeka nodded in agreement. His friend was nothing if not diplomatic. Nonye knew better than to interrupt him when he was in a meeting with his special adviser except if the reason was of utmost important and urgency.

"Amobi, thank you for your time. I'll speak to you later." Emeka nodded his head, discharging Amobi and his personal guards from his presence.

When they left the room, Nonye nodded to the girl.

The moment he turned to look at the girl again, his gaze was riveted to her. She was indeed the most beautiful maiden he'd seen. Raven-colored hair—braided, twisted and decorated with beads—was arranged in a pile on her head. The heart outline of her face framed almond-shaped beguiling brown eyes, a small nose, and full sumptuous dark lips. Her skin glowed like raw umber clay and the decorative uli on her body enhanced her beauty.

From her attire, he deduced she was an unwed maiden.

Several rows of elephant tusk beads hung around her neck partly covering her full breasts. More beads hung around her waist, accentuating her slim midriff. A thick-woven skirt the color of fresh okra flared over her round hips and stopped just above her knees. There were more stringed beads on her lower legs and ankles. Each time she moved they jingled like gourd rattles.

She was dressed similar to a young bride on her wedding day.

Emeka wondered what she was doing here. Does she come to seek my blessing? Somehow the thought of her marrying some unknown man had his chest constricting again in jealous rage.

Who is she?

The girl approached his chair, one hesitant step after another. Within touching distance of his seat, she halted and lowered her body in a slow awkward curtsy.

She didn't have Nonye's grace and poise. Still, the curve of her bowed spine was sensuous. Seductive. The embers of desires sparked again in his loins.

When she rose and straightened her spine, instead of looking back up at him, her stare fixed to the ground, her eyes shielded by long black lashes.

Then it hit him.

That gesture. He'd seen someone else do it often. Nonye's handmaiden.

In his mind's eye, he shook his head. It couldn't possibly be her.

"My prince, I want to present Ezinne to you. She will be your companion while I'm away from you."

Astonishment warred with aspiration. For a moment he said nothing. All he heard was the whoosh of his blood in his ears as it raced from his head, across his body, filling him with aching need.

His body prepared for a mating that should never be. His mind knew it would never be.

With the knowledge he garnered the strength to control his body's reaction to the news, to the girl. Under his scrutiny Ezinne seemed uncomfortable. She shifted from one foot to the other, her initial confident air evaporating.

"What do you mean, my 'companion'?'" he asked, forcing his stare to move from the girl to Nonye, who hadn't lost her ability to beguile him as she caressed his hand.

"She will be my stand-in; helping you with all the tasks I usually perform for you, my prince." Nonye's lips curled in the seductive smile he'd become accustomed to, in the past two months, since her arrival.

"All the tasks?" he asked, raising one eyebrow and turning back to face the girl, whose cheeks now had two dark spots, the size of quail's eggs. Her uneasiness seemed to increase, her fingers now pulled at the edge of her skirt fabric in an erratic motion.

Did Nonye realize what she was suggesting? Did the girl agree to this arrangement?

"Yes, my prince. All the tasks." He could see Nonye nod her head from the corner of his eyes. "She is my gift to you to make up for my long absence from Umunri."

"You needn't worry, Nonye. Four weeks will soon go quickly, and you will be back home. So I don't need a companion."

He didn't even want to contemplate the kind of temptation his wife was presenting him with. The kind of temptation he had fought for weeks, since Nonye arrived with Ezinne in Umunri.

"But sixteen days is a long time for my prince to be alone without a woman's comfort," his wife said as she continued to caress his arm. "Ezinne is well trained, and you'll be pleased to know that she is also untouched. Of course, if you have no wish for her in your bed, then let her still perform the other tasks for you, please. It will ease my conscience while I'm away."

Nonye squeezed his hand, her eyes pleading with him.

Emeka understood his wife. She was a woman accustomed to getting her own way. Knowing how to win people's—especially men's—attention was part of her upbringing. She'd been groomed as a political mate and diplomat—the wife of a future king.

In most cases, he indulged her. If she made a request, he granted it.

This—this was too much to ask him.

"And is this what she wants as well?" He turned back to the girl. "Ezinne, do you want to do this? To be my companion? To serve me in every way possible?"

He wanted to spell it out so she was absolutely sure of what she was consenting to.

"Of course she does," his wife replied. "It is her duty to serve you as her prince and master."

"No, Nonye, I want to hear it from her lips. I'm only going to agree to this... arrangement" —he waved his hand in the air— "only if she confirms to me here and now that she wants to do this from her heart. So, Ezinne, what will it be? You don't have to do this. I will not be angry with you if you say no, and no harm will befall you. Tell me the truth."

He watched Ezinne closely, focusing on her eyes, curious to find out her response. He wanted to know from her body's reaction what she truly thought.

Brown eyes with flecks of gold dancing in their depths stared back at him. Right now they shone brightly as they focused on him without wavering. Her shoulders straightened as she seemed to stand taller. Her once fidgeting hands were now folded before her and stilled.

There was none of the cowering handmaiden who usually served their dinner in her. The way she stood, one could be forgiven for thinking she was a highborn princess and not a lowly servant.

"If my prince so wishes, I want to serve as his companion." Her voice was clear and confident, warm and enticing. It traveled through his body, dissipating vibrations down his spine.

He released the breath he hadn't realized he was holding in expectation. The musical tone of her words did things to his body he hadn't realized a woman's voice was capable of doing.

In that moment he forgot who she was. Despite knowing better, he allowed himself to be seduced by utterance. What would it feel like to trace her lush lips with his tongue? To taste and drink from her body?

Somehow he knew it wouldn't be enough to taste her. He would want to claim her as his. Since he'd first glimpsed Ezinne's beauty, he'd barely been able to control his body's response to her. And he never looked at other women since Nonye.

Still...

"You are sure about this?" he asked again, wondering why she agreed to do this. No maiden would choose this for herself, surely.

He understood Nonye's reason for planning this. Sometimes wives arranged concubines and even second wives for their husbands. It was a tactical move that guaranteed control of her rival. It was also a way of growing the man's wealth as it produced more hands to work in the farms.

For the royal house, it meant more sons to secure the family line and ensure the crown passed along from one generation to the next.

Still he couldn't understand Ezinne's motives, and that annoyed him. As the next in line to the throne, he liked to understand the people around him and what moved them.

In the months Ezinne had been in his household, he knew little about her except as the girl who served Nonye. Now he was supposed to accept her as his stand-in companion, even as a bed mate, without knowing her true being?

"Yes, my prince." Ezinne nodded, this time lowering her body in a brief bow.

"So be it," he snapped, turning away from Ezinne.

With a short nod of his dead, he ended the matter. White hot rage flowed through him. He gripped the hard arms of his chair. The alternative was to stand up and shake the truth out of Ezinne.

In his bones, he sensed something wasn't right. He hated being in the dark—without control—over anything. He was angry with her for saying yes, for now putting him in a position where he would have to actually go through with the arrangement.

He'd given her the chance to back out, and she 'hadn't taken it. Why?

Ezinne didn't appear to his as a social climber. At least he hadn't equated her with one previously. One day she would be married to her own husband. So why would she want to offer herself to him if she was untouched as Nonye had claimed?

The whole situation was preposterous. Didn't the girl have her own mind? Had she allowed his wife to manipulate her into doing her bidding? Had Nonye coerced her?

Nonye squeezed his hand one last time and arose from her seat. "Thank you, my prince. Do I have your permission to take my leave? I need to finish my packing as I'll be leaving in the morning. I'll be back later with your dinner."

"Of course. I'll see you later."

Nonye walked past Ezinne and headed toward the door.

Ezinne stood on the same spot for a brief moment, her eyes lowered. When she looked up at him, he saw a flash of anger in her eyes, her lips pursed with distaste. It rammed into him, disorientating him for a moment. He blinked several times not quite believing what he'd seen. What does she have to be angry about? I granted her wish, didn't I?

With her shoulders straightened, she swiveled and followed Nonye out of the room, her back turned toward him. Something she'd never done before; something she wasn't allowed to do.

Instead of raising his anger, her actions excited him, his sense of guilt and caution thrown to the wind. Whatever game Nonye and Ezinne had instigated, he would play along. Maybe it was better this way.

This was fate. The gods had presented him with Ezinne. Who was he to turn it down? He wanted to find out more about the fiery maiden hidden beneath Ezinne's demure exterior. His outlook for the next four weeks brightened.

Chapter Four

Ezinne stood outside the door to Prince Emeka's private rooms, bracing herself. It was the day after she'd been offered to him as a companion. Even thinking about it still made her blood boil with anger. Yesterday she couldn't believe that he'd agreed to the whole ridiculous plan. But yes, it was actually happening.

Nonye had left for Umulari with her convoy earlier in the day, leaving Ezinne here in Umunri to cater to Prince Emeka's needs. A warm shiver slid down her back, and her hold on the wooden tray of food tightened as she continued to hesitate.

The guard standing beside the doorway glanced over at her before staring straight ahead as he normally did. She wondered what he must think of her, standing at the threshold quivering because she had to take food in to their master.

She had managed to avoid the prince all day, refusing to go to him until he summoned her. However, he hadn't ordered her presence. Now she couldn't avoid him any longer as she was the one scheduled to provide his evening meal. She could ask someone else to do it, but that would mean admitting she was a coward.

A coward, she wasn't. Furious, she was.

Allowing the anger to bubble and rise within her, she stepped forward through the door frame into Prince Emeka's main chamber. He wasn't in the first room. With fraying nerves, she flicked her eyes to the door leading to his sleeping chamber. Then, she swiped her lips with her tongue in a nervous movement.

"Who is there?" Prince Emeka's strong, grave voice rumbled from the other room.

She was wound so tight with worry, hearing him speak nearly made her leap out of her skin. The tray in her hand wobbled, the dishes doing a precarious dance. Nothing fell off, and Ezinne thanked the gods. The last thing she needed was an embarrassing scene to top everything else.

Telling herself she could do what was required, she coughed to clear her throat.

"My prince, it is me, Ezinne. I brought your dinner." As fate would have it, she spoke clearly and showed none of her nervousness.

"Put it on the table. I'll be out shortly," was his calm response.

Ezinne took it as a good sign. Hopefully he wasn't angry with her for avoiding him all day. She laid out the bowls of food on the table and the gourd of water.

When she was done, she stood by the table unsure of what to do next. She wasn't used to working as a companion. Was she allowed to sit in the chair at the table or sit in one of the other chairs where Prince Emeka and Princess Nonye usually sat? Nonye wouldn't be happy if Ezinne sat in her chair. She knew that for sure. So she chose to stand instead.

The prince walked out of his inner chamber. Their gazes connected, his black eyes rooting her to the spot.

Mouth dried out, she swallowed hard, her saliva feeling like stone it went down her throat.

Everything else receded to the background. All she could see was him, looking resplendent in a light blue flowing caftan. It was made with soft material that seemed to shimmer in the light. Navy thread embroidery ran around the neckline and seams.

Majestic. Powerful. Tall. There were no other words to describe him. Even in the privacy of his quarters his authority overwhelmed her. There was no detracting from whom he was—the crown prince.

His outfit wasn't traditionally Ibo, covering him from neck to feet. However it didn't hid the strength of prince as it seemed to caress his skin like a stream of water. Her gaze moved to his chest, the embroidery pattern formed a v shape down from the collar, exposing copper-colored skin.

Strangely, she envied the fabric its closeness to his skin. What would it feel like to feel the whisper of his skin again hers?

The sound of coughing brought her back from her musing. Now aware of her surroundings, she lifted her gaze, meeting his knowing gaze that seemed to glitter with amusement.

Heat singed her cheeks. Embarrassment and self-awareness overrode her mind.

"My prince." Suddenly recovering her comportment, she curtsied in the usual formal manner and lowered her gaze to the floor. The black spots on the leopard skin carpet wavered, seeming to mock her.

What had she been thinking? She was in the presence of the heir to the throne of Umunri. A man beyond her reach and station. A man in charge of everything within his realm. Her master.

Granted, Nonye attendance always acted as a buffer between them. Now it was just the two of them—alone—in large room. For the first time in a long time, she felt vulnerable and ill at ease. She didn't like the feeling of being helpless and exposed to someone else's control.

He seemed to consider her in silence because he didn't say anything in response to her greeting. Though the urge to look up plagued her, she kept her gaze lower and her body stooped as was required until he gave her permission to rise.

She'd wondered if she had offended him. Yesterday she had been brazen by turning her back on him as she left his obi. It had been a moment of madness, knowing he could've instructed his guard to take her out into the courtyard and whip her for insubordination.

Perhaps her punishment still waited.

Her anger returned. Her grip tightened on the back of a chair, her short nails digging into the hard wood, inflicting pain on her fingers.

Let him mete out a reprimand for her actions. It wouldn't change her mind or make her yield to him. She had only one purpose for being here. She would fulfill it and move on.

"Rise, Ezinne," he said.

The intense timbre of his words resonated, doing odd things to her insides. She'd heard him speak before. Still, being alone with him seemed to heighten the effect of his voice on her body.

She straightened but kept her eyes lowered. She needed to gain back control of her body. If she kept her eyes lowered, away from him, she could keep her body in check.

"Look at me," he said in a snappy and low... dangerously low tone.

Was he annoyed?

Slowly she lifted her chin, her stare connecting with his once more. His lips were pursed, confirming her suspicions of his irritation.

Anxiety and excitement caused her heart to thump against her chest. Instinct told her to look away. This was the prince. He was capable of crushing her with a snap of his fingers. She should heed the warning.

Instead, she refused to look away and held his gaze. Infuriation crept up her spine at a snail's pace. She would not be intimidated.

"When you are in my presence, you will look at me directly," he continued.

"As you wish, my prince." She nodded and curtsied briefly still maintaining his gaze.

"And when we are in private like right now, you will use my given name, Emeka."

Doing that would mean accepting this whole arrangement as his con—companion. She couldn't do that. She wouldn't do that.

"No, my prince. Regardless of where we are, you are still the Crown Prince of Umunri, and I'm just a servant in your palace. I can't address you by your given name. It is improper."

"That may be so. But for the next four weeks, you are here to grant my every desire as my concubine."

A soft gasp escaped her lips. The way he said the words conjured up images of the two of them intertwined. Heat traveled through her body. She noticed that his lips were lifted in a half-mocking smile; both eyebrows raised, daring her to refute his words.

Sure she'd agreed to this arrangement, but she wasn't going to let him treat her like some woman with no scruples. She was doing this for her own reasons, even if he'd never know them.

"I'm not your con—" She broke her gaze with Prince Emeka. Cringing, she couldn't even bring herself to say the foul word out loud, thinking it would taint her.

He took an imposing step toward her. Panicked, she backed away.

"You were going to say what? That you are not my concubine? That Nonye didn't promise you some sort of reward to keep my bed warm for the next few weeks. That you are not looking forward to the prestige that comes along with claiming you have been bedded by the Crown Prince of Umunri. Or you want me to believe that you agreed to this charade out of the goodness of your heart?"

"I—"

He lifted his hand, stopping her speech.

"I have no wish to hear your lies. Sit down. Let's eat this meal before it gets cold." He pulled out his chair but stopped when she didn't move.

Gripping the chair in front of her tighter, Ezinne bit her lip to control the anger bubbling in her belly, but it erupted before she could put a lid on it.

"I'm not a liar. Neither am I your concubine. In the next four weeks, I'm here to serve you in every capacity as your companion. But I'll not 'keep your bed warm' as you aptly put it. I'll not bed you, even if there were no more men in the whole of Umunri."

"Bravo." He clapped. "Finally, you show your true colors. That's more what I was expecting, and I like it. Since you've got that out of your mind, can we eat dinner?"

He remained calm and sat down. Now that the haze of anger had passed over her, Ezinne stood still in shock. She was expecting Prince Emeka to be angry and lash out at her or order her punished with several stokes of the whip.

He appeared far from angry. In fact he looked decidedly amused; his face widened in a broad smile that dimpled his cheeks, his eyes glimmered with barely concealed laughter.

What is going on here? Why isn't he angry? The truth was she wanted him to be angry. She had hoped she would provoke him and get to see his true personality. Because she knew that once he punished her, the feelings that had been rising within her would subside and she would hate him. She wanted to hate him just as she hated every other man. Men were all alike. Brutal, unforgiving, and selfish.

As she stood rock still watching him, she sensed there was something different about him. He wasn't like all those men. She'd sensed it the first time she'd met the prince. She hadn't paid much attention to it in the past because she'd focused on doing her duties. Now that she was stuck with him for the next four weeks, her awareness of him was rising by the minute.

"Ezinne, sit down, or I'll sit you on my lap and feed you myself. Maybe that's what you'd prefer?" He raised one eyebrow in an acerbic query.

Ezinne bit her tongue to stop from retorting. She had already insulted him once tonight. She really didn't want to push her luck. While she didn't mind being whipped for being insolent, she certainly didn't want the humiliation of sitting on his lap for the rest of the evening.

Heaving a sigh of resignation, she walked to the other end of the table to sit down. The farther away from him she sat the better.

Emeka shook his head. "No. Sit over here." He patted the seat next to him.

She stopped. "But that's Princess Nonye's seat."

"You're standing in for her, aren't you?"

Frowning to show her displeasure, Ezinne moved to the chair on Emeka's right-hand side. She felt odd sitting at the table where she'd served food for the past few months and could only watch from the shadows. Now she was seated next to the prince, in her mistress's chair able to observe everything as the princess would have been able to.

Remember you station. This is only for a short interval.

She kept her eyes fixed on the food as she started dishing it out into the plates.

Before they started eating, she passed him the large bowl of water to wash his hands. She refused to look at Emeka as they ate in silence. Her tongue didn't seem to be functioning correctly as she didn't taste the food flavors. It wouldn't have mattered if she was eating chaff.

No one would believe that sitting next to the prince and eating dinner was not filling her with joy as it would any other woman or person. Instead she was filled with apprehension, worried about what the night would bring.

Would he ask her to his bed tonight? Though she had claimed she wouldn't bed him willingly, he was within his right to force her since she had already agreed to the arrangement in front of a witness. She would be unable to do anything about it. Even if she called for help, no one would come to her rescue. He was the crown prince after all.

"I never realized you were this stubborn."

Without thinking, she lifted her gaze and looked at Emeka. The serious expression in his cold, hard eyes had her worried. All the humor was gone from his face.

She lifted her shoulders in a defensive shrug, unsure of what to say, unable to tell what he was insinuating. She returned her stare to the bowl of food on the table.

Obstinacy was a family trait. He would have to live with it if he wanted her here until his wife came back.

"Are you usually this way?" he asked, his tone blunt. "Or have you reserved this special performance just for me? I know you don't disobey orders from your mistress. Otherwise we know she would run out of patience very quickly."

Nonye was her burden to bear. Ezinne tolerated her for a reason. She didn't have to bear the prince.

Ezinne still refused to look back at him. Being this close to him affected her in an adverse way. Affected her judgment. She needed to keep control of her senses.

"In the space of a little while, you have insulted me, disobeyed my request, and continue to behave with a bad attitude. Are you going to continue that way till your mistress returns?"

Why wouldn't he just drop it? She just wanted to get on with the whole ridiculous affair with the least effort required. Her wish was for it to end soon.

In any case, it was his fault that she was here. All he had to do yesterday was to say "no" and none of this would have happened.

Yet he'd asked her to choose. As if she held any sway in the world. Of course she had to say yes. She'd promised Nonye and couldn't go back on her words.

Before they'd arrived at his obi, she'd prayed with utmost most fervor to the gods for Prince Emeka to refuse and call the whole thing off. But he hadn't.

So tough, but she wasn't speaking to him unless it was absolutely necessary.

"Answer me, woman!"

She flinched and snapped her eyes up. She couldn't miss or ignore the hardness of his voice as if reinforced words with iron. This time he did look riled, a vein pulsing on his forehead, his black eyes piercing through her.

"If I have a bad attitude, it's your fault for making me do this," she retorted, glad to finally get it out of her system. He might as well know it was his fault.

Prince Emeka burst out in a chuckle, yet it lacked real humor. "What? My fault? How do you figure that? I gave you a choice and you said yes."

"The choice you gave me was an empty one. Sla—" Nonye had banned them from referring to themselves as slaves since Prince Emeka had announced there were none in Umunri.

All her life, she'd been treated as a slave. The truth was, regardless of her location or job title; she still felt like one—dominated by her mistress and bound to serve without recompense. She was a slave.

But knowing the prince hated the word, she revised her statement.

"Servants do not have choices," she started again. "They do whatever their mistresses or masters require of them. I couldn't possibly say no to my mistress. You on the other hand are the master. You choose your own destiny. You could have said no to this whole debacle. Instead you had to say 'so be it,'" she said mimicking his speech tone from the other night.

Prince Emeka stayed silent for a little while watching her with an expression she couldn't read. He looked neither angry nor happy. Then he washed his hands in the bowl, drying it on the piece of cloth before turning back to face her.

"Ezinne, I think I need to clarify a few things about me, the palace, and Umunri in general," he started. He looked away, the line around his lips tightened. When he looked back at her, she saw sadness flicker in the depths of his eyes, and then it was gone.

"There are no slaves in Umunri. My father set all them free when he started his reign two decades ago. We only employ servants in the palace. Everyone is paid for their work. It is their choice to work here. If someone is unhappy with their job, they are free to leave. I certainly don't wish for unhappy staff."

He paused, his gaze assessing. It was as if he was referring to her as an unhappy employee and expected to make her complaints known. Her nervousness returned. She pulled at an invisible thread on her skirt.

"I know that things were different in Umulari, but you now live in Umunri, which makes you a citizen in this kingdom. You are subject to our laws which say you are a free woman. If you have no wish to be here, you are free to leave when you want. No harm will befall you. I swear it on my life."

Surprised at his grave oath, Ezinne couldn't say anything for a while.

Could he really be serious? No one swore on their lives with jest. The consequences could be devastating. He had no reason to reassure her. He was the prince. She had to accept his words as law.

"I have no wish to leave, my prince," she said finally when she got her voice back.

"But you have no desire to share my bed. Is that correct?"

"Yes." She nodded. She lowered her lashes to shield her eyes, afraid he would see the truth in them as her body quivered with the thought of feeling his skin against hers.

She felt his warm smooth hand under her chin, lifting it till she had to look into his eyes.

"Then you need not fear. I have never forced a woman into my bed. I'll not start with you." He paused before continuing. "I want to look into your eyes when you talk to me. And you should always speak you mind. Can you do that for me?"

"Yes, my prince." Her voice was barely above a hoarse whisper as she struggled to speak.

Having his hand on her flesh started a fire on her skin that burned all the way down to her belly. The temptation to lean into his hand, to have it brand her grew to a frightening level. His thumb played an arrhythmic beat on her chin and the will to withdraw from his touch left her.

He pulled back his hand and clapped them together to summon the guard at the door.

"Get someone to clear the table," Emeka said when the man came into the room. The man walked out, and a few minutes later, two servants came in and cleared the dishes from the table.

Usually at this point, Ezinne would help to clear the table while the prince and princess retired to their lounging chairs for the evening. Tonight, Emeka stayed seated at the table until it was cleared. When the servants left the room, he turned to Ezinne.

"Let us make a new arrangement," he said. "For the next few weeks, all I ask of you is that you share the evening meal with me. During the day, you can do whatever pleases you. Take up whatever activity you wish to pass the time. Learn a new craft if you like. You can learn to weave cloth or baskets. You can learn to paint or sculpt. We have the best master trainers in this palace who will teach you whatever you wish to learn. Simply tell them you were sent by me. In the evenings you will join me for the meal so that I can have someone to converse with. After that you can go to sleep in your own bed. Is that agreeable with you?"

Her mouth was agape for a moment as she processed the prince's words. She couldn't believe what she'd heard. No one had ever offered her such a lifeline. An opportunity to learn a skill she could use outside the palace. Something she had always yearned for. She almost leaped out of her seat with gladness. In Umulari she hadn't been allowed to learn any skills outside of those required to do her job.

"Really? You would let me learn a new skill?" she asked, her tone hesitant, unsure if she'd heard correctly.

"Of course. It is my way of making up for the inconvenience of my company until your mistress returns. As I said already, everyone is compensated for their work.

As your work is to keep me company, learning a new craft is your compensation. So, is it agreeable?"

"Absolutely agreeable, my prince." She couldn't help the smile spreading on her face. Overjoyed with finally getting an opportunity that could get her out of her mistress's hold, she stood up and hugged Emeka, tears clouding her eyes. "Thank you. You don't know what that means to me."

"It's not a problem," he said, patting her shoulders, his gentle touch stimulating.

Realizing what she'd done, she withdrew at once. "I'm sorry, my prince," she said and knelt down to beg his forgiveness for touching him without invitation.

"Stand up, Ezinne. Don't be afraid. You are allowed to touch me. After all you are my companion."

She breathed a sigh of relief that he hadn't used the other word he had used earlier. Standing up, she thanked him again.

"And another thing, since we've come to a truce, I'll request that you use my given name when we are in private. Can you do that?"

She hesitated but thought that since he'd been generous enough with her the least she could do is carry out his request.

"Yes, my pr—Emeka."

He smiled at her. Her heart leaped with joy at the beauty of his smile, his cheeks sinking into dimples. He stood and walked over to his lounging chair. She waited by the table unsure of what he wanted her to do next.

"Thank you for your time this evening. Have a good night. I'll see you tomorrow," he said when he sat down.

"Wh-what about your massage?" she muttered, remembering Nonye always gave him a massage every night.

"I don't think that's a good idea under the circumstances. Tomorrow I'll arrange for the palace masseuse to do it until Nonye returns. You can go. Good night."

"Thank you. Good night." She tried to keep the disappointment out of her voice. The dressing up and decoration she'd gone through to be transformed from servant to seductress hadn't worked. The prince didn't desire her at all. He no more wanted her in his bed than she wanted to be there.

Still, she knew that was a lie. Her mind might not want him, but her body clearly did. The sensations he'd invoked within her matched no other she'd experienced in the past. While she might not have Nonye's adept knowledge, she certainly knew what it felt like to yearn for a man. Her longing would never be fulfilled so there was no point dwelling on it.

Giving him one last quick glance, she walked out of his quarters, guilt washing over her. Somehow she didn't think it fair that all she got to do in the new arrangement was sit down to dinner with him while he was rewarding her with something so important: her dignity and self-esteem.

The evening had not gone the way she'd anticipated. In truth she still wasn't sure what to make of the prince. There had to be a trap somewhere, and she knew it would hit her sooner or later.

In the meantime she planned to make the most of the opportunity before her. Learn a craft she could use so that when she decided it was time to move on from Nonye, she would have something to fall back on. The future suddenly seemed like something to look forward to.

Chapter Five

"So how is your training going?" Emeka asked as they sat down for dinner four days later. Ezinne sat in the chair next to him.

The prince had kept to his word and informed the master trainers of her wish to learn a craft. She had chosen fabric weaving. The intricacies of making fabrics had always fascinated her. Though it was a male-dominated skill, Emeka had given the master trainer permission to train her.

"It is slow going at the moment. But the teacher is a very patient man. I'm grateful for his fortitude," she replied.

"Well, he told me you were doing well," Emeka said in between chewing his food.

"He did? You asked him?"

She was surprised that the prince would take time out to inquire about her progress. Another new thing she was learning about him. He took a keen personal interest in the people around him regardless of their station in life.

"Yes, I did. So many things about you fascinate me. I also wanted to make sure he wasn't being too hard on you."

Did I just hear him right?

"My prince, there is nothing fascinating about me. Your time is surely better spent on matters of state." In reflex, she lowered her gaze to the table. Many years of being told she was nothing and no one of interest had been ingrained into her being.

"What now?" he asked sternly. "Are you trying to raise my ire this evening?"

Worried, she looked up and met his gaze, wondering what she'd done wrong. She realized he was feigning anger when his onyx eyes sparkled with laughter.

"No, my prince."

"Then look at me and stop this 'my prince' refrain. I thought we've already agreed you will always call me Emeka when we are in private."

"Yes... Emeka." She rolled his name on her tongue as she said it. It still felt strange referring to him by his given name even after four days.

"That's better."

He took her hand in his. His touch was soft, encompassing as he folded her hand into his large ones. Still, she felt the edges of roughness in there too—the hands of a prince who worked with his hands as well as his mind.

The spark of warmth generated spread tingles through her body. They hadn't had any physical contact since the first night at dinner. In that time, she had yearned to feel his skin against hers again. She prayed he would touch her.

Spending time with him every evening was turning out to be the highlight of her day regardless. But now that he'd touched her, the caress wonderful, a warm glow surrounded her. She felt connected to him and not just physically. It was as if she was meant to be here with him every night, talking about politics or whatever else pleased him.

"Ezinne, you are a beautiful woman."

She looked up at him. His black eyes glimmered with sincerity, she couldn't believe his words. Everyone else thought she was ugly, so he couldn't possibly be right.

"I'll have to disagree with you on that. I'm not beautiful. I don't have the grace or poise that my mistress has. She is beautiful," Ezinne said with confidence.

Emeka brief chuckle rumbled through her. She loved hearing him laugh, especially the way his eyes sparkled in the light. It always put a smile on her face.

"It makes you even more beautiful, that you don't know how beautiful you are," he said in a light tone. "I have observed you the last few days. I noticed the way the men around the palace stare at you each time you walk by. They would all like to claim you."

She shook her head, not believing what he was saying. He didn't find her attractive even after all the efforts she made daily on her appearance.

"It's true. You are also intelligent and naturally gifted."

"Now you jest."

"I do not," he answered, his voice hard and somber. "The trainer informs me you have been making suggestions of how to mix the threads to create new fabric textures. And this is only after a few days of learning. I already know that you are strong-willed. No one can bend you to their will unless you allow it. All these things make you very fascinating. I want to find out so much more about you. However, it seems you don't like talking about yourself."

He was correct. She never talked about her life or her past to anyone. The mere thought of her existence made her feel low and dejected. The least said the better.

"There isn't much to say. My life isn't as interesting as yours," she replied.

"But I want to know about you, your parents, what you were like as a child," Emeka insisted.

"I don't have parents. My mother raised me, but she died a few years ago. I had a reasonable childhood. Some would say it was even privileged because I lived in the palace servant quarters and got to play with the princess," she said with haste, hoping to end any further discussion.

"So you and Nonye grew up together?"

She sighed in resignation. It seemed Emeka was not ready to take a hint. Maybe it was better to talk about it now and get it done with. But there were matters even she couldn't talk about, regardless of how much he probed. Dark troubles locked in the recesses of her mind and best kept hidden away.

"Yes. At one point we were the best of friends, always playing together," she said, focusing on the lighter subject.

"So what happened?"

"When her mother, the queen, died, the king decreed that the slaves should be kept away from the main palace residence. That meant I wasn't allowed to go to see her anymore."

"Didn't she come to see you?"

"She did a few times, but her father found out and banned her outright," she said in a nonchalant tone to keep the cheerlessness out of her voice. However, misery sat heavy in her belly like a boulder.

"I was punished for daring to play with the princess. He told her she had to focus on learning how to be a princess, that slaves would taint her. By then I was learning to serve as a handmaiden. When she became of age, I became her servant."

"I'm saddened that you experienced all that. It's the kind of practices that my father has worked to stamp out in Umunri. It hasn't been easy, but I think we are finally there." Emeka's smile was tinged with gloom, his eyes lost their spark. He stopped eating and washed his hands.

"You see, that's why I don't like talking about my life. It is depressing," she said as she washed her hands as well. She'd lost her appetite.

"I know what you mean, but sometimes we need to say the words out loud to someone else so that they don't depress us to the point of the grave," he said, leaning back into his chair.

"But for some people, the grave is a more appealing prospect than the life they lead."

Abruptly, he sat up with a frown marring his face. "Don't say that. I hope you're not referring to yourself." He moved his hand to cup her face, his palm under her chin. "Promise me you're not thinking of taking your own life."

"No." Her smile was weak as she fought the tears building within her. There had been times when she'd thought death would be better but not anymore. "I have no wish to end my life."

Shrugging to hide the wretchedness wrapping its cold fingers around her body, she tried to move her head, but he held it still. She closed her eyes to stop the tears, but they broke through her lashes dropping onto her cheeks.

Emeka's warm breath fanned her cheek before she felt the light brush of his thumb and fingers wiping her tears away. His touch was comforting. Stimulating. Tingles like sparks of fire spread from her cheeks to pool in her belly. She opened her eyes and looked into his. His dark eyes shone with warmth and compassion.

"No more tears, Ezinne. The past is gone. It can't hurt you anymore, I promise," he said, his voice low and gruff, full of emotion.

She nodded, grateful for his kind words. The fondness and warmth in her heart bloomed fully. Her core ached for this man—this prince, the most wonderful man she had ever encountered. Even with his power and strength, he was still kind, generous, and gentle. The kind of man she had secretly yearned for but feared didn't exist.

Yet she knew she couldn't have him. He was someone else's husband. She couldn't betray Nonye, even if the princess didn't appreciate him. It wasn't Ezinne's decision to make. The gods had already decided who would spend the rest of her life with Emeka, and it wasn't Ezinne.

"If you could have anything, I mean anything, what would it be?"

His profound question roused her out of her reverie. She looked up at Emeka, He watched her with concentrated focus. Confused, she squinted at him. "I don't understand. What do you mean?"

"What is your greatest desire? Say it and I'll grant it."

She sat back in thought. Right now, her greatest desire was to be in his arms, to have him soothe the ache within her.

Even she wasn't stupid enough to openly admit she desired another woman's husband. More so when the man had no desire for her. Especially a woman like Nonye who would invoke the demons from the underworld to torment her if she dared show any disloyalty.

So she went for the relatively safer option.

"I desire freedom more than anything else," she said with a joviality she didn't feel, knowing that even Emeka couldn't grant her that wish.

"Then you have it. You are free to do whatever pleases you. If you want to leave the palace and go live somewhere else, you can do that," Emeka said, smiling as if he'd achieved a great feat.

Sadness squeezed her chest. If only it was that easy. She reached out and took his large hand in hers, squeezing it, reveling in its strength and warmth.

"Thank you so much for granting my wish. Someday it may actualize. But for now, I'm not free until Nonye grants my freedom too."

Looking displeased, he moved his hand away. "What? In Umunri, I'm your master, and my word carries more sway than Nonye's. So as I've granted your freedom, you are free from this moment onward."

She shook her head knowing he wouldn't understand. "In Umulari, all the slaves are made to take an oath binding them to their masters or mistresses. I'm bound to Princess Nonye by an oath only she can break or my life is forfeit."

Emeka sat back, looking shocked, the frown on his face deepening. Overwhelmed with gloom and needing to get away, Ezinne stood, the sound of the hardwood chair scrapping the stone floor, jarring her nerves even more.

This was the reason she didn't like thinking or talking about her life. She always ended up wanting to end it all. What kind of life was it to be bound to someone when you would rather be free as a bird?

"Please excuse me, my prince, but I need some air."

He grabbed her hand, searing her to the bone. She could barely stand straight, her knees wobbled.

"Don't go. Let me help you."

She could hear the pain and shock in his voice. But she couldn't stay here. She would end up begging him to take her in his arms and soothe her pain. She couldn't do that.

"No one can help me. I'll stay if you insist, but I'd rather not be here right now."

"I understand. You can go. Good night, Ezinne" He nodded, releasing her hand.

"Good night, my prince," she said and fled the room without looking back.

***

Emeka sat in the same chair without moving after Ezinne left. He couldn't believe what Ezinne had told him. Yet in the back of his mind he knew she wouldn't lie to him. What reason would she have to tell a falsehood about something like this when she knew he could verify it for himself?

The people of Umulari made their slaves take oaths before a shrine that permanently bound them to their masters.

It was quite unbelievable. It was bad enough that they had slaves, a practice he abhorred. He believed every individual should be free born, free to choose their own destiny, not under anyone else's yoke.

He had thought that with his marriage to Nonye, he could show the people of Umulari how they could make the lives of their citizens more stable by freeing slaves. Now it seemed the problem was more deeply rooted and wouldn't be easily wiped out.

Still he had to do something about it. He couldn't simply fold his hands and watch injustice from afar. First he had to start with Nonye. Ezinne was a human being and should be allowed to exercise her free will without being forcefully bound to her mistress.

Nonye needed to start learning to behave like a citizen of Umunri which she now was by virtue of their marriage. She was not permitted to keep slaves, and he had to ensure that all slaves bound to her were released from the oath as soon as she returned.

Even when he'd decided what he was going to do, he remained unmoving in his chair. He should call out for the table to the cleared off the dinner crockery. Instead, the vision of Ezinne with tears rolling down her cheeks tormented him.

The sight had torn his heart in half. Unexpected, the intensity of his feelings for her had unraveled when she'd finally broken down in front of him. Pain had seared through his body like someone had whipped his bare skin.

The need to take her into his arms had all but overwhelmed him. He'd wanted to take her into his arms and console her—to make everything alright for her. Latent possessiveness had warred with doing the right thing.

Taking her into his arms wouldn't have been the right thing to do. Not when he'd wanted to press his lips against the softness of her cheeks. Swipe the saltiness of her tears with his tongue. Taste the juiciness of her sweet lips.

No, he wouldn't have stopped at just holding her. Not from the way his manhood throbbed at just the memory of Ezinne. Without shame or honor.

Wiping her tears with his fingers had been the honorable thing to do.

He had to find a way to squash his growing feelings for Ezinne. For the past four days he'd looked forward to every night they had spent together eating and talking. He'd even cleared his schedule to ensure he had enough time to prepare for her arrival.

Each moment with her, learning something new about her was without equal. She was an amazing woman, strong and brave. One he longed to connect with on every other level.

Still, it wasn't possible. He was bound to another. Yes, he could take a concubine, but what kind of man would that make him? He was a leader who showed his people a better way of living, to stand above the murk, the dredges of society. If he couldn't control his desires, what right did he have to set himself apart and lead as the future king?

Leadership meant sacrifice and this was his sacrifice. He couldn't have Ezinne, though he'd desired her from the moment he'd first met her when she arrived in Umunri. No matter what, service to Umunri came before personal gain.

Furthermore, she didn't want him. She'd said so. It was best that way. If he ever felt tempted to disregard his duty to Umunri, he would never force himself on a woman.

As the frustration rose within his body, he stood and walked out into the clear moonlit night. His personal guards followed him. He stopped them. He wanted to be alone with his thoughts.

Walking through the tall palm trees surrounding the palace, the silver beam lit his path. The air filled with night sounds: an owl hooted, crickets chirped, and the leaves rustled as he brushed against them.

He headed for the palace lake. It was set against rocks that rose into the sky with a waterfall descending in cascades. Legend had it that the pool was carved out by his great ancestor, the first king of Umunri.

When he arrived, he realized someone was swimming in it. No one was permitted here except members of the royal family. He knew his parents and sister had already retired for the night.

He moved closer to the water, ready to call out the trespasser, the round moonlight reflecting off the water. The person stood up. He realized it was a woman, her back turned to him, her long black braids cascading down her back all the way to her hips. The rest of her was below the waterline.

He stood, riveted to the spot. Something about the woman gripped his attention. At the back of his mind, a voice told him to turn around and go back to the palace. But he wanted to see her face, though he already had his suspicions.

She turned around and gasped. "My prince." The sound of her soft voice flowing through him, twisting his insides like it always did. Ezinne.

In the moonlight, she looked even more remarkable. Like a water goddess, her wet hair cascaded behind her, her ample breasts in full view, her nipples taut and pointing toward him. Water ran in between her breasts down her flat belly.

Immobilized, he watched her, his mind unable to think coherently. His body didn't fail to response to the temptation displayed in front of him; the rush of heated blood swelling his manhood to the point of pain.

When she moved in his direction, he was jolted into action as he became ashamed of his inability to control himself.

"I'm sorry," he said and turned around, intending to walk away. He stopped when she spoke.

"I should be the one apologizing. I know I shouldn't be here. But I was restless and needed a swim. I didn't want to go to the main stream this late at night."

"It's not a problem. You have my permission to use this pool whenever you want to."

"Thank you," she said softly.

He took another step away, but her voice stopped him again.

"Please don't go. I know I'm not as beautiful as Princess Nonye, but am I so repulsive that you cannot bear to look at me?"

Seeking first to reassure her, he turned around without thinking. She was standing a few paces from him and had now wrapped her skirt around her hips. But she remained bare of any covering on the rest of her body, her beads and trinkets all still on the ground where she'd left them. Her dark skin glistened in the silver light. He yearned to touch it, to feel its texture against his skin.

"You are very beautiful, Ezinne." He could hardly recognize his own husky voice as his emotions clogged his throat. This woman affected him like no other. He had to stiffen his stance so as not to walk over to her and take her in his arms. Couldn't she see the evidence of her impact on his body?

"Who is the liar now? You have barely looked at me nor touched me in the past week. I'm obviously not that—"

Nasty words. He couldn't let her finish them. I took two short steps to reach her. He cut off her words by pulling her into his arms and crushing her against his chest.

"You are the most beautiful woman I know. There, I said it." He never thought he would do this. He was not a weak man to allow emotions and lust to overwhelm him. But here he was doing the thing he'd sworn he'd never do— comparing another woman to his wife. His mind warred between guilt and protectiveness. Somehow, he felt as if he was betraying his wife by telling Ezinne she was the most beautiful. But there was something about Ezinne that made him want to shield her from pain.

Still, it seemed his words alone were not good enough for her. Ezinne shook her head against his chest.

"No."

He lifted her head, muffling her word with his kiss. The one thing he had wanted to do for days and had told himself she wouldn't want. However, she put up no resistance, her pliable lips opening willingly when his tongue probed them. She welcomed him into her warm, sweet mouth. She tasted of oranges and mangoes, sweet and succulent. Her tongue touched his, matching his movements.

When she slid her tongue into his mouth, all sense of the world fled him. She became his world. He tasted her, inhaled her, and touched her. She seared him in return, branding not just his body but his heart.

With one hand holding her neck, the other roamed her body enjoying her feel. Her skin was firm and smooth on her back, but when he touched her breasts, they were yielding and heavy, overflowing his palm—perfect globes. He wanted to taste them; he wanted to taste all of her. She whimpered when he moved his lips to her neck, kissing her collarbone and inhaling more of her clean scent.

Her sounds roused him from his lustful haze. He lifted his head, trying to clear the fog of desire from his mind. He shouldn't be doing this. It was wrong.

She opened her eyes, their brown depth filled with longing.

"I have never lied to you. I never will. You are beautiful. Don't let anyone ever tell you otherwise." He stepped back creating some space between them. He needed a cold, vigorous swim tonight, but he would see her returned to the palace before returning. The last thing he needed was to show her the evidence of how much she affected him.

"Pick up your things, and I'll escort you back."

She nodded before squatting to take her things. They walked to the palace gates. He bid her good night before returning to the pool. He would be swimming a few lengths if he wanted to get any semblance of sleep that night.

Chapter Six

"My prince, our spies inform me that Oshaji is preparing for war with Umulari. The king of Oshaji has blamed Umulari for the abduction of women and children, so they plan retaliations."

Emeka was in his obi in conference with Amobi and Ikem the chief warrior and the head of the intelligence team. For a while, there had been rumors of war looming against their neighbor in the east, Umulari. Emeka had ordered the spies to investigate and report back to him. Ikem was here presenting their findings.

"This is a serious matter. Are you sure of what you're saying?" Emeka asked, his demeanor calm. Ikem had never misinformed him in the past, but the implications of the news were dire. He had to be absolutely sure.

"I'm very sure, my prince. Our sources have always been correct with their information. I have no reason to doubt this," Ikem replied with confidence. He was a great warrior leader, so Emeka felt comfortable with the man's information.

Yet this was not good news for the people of Umunri.

"My prince, you realize if Umulari goes to war, then by virtue of our relationship with them, Umunri will be at war too. Their enemies have become our enemies by proxy," Amobi's grave words confirmed Emeka's fears.

"I'm fully aware of this, and it worries me. We have worked so hard for peace to be dragged into war at this moment. This news will not please my father at all."

The king while still strong in his mid-forties was aging in relative terms. He had hoped that Umunri would not be at war for the rest of his reign. It seemed that was about to change.

"No, His Majesty will not be pleased. But we cannot renege on our deal with Umulari. We will have to get involved," Amobi remarked as he shifted in his seat to the right of the prince. Ikem sat opposite him to Emeka's left.

"I know. But before we make any decisions to go to war along with the Umulari, we should send a delegation to Umulari and Oshaji to discuss their grievances and negotiate a peace treaty between them before things escalate," Emeka said. There had to be a solution that didn't involve hostilities between their neighbors.

"I agree. We should work on diplomatic efforts first. War should be a last resort." Ikem nodded when he spoke.

Emeka was glad that even the most fearsome warrior in the land was not bloodthirsty. For the years preceding and in the first few years of his father's rule, Umunri was constantly at war with its neighbors. Every grown man was trained in warfare skills.

However, a few years ago, his father made the decision to stop all hostilities and started to negotiate peace treaties with all their bordering neighbors. For the past five years, there had been no wars with their neighbors. The warriors had lost their thirst for blood. His father's legacy had taken root within Umunri, and Emeka would do all he could to protect that legacy.

"I think that's best too," Amobi agreed.

"When the delegation is agreed, I'll arrange for the guards to go with them. It is not a safe time to travel especially if there are random kidnappings going on in the bordering kingdoms," Ikem added.

"Thank you, Ikem. I'll speak to my father later today. I know he will want to arrange a meeting with the elders too."

Emeka paused, frowning for a moment as a thought occurred to him.

"My wife is currently in Umulari and is due back in two weeks. I'll have to arrange for extra guards to go and bring her home."

"Perhaps it is best to leave her there until the investigations have concluded," Amobi said.

"I'm not so sure that's a good thing. I'd rather have her here where I know she's safe. While she's there and with all this uncertainty, I'll be restless." His frown deepened as guilt spread through his body. If anything happened to Nonye, he would feel responsible knowing how he felt for Ezinne.

Amobi tried to reassure him. "She will be safe in her father's palace for a few more days. War hasn't broken out yet. But it is probably not a good time to travel until we ascertain what is actually going on."

Uneasy, Emeka shifted in his chair. He wasn't reassured. His conscious warred with the need to make the right decision. He knew why he wanted Nonye home. If she was back here, he would no longer be tempted with Ezinne. He would have Nonye to lavish his attention on instead of Ezinne.

The last few days had been torture. He'd had to limit the time he spent with Ezinne, sending her off to her room as soon as the evening meal was done. Not wanting to prolong the agony of seeing her and not being able to do anything about it.

The more time he spent with her, the more irresistible she became. His restraint was gradually slipping. The affair between them wasn't just lust. And that made it even harder.

There was brazen passion. Their kiss the other night confirmed it. He wanted Ezinne so much he physically ached most of the time.

Still, there was something else—deeper, heart-warming, soul-searing. That was what scared him.

If it was only a matter of bedding her, it wouldn't be too bad. After all, it was what Nonye had arranged. If his wife didn't return home soon, he wasn't sure he would be able to hold out for much longer.

Having Ezinne in his bed for a few days would never be enough.

Every night Ezinne haunted his sleep. She visited his dreams and stayed in his bed. Often, he tasted her sweet lips and filled her soft slick depth with his hardness. Always, he woke up sweaty and frustrated.

No matter what, he needed his wife home soon. He had to find a way to bring her back and end this madness because he was gradually going insane.

"Ikem, what do you think? Is it safe for Nonye to return, or should I leave it for now?" Emeka asked the man who knew best in matters of security.

"My prince, I would suggest that we restrict traveling to only those who need to travel. However, if you would rather have your wife home sooner, then I'll go myself to guard her journey home."

"Thank you, Ikem. I'll think about it and let you know my decision. No matter what happens, I'll need her home before the New Yam Festival. But first, you owe me a sparring match." Emeka laughed to ease the tension in his obi. War was not an easy topic to discuss.

"Whenever you're ready." Ikem boisterous laughter echoed in the chamber. "I've been looking forward to getting you into shape."

When he was younger, Emeka trained and exercised with the warriors. Now he kept his exercising to sparring weekly with his guards or Amobi. He loved sparring with Ikem but these days the warrior was usually busy with other assignments.

Since he had him around today, Emeka wanted to make the most of his presence. Sparring with the best warrior in the kingdom was good exercise and should help him work out his mounting frustrations.

"You can ask Amobi. I won our last match. You better watch out," Emeka replied. He laughed with equal animation.

Standing, he gestured to his guards to bring his weapons. He stripped off his ceremonial robes and trinkets down to his loin cloth. The palace head guard handed him his machete still in its scabbard. Emeka unsheathed it and took his shield.

"We are using live weapons?" Ikem asked, looking surprised.

"Yes, are you afraid, Ikem? Don't tell me our chief warrior is afraid of sparring with live weapons." Emeka laughed again as he teased the warrior.

"Afraid? Never. Let's go."

They both walked out to the courtyard in front of the palace where they were to begin their match.

***

Ezinne sat at the loom in the large weaving hut. It was a hot day outside, yet the hut was always cool, the mud wall absorbing the heat from the scorching midday sun. Her mind wasn't on the activity at hand but back at the waterfall where Emeka had kissed her a few nights ago.

She had relived the kiss every day: the feel of his firm lips against hers, his warm wet tongue invading her mouth, the hardness of his body against hers, the tingling sensations that spread through her body, the feeling of being lost and home at the same time.

It had been a wonderful kiss, more than she'd ever imagined it to be. Not that she'd had enough kisses to compare it with. She'd had a man slobber her with his sloppy kiss and stick his large tongue in her mouth. That experience had been revolting, and she'd had to prevent herself from throwing up.

Emeka's kiss was eons above that one. It had elevated her into another realm she hadn't been aware of—one of bliss and pleasure, one of heightened awareness and a growing ache deep within her.

Above all, she wanted to taste his lips again and feel his body next to hers. She wanted him to make love to her, to surrender her body and soul to him. She had never wanted a man that way before.

"Come and see. Prince Emeka is sparing with Ikem, the chief warrior."

The distant words roused Ezinne from her deep thoughts. The mention of the prince's name had her ears pricking up with alertness. The person was outside but close to the loom hut. She recognized the voice as one of the palace servant girls, Oma. From the corner of her eyes, Ezinne could see the master weaver standing over her shoulder watching her actions. She paused, wanting to hear more of the conversation going on outside.

Another female Ezinne didn't recognize immediately responded. "Really, Ikem is a fearsome warrior. The prince is brave to face such an opponent. But we know they don't practice with real weapons so no harm with befall him."

"No. Today they are using real weapons. If you doubt me go and see for yourself. They are in the courtyard," Oma said.

"I have to see this for myself," the second speaker replied.

The sound of footsteps fading told her the conversant had moved away. Panicked, her heart constricted in fear.

Emeka was sparing with real weapons! Why would he do that?

She'd never seen him practice with the warriors before, but she'd heard they always used the blunt wooden practice weapons not the sharp metal ones. Distracted, she missed a line of thread in the loom as she fumbled with worry.

"Ezinne, are you all right?" The master weaver stopped the loom and put his hand on her shoulders.

"I'm sorry, but I don't feel very well. Do you mind if we end today's lesson early?" She looked up at him, hoping he'd let her go. She needed to get out there and see what was going on.

"It's not a problem. We can continue when you feel better. Go and see the palace *dibia* so she can give you something to treat your ailment."

"Thank you. I'll see the dibia if I feel worse than I am right now."

She stood and walked out of the hut. The hot earth singed the soles of her feet, reminding her they were bare. Out of habit she'd forgotten the leather slippers the prince had given her in the loom hut. In only a short while, her feet had become accustomed to wearing them when she would normally walked bare-footed.

Footwear was only won by those who could afford it— nobility, titled people or wealthy merchants. It was another gift from Emeka that raised her from the status of a servant to a consort.

She collected the slippers from where she'd abandoned them, put them on and headed toward the courtyard. She prayed what she'd heard wasn't true. Fear of the prince getting injured in quickened her pace. Cold sweat broke out on her skin.

The palace was made up of rows of courtyards bordered by buildings. Each courtyard represented a unit. When you arrived through the archway into the palace, the first building was the King's. His obi stood majestic and imposing at the front; murals of different scenes across the kingdom were painted on the outside and bronze statues of the gods formed a column outside it.

The images were striking, giving the impression to a visitor that the gods lived there. At the back of the building there were other long houses to the left and right, forming a private courtyard of his dwellings.

The next set of building were the prince's, the construction mirrored his father's—his obi at the front and private dwellings at the back. Behind the prince's quarters were the barracks, servant quarters and service huts, where the loom hut was located.

So it took little time for Ezinne to arrive at the prince's courtyard. A small crowd had already gathered. It seemed everyone was interested to see a fight between the prince and the fearsome chief warrior. She heard the sound of clanging metal, and her stomach dropped.

It is true! They are fighting with live weapons!

The idea of men fighting or war in general, caused fear to ice her blood. Her mother had told her awful stories of how their village had been raided by warriors and she'd been abducted and turned into a slave in Umulari. Ezinne had been glad to find out that Umunri was a peaceful kingdom.

As she couldn't see the fight properly from where she stood, she moved around the crowd trying to find a vantage position from which to watch. She caught glimpses of metal reflecting the sun's rays as the crowd cheered the combatants.

She noticed a gap in the crowd ring and walked to it. When she saw the two men, she felt faint for a moment. Both men faced each other off, weapons raised. Their chests rose and fell with heavy breathing, and their dark skins gleamed with sweat.

While they were matched in height being tall men, the warrior Ikem was heavier in muscle definition, one side of his torso covered in tribal tattoos.

Yet her eyes were drawn to Emeka. She had never seen his body uncovered before.

He had broad shoulders, a lean waist, and powerful legs. He was more athletic than bulky which surprised her. As a prince she had expected the flabby tell-tale signs of good living around his midriff but there was no flab in sight. He was all lean muscle. He had the frame of a working man.

The instant response of her body caught her in surprise; her breasts felt heavy and sensitive, her skin flushed, and heat pooled in her belly, filling her with excitement and longing.

Yearning seized hold of her. She wanted to move closer, to rub her hands over his slick skin, to feel the pulsing of his heart against his chest. She bit her lips to quell the desire growing within her, knowing it would never come to fruition. He didn't desire her in return. Yes, he'd told her she was beautiful, but she'd felt he'd only said it to make her happy.

As the men circled each other, swinging their machetes, weaving out of the way, deflecting the hits with their shield, she stood there, entranced, suppressing the urge to scream every time Ikem swung a blow at Emeka. Her heart jolted each time. She told herself to be brave. It was only a practice fight, not a real battle.

Emeka appeared to be a good fighter. From the way he deflected and returned the strikes, he looked like a skilled warrior. It felt strange to watch him in a bout. Since Nonye's departure the man she'd come to know and admire was gentle, considerate, responsible, self-disciplined, and sympathetic to others. He'd shown those characteristic in his actions toward her and the decisions he'd made concerning other citizens of Umunri.

Yet watching him fight, she saw a brave, decisive, and strong man too. It seemed contradictory that a gentle man would also be strong. But he was. She guessed it was why he was such a good prince, a king in waiting. It was obvious his people loved him.

She loved him too.

She'd never thought it would happen. That she would ever meet a man she admired enough to love. Her hatred of men started with the man who sired her and abandoned her to all the other men who had abused and mistreated her in one way or the other. She'd had nothing positive to think or say about a man until she met the prince.

Of course she hadn't believed he would be any different from the other powerful men she'd encountered. But his actions from the first day she arrived in Umunri had been without reproach.

Though she'd been wary of him, slowly, unknowingly, he'd taken down the protective wall around her mind, one stone at a time. Now she had nothing to fight him with. Nothing to hold against him. Except that he was Nonye's husband. Even that defense didn't hold sway with her any longer.

The fear she once held about her mistress was gone. Somehow during her interactions with Emeka, she no longer feared Nonye's wrath. He'd taught her to be brave and confident. He'd given her back her self-esteem. When he looked at her, he made her feel strong and intelligent.

All her life she'd submitted to the wishes of other people, never doing anything for herself. She had always been loyal to Nonye even when the other woman was being nasty.

Didn't she deserve something back? Why was it that Nonye deserved the prince and Ezinne didn't? Especially since Nonye was probably in Umulari at this very moment having an illicit affair with Dike. While she couldn't be sure, she knew it was a high likelihood. Nonye had practically said so herself.

It was Nonye who had insisted Ezinne become Emeka's concubine. While she hadn't been in agreement with it at first, now she wondered if it was the only way she was ever going to get a chance with Emeka.

He could never love her. She was a servant to his princess. She accepted it.

A man's love had never been her aspiration.

Loving Emeka made her happy. Showing him would make her happier. If getting into his bed would allow her to express how she felt about him, even a little bit, then she'd take that chance. Nonye would be home in a few days and then their affair would be at an end.

Observing the fight, she moved closer to stand in front of the crowd. When Emeka turned, their gazes connected. His black eyes held surprise for a brief moment before sparkling and his lips lifted in a smile. In the moment of his distraction, Ikem seized his opportunity and struck, swinging his machete at Emeka.

Instinctively, Ezinne screamed with terror as the blow bounced off Emeka's shield he'd raised a tad too late. It connected with his shoulder before Ikem pulled back his machete. When he lowered it, Ezinne noticed blood on its sharp edge. Feeling faint she wanted to run to the prince. She took a step toward him. He held her gaze coolly and shook his head, halting her movement with his silent command.

The rejection she should have felt was overshadowed by the fear that he'd been seriously injured. Blood trailed down his arm as Ikem helped him stand. He remained restrained showing no further sign of injury, while she felt sickness roiling her stomach. His guards came to attend to him, and he walked off toward his private quarters.

As the crowd dispersed, everyone muttering about the fight and how brave the prince was, Ezinne couldn't move her feet. Her body vibrated with tremors. She had never been this scared before.

Seeing the blade connect with Emeka's shoulders had nearly knocked her over with fright. Guilty joined the other emotions spiking through her mind. She'd distracted him enough for Ikem to strike.

The urge to go to the prince straightaway made her take a couple of steps in the direction of his chambers. She cared not about what anyone said.

Gods! The man she loved was injured. She should be with him.

But he'd indicated he didn't want her there. It would raise too many questions. She understood his need for decorum and secrecy. She would respect his wishes for now. However, she would go to him this evening; nothing in the world was going to stop her.

She turned back and headed to her dwelling, the matter resolved in her mind.

Little opportunities came along in her life. She needed to make the most of this one. Tonight she was going to tell the prince how she felt about him, no matter the consequence.

Chapter Seven

For the rest of the day, Ezinne was listless. Her concentration swayed from one matter to the other. Thought of Emeka overshadowed all else. As she didn't have any menial chores to do, she went back to the loom hut. But even that didn't keep her concentration for long. The day dragged on too slowly for her.

At intervals, she walked past Emeka's quarters whenever she could, hoping to catch him in a quiet moment. It seemed he was having a busy day because he didn't come outside again. Once, she caught a glimpse of him walking to the king's obi, his footsteps hurried. He didn't look in her direction. She wasn't sure if he knew she was there.

Later that day, she saw some of the elders of the high council arriving at the palace. There was a sense of urgency in the air as people hastened to get to the king's obi. She wondered what the commotion was about. The palace had regular visitors, but she'd never seen so many people arrive at the same time. She assumed there were important matters of state to be resolved.

Would Emeka discuss them with her later tonight? While he discussed most things about his day, he never talked about weighty issues. Political wrangling was not for servant ears.

As evening approached, she decided to have a bath in preparation for seeing Emeka. She wanted to make herself as appealing as possible to him. Tonight she was going to present herself as a concubine. She didn't know how he would accept it, but she had to try. Time was running out on her. She only had a few days with Emeka until Nonye's return.

When Nonye returned, Ezinne would request to be sent back to Umulari. While going back to Umulari didn't appeal to her, it was the sacrifice she needed to make in exchange for the time with Emeka.

Otherwise, staying on would mean dying slowly. To have to sit back and watch Nonye with Emeka, knowing Nonye didn't care for him as much as Ezinne did, unable to say or do anything. And worse, having Nonye treat her like she was nothing again. It would be an unbearable torture.

Putting the harrowing thoughts out of her mind, she went to the main stream used by the villagers. Though Emeka had granted her use of palace bathing facilities, she still felt awkward about using it. The stream was a longer walk but she needed the time to calm her nerves so she didn't appear too eager when she arrived at Emeka's chambers.

Due to the day being mostly gone, there were less bathers using it—only two other people, servants from the palace. She got distracted chatting with them and didn't notice the time pass.

It was dusk by the time she returned to her quarters. She dressed with care, choosing the best clothes from the ones Nonye had left her. Instead of twisting her hair up in the formal way, she wrapped it in a loose knot at the back of her neck to provide for ease when she wanted to loosen it later.

She put on her trinkets but didn't use the heavy neck beads. Instead she chose the waist beads and left her chest bare. Her breasts were full and firm and, in her opinion, her best assets. She didn't want them covered up. The skirt she wore was heavy woven cotton in emerald green color that worked well with her skin tone.

On arrival the prince's dwelling, she hesitated for a moment, her boldness fled. Emeka was the Prince of Umunri, and she was a slave girl. Did she really dare to win his heart or even his body? Would he stoop so low as to claim her even temporarily? The guard at the entrance coughed, jarring her into action, and she stepped into the main chamber.

Emeka sat in his lounging chair. He looked neither happy nor displeased to see her—not his usual welcoming demeanor. Winged creatures seemed to flutter in her belly. Her uncertainly increased as she walked toward him, each step hesitant.

He didn't get up or say anything as he would normally do whenever she arrived. She sensed instantly something terrible was afoot. She studied him trying to comprehend his behavior.

Tonight, he wasn't in a long caftan as he usually wore. Instead he was in a purple toga wrapped over his uninjured shoulder and around his waist. A tight piece of cloth surrounded his injured shoulder. It looked clean. She assumed someone must have tied a fresh cloth after his evening bath. She realized the change in his evening attire was best so as not to aggravate his injured shoulder.

Still, she worried about the extent of his wound and how much it must hurt him. She wondered if it was the reason for his unusual mood this evening.

She knelt before him, placing her hands on his knees. "My prince, how is your shoulder?"

"You are late," he stated as if he was making a simple pronouncement in the palace court.

She looked up at his face but couldn't read his expression. Was he angry with her? She noticed the vein ticking on his jaw and realized he wasn't pleased though he appeared calm.

"I'm sorry. Please forgive me. I—"

"It's done now. Let's eat." He interrupted her speech. Brushing her hands off his knee, he stood and strode to the table.

Shocked, she remained kneeling, unable to understand the reason for his uncharacteristic ire. He had never snapped at her before and was usually quick to forgive her when she stepped out of line. But the rage she sensed within him was beyond any she'd experienced before.

With as much grace and serenity as she could muster, she rose and walked to the table. He was already seated which was also unusual because he always waited for her to sit first.

"My p—... Emeka," she caught herself before she used the formal phrase. "Have I done something to offend you? I promise I'll not be late again. Whatever it is I've done please forgive me. If you tell me, I won't do it again. I promise."

The earlier winged creatures in her belly seemed to have undergone some metamorphosis into slithering worms. Her initial nervousness turned into sickness.

Disappointment with herself for causing his upset made her ill. More than anything, she wanted Emeka to be pleased with her, especially tonight.

"There is nothing to forgive. It isn't your fault. It is my fault for thinking I could expect more from you, for thinking there was more to us."

Pain seared through her like someone had pushed a knife into her stomach. Her eyes stung with banked tears. "But there is more to us. I want there to be more to us. You mean a lot to me, more than I can put in words. Why would you think any different?"

"Ezinne, this is hard enough as it is. Let's just leave it and eat." He dismissed her words with a wave of his hands and looked away from her.

His rejection hurt the most. It also angered her, raising her quick temper. Agitated with her pulse racing, she spoke, forgetting her place.

"No, we cannot leave it. If I have offended you, don't I deserve to know what it is? Or does a lowborn concubine like me not even warrant a fair hearing?"

The vile words left her lips before she could call them back.

Emeka sat up. His grip on the table tightened, turning his knuckles a pale color. His eyes changed to fiery onyx flashing his anger at her.

"Stop this nonsense, Ezinne." The growl in his voice reminded her of the sound of a tiger warning off intruders. Her instincts told her to take caution, but she ignored it.

She'd had enough of not being given a voice, not being heard. For years she'd kept quiet in Umulari. Emeka was the one who told her to always speak up. He was going to hear her out whatever the consequence.

"No, I won't stop. Would you rather I strip now so you can call the guard to whip my back until it is welted and red with my blood?" she continued, ignoring his warning.

Pushing back his chair, Emeka stood. The sound of the wood against the stone floor screeched in her ears. He paced the room like a confined wild animal. Had she pushed him too far. When he stopped by the table again, he appeared calmer.

"Is that the way you see me? Like some depraved, bloodthirsty tyrant, a man with no conscience?" Though his voice was serious and mollified, his eyes looked troubled and uncertain.

Shame and guilt washed over her, churning her stomach. This man who had treated her so compassionately was not a tyrant. She was ashamed she'd made him think so.

"I thought you were that way two months ago when I first came to Umunri. But the past few days with you have shown me otherwise. I believe you to be a fair man. It is why I'm surprised by your irrational behavior tonight," she replied, hoping he would explain what was going on.

"If I'm behaving irrationally, it is you who drive me to it, Ezinne." He stared at her as if unsure of what to do. There was no anger in his eyes. She could have sworn he looked at her with tenderness. Then he growled again, scrubbing his face with his right hand before turning his back to her.

For a moment, she was stunned. Had she heard him right? Could it be that he felt something for her but was trying to hold it in? He was a man of veracity. He lived his life openly. So she understood why he wouldn't want to put his honor in question.

But surely there was a way forward for them. They were not doing anything that wasn't already approved by Nonye, except maybe Ezinne falling in love with Emeka. But that was her risk to bear, not his.

"My prince, Emeka, please. Tell me what bothers you. I know I fall short of what you deserve, but I'll listen and atone for whatever offense I have caused you. Please." She lowered her voice and walked to him. Lifting her hand, she touched his rigid back seeking to calm his unrest. The muscle twitched under her fingertips.

Unhurried, he turned around. She looked up at his face. In his eyes, she saw his torment. A lump lodged in her throat choking her. She swallowed hard.

This man cared for her more than any man ever did. Before she could say anything, he pulled her with his unbound arm to his chest and fused their lips together.

Emeka was kissing her again!

Did she dare to believe it? Was she in dreamland? Let no one wake her if she was. The thing she'd prayed for was happening, at last.

At first gentle, his tongue swiped across her lips, teasing her. Then he probed for entry. She parted her lips, this time more confident after their encounter at the poolside.

He tasted divine. His tongue masterful in her mouth, sensation exploded through her body. Heat flowed in her veins. The world tilted. Her knees wobbled as if the ground beneath her feet quaked.

Tighter, he held her to his hard body. His large hand splayed across her round bottoms. The swell of his manhood pulsed against her belly. The feel of her sensitive breasts and taut nipples on his chest—hard contours and bristly hairs—wrecked havoc on her already overloaded emotions. She wanted more of him. Wanted the fulfillment of the pleasure the kiss promised.

The ached in her core deepened. A strangled moan escaped her lips when he lifted his head.

They stood still staring at each other as their chests rose and fell, needing more air than the room seemed to have.

She gulped in air, feeling light-headed. His eyes burned with flames of desire. He looked like a man who wanted to claim her. A warm shiver traveled down her spine. His hand moved up her back, massaging it.

"Ezinne, I want to love you the way a man loves a woman. Yet I'm torn because I know this can only be for a few days more."

More warm tingles spread through her as joy filled her heart. His words pleased her to no end. He desired her. That was enough for her. Tilting her head, she beamed him a smile of pure delight.

"A few days are more than I ever hoped for. I have yearned for your love, Emeka, for you to soothe the ache growing within me with your touch and your body."

"You have?" He studied her with a curious expression, his lips tilting up in a glorious grin.

Lowering her lashes to conceal her eyes, she nodded in response. She was unable to speak as her throat clogged up with emotion.

He let out a heavy breath, the warm air fanning her cheeks. He smelled of the clean night air after rain. Leaning his head against hers, he whispered against her skin in a husky voice. "You deserve so much more than a few nights in my bed, Ezinne. I want to give you the world."

She nearly wept with joy. She'd never been this happy. No one had ever said anything like that to her. Pulling her head back, she cupped his chin, loving the feel of his bristles against her palm.

"For me, a few nights with you are better than nothing. I want to make the most of the time we have left together."

Darkness flickered through his eyes, his smile turned wry as he shook his head.

"You don't understand. Making you my concubine goes against everything I stand for and my honor as the prince of Umunri." He paused and let out a grave sigh as if resigned to fate. "I'll summon Nonye home immediately, and she will unbind you from your ties with her. Then I'll make you my wife."

A chill went through Ezinne, goose bumps mottling her flesh. She pulled away, shaking her head. Untangling her body from Emeka's, sadness overtook her and all her pleasure for his kiss evaporated. She moved to the table.

Already, she had lost her appetite. But she needed a place to sit so she didn't topple over from the tremors that racked her body. After sitting down, she lowered her head into her hands.

"Ezinne, what's the matter?" Emeka walked to her and sat beside her. He pulled up her chin. "You look less than happy. Is the thought of being my second wife that disagreeable?"

Heaving a sigh, she tried to smile but couldn't. Misery wrapped its claws around her body, pulling her shoulders down.

"I cannot be your wife," she said, the words simple yet heavy on her tongue. She didn't even want to think about it. Why did he have to bring it up?

"Why not?" Emeka frowned, his eyebrow raised in unbelieving query.

"Look at me. I'm a slave." His frown deepened, and he looked like he would retort but she continued. "Yes, I know Umunri doesn't have slaves, but it doesn't change who I'm. You'll put your future as king in jeopardy for even thinking it. I cannot allow it. Princes don't marry slaves."

"Who says? As prince I can choose my own wife," he countered with confidence.

"Just the way you chose Nonye, right?" She had to make him see sense.

"I could have disagreed with that marriage if I'd wanted to. Anyway, that has nothing to do with this. Knowing the sacrifice I made for Umunri with Nonye, there's no way they can decide for me whom I marry next. And I choose you. So stop arguing and agree to it."

She shook her head. He was just as pigheaded as she was. She would have laughed if the matter wasn't so grave. "I'm not at liberty to agree to a marriage with you. It is for my mistress, Nonye, to decide if I'm to marry and to whom. I know she'll never allow it."

"I'll command her to. She cannot have a slave in Umunri. She'll do as I bid her," he snapped, his annoyance at her disagreement to his proposal obvious in his tone.

There was nothing she could do. Her hands were tied. It wasn't her decision to make.

"It shows how little you know her."

His gaze flicked toward her, and his forehead furrowed. Seeing his response, she wished she could call back the words.

"What's that supposed to mean? Is there something I should know? Something you're not telling me?"

Letting out a resigned sigh, she lifted her shoulder and shrugged. It wasn't her place to tell tales about Nonye. She still owed her mistress some loyalty regardless.

"There's nothing to tell. It's just that Nonye won't be happy to have me as a rival wife," she said, hoping to appease him and halt further questions. "When she made this arrangement, I was to be your concubine for a limited time, not your wife. I don't see that she will change her mind easily."

She paused for effect.

"If anything, she will blame me for seducing you and trying to wreck her marriage. I don't want that on my conscience. If you care about me the way you say you do, drop this thing about making me your wife. It will not end well. Please."

She held onto his arm, hoping he would grant her this one request.

He placed his hand on top of hers. The warmth of his palm permeated hers, soothing her. "Is that really what you want?" he asked his tone gentle.

"Yes."

"If it makes you happy, then I'll not raise the matter again. But I still intend to get Nonye to release you. You will become free."

Relief slammed into her, the breath she'd been holding let loose.

"Thank you."

Now that they'd resolved their disagreement she could continued with her plan for the night.

"I noticed a lot of visitors in the palace today. Was there a meeting of the council?" she asked.

Despite the strength of her feelings for Emeka, the distrustful side of her still wanted some reassurance. Would Emeka be forthcoming about grave matters? Or did he just lust after her body?

"You are quite observant. Yes the ruling council had an emergency session today."

"It sounds serious. I hope all is well in Umunri."

Emeka assessed her for a moment as if weighing up how much detail to divulge. "This is not a matter for idle chatter in the market square. Do you understand?"

"Yes, my prince." She replied without thinking.

"I'm telling you this because I think you should know. There is a threat of war at Umulari. And Umunri could be dragged into it if not resolved diplomatically."

"Dear gods," she gasped. "I hope it doesn't come to pass."

Though Umulari held bad memories for her, she didn't wish it citizens any harm.

"I hope so too," he replied in a grave voice. His brows knotted together in a frown.

"Forgive me, my prince. I have not been a good companion." She rose and stood behind him.

"Nonsense. You've been more than good except when you refuse to use my given name," he teased.

She placed her palms on his cool back. "I'm serious. While you have grave matters to contend I have burdened you with trivial issues and given you little pleasure. What kind of companion does that make me?"

She kneaded his tense back muscles starting from his neck downward, avoiding his injured shoulder.

"One that is very skilled with her hands." Emeka's pleased groan vibrated through her belly.

"Where did you learn to do that?" he asked before releasing another grunt of contentment.

"I was trained when I learnt my duties as a handmaiden."

"What else did you learn how to do?"

She tensed, her hand froze on his skin. "I refused to train as a pleasure maiden. It was one of the options but being a palace courtesan didn't appeal to me." Her words sounded stiff.

Emeka rotated in his chair to face her. The concern in his eyes nearly floored her. She clutched her palms together.

"That wasn't what I meant, Ezinne. I was taken aback with how good a masseuse you are," he said. "Come and sit down. At this rate we will never eat dinner."

"There are other things I would rather do." She knelt beside him. "Let me show you my gratitude for everything you've done for me in the past few weeks, especially releasing me from my bonds."

He pulled her up to sit back on the chair. "You don't owe me anything. Freeing you is an obligation I owe you as a citizen of Umunri. It is your right, not a privilege."

"I know." She caressed his arm with her fingers, hoping it would have the desired effect. She kept her voice low, sultry, as she'd seen Nonye do several times. "But you've done so much for me. You've given me so many gifts. I want to give you something back. I know it is nothing compared to what you own, but it would please me if you accept my gift."

He caressed her face with his other hand. Warm tingles spread through her, pooling at her center "Whatever it is, I accept it." His voice reminded her of feet crunching over gravels, the vibrations reverberating through her body.

His words encouraged her, her fear of rejection fading. She wasn't a naturally seductress, but she moved her lips in a smile she hoped had the desired effect.

"My gift to you is all I have and precious to me. It is the heart of a slave, lowborn, worth nothing. It is my love blooming without conditions. It is my body that yearns for your fulfillment. It is all that I am."

His eyes picked up the flickering of the lamp and sparkled, his lips uplifted. He pulled her onto his lap. His thigh felt firm and strong beneath her yielding bottom. "You honor me with such a precious gift, my love. Do you not know what you mean to me?"

Taking her hand, he placed it on his chest above his heart. She felt its strong erratic beat echoing the rhythm of hers. Her stomach churned with excitement.

"Do you not know that being here with you at the evening meal is the highlight of my day? Do you not know that I count the moments until I see you? That I dream of you every night?"

"If it's so, then show me. Tonight, make me your woman."

Without saying another word, he winced as he lifted her into his arms and carried her into his sleeping chamber.

Chapter Eight

Emeka stepped into his bed chamber with Ezinne, all thoughts of dinner out of his mind. His eyes focused on the loveliness of the woman in his arms. His pulse raced with expectancy, his body primed with desire and hardening by the moment.

In his mind the war waged on; delight against despair. He wanted this woman in every way possible. It seemed she wanted him in return. She had offered herself to him. It still felt like he was letting her down by this half measure. This temporary contentment.

They only had a few days but he wanted forever. They would only be sharing his bed but he wanted to give her his home. He would be worshiping her body but he wanted to be bound to her heart.

She deserved a place of worth in his life.

Gently, he lowered her. Her body slide down, soft curves touching firm flesh. A groan erupted in his throat. A haze of lust blanketed him. When her feet met the floor, she looked up at him. Her brown eyes burned with flames of longing, flames he knew matched his.

He gazed upon her lips; full and firm. They were inviting, sweet and succulent too. When their tongues had danced, her kisses had been that of a woman unexplored, a woman not used to the attention of men.

He couldn't help but compare her tentative touch to that of Nonye's knowing and refined actions. His wife was a woman well skilled in the act of seduction; every stroke and motion intended to lure a man to explore untold intimacies.

However, Ezinne's movements were uncertain and awkward. She remained still in his arms when their tongues mated. Yet her eager response indicated her latent sensuality, waiting to be awakened by the right man.

Was he the right man? Was he doing the right thing? He'd asked her to marry him, and she'd refused. He understood her fears. There were so many things that needed to be resolved before they could ever take that step.

First, Nonye needed to release her from her servile bonds. Then he would have to seek Nonye's consent to take another wife. To take Ezinne as his wife. While it was his right, he would never do it without Nonye's consent. As his first wife, she deserved that respect.

There was a strong possibility that Nonye would not agree to Ezinne as her rival. He could only hope that Nonye saw Ezinne more of an equal than a servant. That would ease matters a little.

He stroked Ezinne's cheek with his fingers, her face soft and warm against his palm. His other arm curved behind her, caressing the bare skin of her back. Her skin was lush, the light scent of coconut oil filtering into his nostrils, warming his blood.

He tilted her chin so he could see her face better in the shadowed room lit only by a low burning torch on a sconce. She let out a soft gasp, her mouth opened, inviting him in.

Without hesitation he lowered his head, eagerly melding their lips. He swallowed her soft sigh as she moved closer to him, her breasts crushed against his chest. Her fervor was nearly his undoing. He couldn't believe that she proffered herself so willingly, so enticingly—such a rare, scrumptious bequest.

Her sweetness surpassed that of sugarcane. She was more intoxicating than fresh palm wine. She was full of the promise of dark surrender and sensual fulfillment. From the first day he'd seen her arrive with Nonye, he'd wanted her in ways so carnal he'd been ashamed of his own wayward thoughts. Now standing with Ezinne in his embrace, he knew he could no longer resist her.

He'd sacrificed so much for his people, always lived his life above reproach. Tonight he might be about to fall from grace. But for once his tortured soul didn't care for rules and principles. It sought a union with this woman in his arms.

Tomorrow there would be a price to pay. For tonight he would indulge in the pleasures he'd yearned for in past two months.

In alternating motions, he caressed her tongue with his and then placed light nips on her lips. Entangling his fingers in her hair, he drank from her lips like a man dying of thirst.

Soft moans of pleasure escaped her lips. The sound was painful and provocative as cavernous hunger swept through his body, swelling his flesh in arousal. His heart echoed in his chest like drum beat in the festivals.

Unable to hold back any longer, he lifted her and placed her on the fur-padded pallet, his actions controlled and tender due to his hurting arm. Her dark oiled skin gleamed in the dim light. The gold in her eyes swirled reminding him of a furnace. There was no mistaking the invitation in the unabashed depths of her eyes. The desire. The tenderness. The love.

A fist squeezed his chest. Ezinne presented herself to him in total surrender. A sacrifice—his sleeping chamber, the shrine of their love and his pallet, the altar of its consummation.

Her readiness touched his soul. Her bold enticement hid the heart of an innocent. A temptation he could no longer resist.

Deliberately he removed his clothing, loosening the toga and letting it drop at his feet. As his hands moved to his loincloth, he noticed that her glittering eyes followed his movements. They stopped, fixated, when he halted.

He lips lifted in a slow smile of pride that she waited for him. Waited to see all of him. Anticipation quickened his motion, his loincloth falling away. His manhood pulsed as if happy to be released from its confinement. She licked her lips, the movement of her tongue across their soft flesh increasing his arousal.

Wanting to see more of her, he bent over and tugged her skirt. He rolled it down her thighs and legs. He took a deep breath. The sweet scent of her arousal hit his stomach, and her juices glistened in the dark curls shielding her hooded gem.

He moved his hand up her thigh, caressing it with tender care. He fixed his gaze on her breasts, the perfect appealing orbs, and leaned over to taste them. At first he licked the soft flesh. Then, he pulled the skin into his mouth, sucking hard. Her soft moans increased when his fingers parted her hooded flesh and he touched her intimate skin.

Suddenly her body went still beneath him. Sensing something was wrong, he looked at her face. She looked worried. Hesitant. She bit her lip and turned her face away.

He moved his hand from her thigh to her face. He turned it back so she would look at him. "Ezinne, what's wrong? Did I hurt you?"

She shook her head, tears glimmer in her eyes. "No, it's not that." Her voice sounded troubled.

He lay beside her and cradled her head against his shoulder, massaging her back in gentle soothing stokes. "What is it that worries you? Tell me and I'll make it right for you."

She broke into a full sob, sniffing louder, her tears dropping onto his chest.

"Ezi m, my precious, don't cry." He held her, speaking in a mellow tone into her hair. His need to possess her was relegated by his need to protect her. He cared for her and was prepared to wait until she was ready.

"If you've changed your mind about joining with me, that's not a problem. I respect your wish, you know." He kept his voice light and teasing to show her there was no need to fear.

"I know but... it's not the problem." She raised her head, her brown eyes filled with doubt as she bit her lower lip. She blinked several times. "I know Nonye told you I'm untouched... it's not true."

Unsure of her exact meaning, he frowned. But her eyes confirmed his fears.

Excruciating pain lanced his gut. He stayed still, his hand frozen where it's been caressing her back.

Ezinne has been with another man? He knew it was unfair to be jealous considering he had a wife already. Yet a part of him had wanted Ezinne all to himself. He couldn't explain it. He only knew the rage building within him.

"Do you mean you have another lover?" Envious, he asked the question, the words nearly choking in his throat as it constricted with pain.

Her eyes turned cold, glittering with insubordination. "No, I don't have a lover. I was raped," she bit out before pushing off him and getting up from the sleeping pallet.

Chapter Nine

"You were raped? Are you sure of what you're saying?" Emeka grabbed her arm, stopping her from moving farther away from him.

Anger already simmered within her blood that he would dare to think she had another lover. The apparent disbelief in his voice broke through the restraint she held on her temper. Ezinne swiveled around, her free hand on her bare hip, her full breasts bouncing with her movements. She didn't care that she stood fully naked with nothing but the rows of beads around her waist.

She cared that the man she loved didn't believe her words. That the man who'd encouraged her to speak up, who'd given her hope that men could be something other than brutal, would question her motive.

"Why would I say I was raped if I wasn't? What do I have to gain? Of course I know what I'm saying." She didn't attempt to hide the contempt in her voice.

The years of suppressing the rage of being violated and unable to do anything about it suddenly erupted in venomous words at the one man she dared to rail against. The person who should know better. The powerful prince capable of crushing not just her body but her heart.

Emeka released her arm. Realizing that their moment of passion was gone, Ezinne moved to pick up her discarded skirt, wrapping it around her hips once more. This kind of news she delivered to Emeka in the middle of their lovemaking was a deal breaker. She'd known she was taking a gamble revealing her past traumatic abuse to him. She could have let him claim her. That way she would keep the memory of what they shared even if he discarded her later.

Now there was a high likelihood he would never touch her again. Rape carried a heavy stigma. Sometimes it was best to live in silence rather than admit one was a victim.

Nonetheless, she'd wanted to be as open with Emeka in the same way that he was open with her. While there were things beyond her control, matters of her body were still within her power, especially where he was concerned. She wanted him to know her in some sense. She could only hope that what they shared was important enough for him to overlook her past.

Emeka sat on the raised pallet, his expression schooled. A vein pulsed on his temple, his hands gripping the edge of the pallet, a sure sign of his rising anger. She glared at him in return even more aggravated that he dared to get angry, her pulse rate rising as her breathing increased.

She was the one who'd been violated! She was the only one entitled to anger.

"Ezinne, this is a grievous allegation. When did this happen? Who is the culprit?" His voice was heavy with the weight of her words. Emeka rose, his body's fluid motions not lost with his haste and he took a step toward her.

She stepped back, not wanting him to touch her, knowing she needed to keep her wits about her. She needed to show him she was strong. If he held her, she wasn't sure her restraint would not crumble or her tears flow.

"It doesn't matter who or what. It has already happened and cannot be undone." She shook her head.

Nothing he could do would replace her virginity. She had sworn not to talk about the incident. It had been the prize for her life.

"Of course it matters. It matters to me. You have been violated, made unclean. This is Umunri. We do not tolerate such abuses. The culprit must be made to bear the punishment. Name him."

There was a deathly calm to Emeka's voice. A cold shiver went through her. She looked up at his face as he towered over her, his body rigid, his clenched fists at his side. In the shadows, his angular features looked wound tight. Intimidating. There was no doubt about the gravity of his words. He meant to punish the culprit! It was impossible.

"It didn't happen in Umunri, and it was a long time ago. Forget I mentioned it." She turned around and walked toward the door.

The intense frustrated growl from Emeka had her frozen on the spot. She heard the rustle of clothing.

"Ezinne, turn and face me."

She didn't miss the commanding tone of his voice. Compelled, heart racing, she twirled around to face him. He now had his discarded clothes back on.

"You have to tell me what happened."

"Why do you want to know?"

He raised his eyebrow in a silent query that dared her to defy him. She hated that he was suddenly treating her like a citizen of Umunri and not like a lover. He'd made no move to touch her or hold her.

"An instant ago, you didn't believe me. As I already said it doesn't matter anyway."

"Ezinne, do you not understand that a grave crime has been committed and that the culprit must be punished? What kind of prince would I be if I let people get away with such offenses?"

This was exactly what she didn't want. Him turning it into a case to be deliberated and ruled upon by the royal court. She hadn't told him to get the offender punished. She'd told him to share a part of her past with him. To show him her true self. Now he was turning it into a campaign for justice.

She exhaled a deep, frustrated breath, telling herself to stay calm. Nothing would be gained by losing her temper again.

"I'll tell you only on one condition. That you promise simply to listen and afterward do nothing about it. I cannot bear the shame of having my disgrace displayed for public viewing."

He shook his head.

"If you don't give me your promise now, I won't say anymore. Do I have it?"

He stared at her for one long moment before nodding. "I promise to just listen. Please sit." He indicated the pallet.

She walked back to it and sat down. He waited until she was seated before joining her. The wood creaked under his weight. He place his hand over hers, caressing the back with his thumb. Warmth spread through her, leaving her feeling safe. For a moment, she reveled in the entrancing sensation.

"Tell me," he urged, his voice rich and tender. She looked up at his face. His dark eyes were concerned. She realized that he was worried about her.

Swallowing a lump down her throat, she nodded, letting her mind roam back to the events of that inauspicious day.

***

Ezinne sat in the room she shared with other handmaids in the servant quarters of the Umulari palace. She'd lived through fifteen New Yam festivals. Her mother, the only close relative she had, died a few full moons previously.

As her mother had been a slave, no special mourning rites were accorded her. Ezinne was the only one who actively mourned her. Princess Nonye had given her a few days off work after her mother was buried.

Today though she had a little time to herself because Nonye had been away visiting her mother's family and had taken other handmaids with her. She was grateful that her mistress had given her the impromptu break. She used the time to catch up on her chores in her own quarters, cleaning and washing her clothes.

"Ezinne, you are summoned to the king's quarters."

She looked up, and one of the royal guards was standing in front of her. Puzzled, she frowned. She'd never been summoned to the palace before except by Nonye.

"Why?" the word spilled from her mouth.

"Do you dare to question the king's summons?" the guard questioned her in a threatening manner.

"No, of course not. I'm sorry." She sprang to her feet with haste, hoping not to raise the wrath of the guards and the king himself. The guard walked off, and she followed behind, jogging to keep up with his fast pace.

When they arrived at the king's quarters, she was ushered into his obi. There was another man with him, a statesman she knew as Ichie Uwaluru. She knelt in front of the king and lowered her gaze to the ground.

"Is this the girl?" Ichie Uwaluru asked. She could hear the leer in his voice. She wondered what was going on, but she could never ask. Her status in life was to obey orders and do other people's bidding.

"Yes, this is the one," the king replied. "As you can see she is well endowed and ripe for picking."

"She sure is." She heard something that sounded like the smacking of lips. From the corner of her eye, she looked at Ichie Uwaluru. He had a shameless smirk on his face. And he was old enough to be her father! Her grandfather even.

She stayed kneeling unsure of what was transpiring between the two men, telling herself to stay strong. She could withstand whatever it was.

"She is my gift to you to ensure I get your continued support. Kanu, take her to the palace courtesan so that she can be prepared," the king said.

The king's guard walked forward, indicating she should stand up and follow him. Without protest she did, all the while praying that the gods would rescue her from what awaited her. She didn't fully comprehend it until she arrived at the courtesans' quarters. The ladies bathed her and dressed her up. She was then taken to a sleeping chamber. The decorations were luxurious, the bed and floor covered in soft fur and fine fabrics. She wondered who slept there. Soon enough her silent query was answered when Uwaluru arrived at the chamber.

"My sweet," he said, smiling at her. "You look so beautiful."

"What am I doing here?" she asked with boldness as her temper rose. She couldn't believe that the king would give her away to a man this old. She was a slave, but this was below her own expectations for her life. She had dreamed of all the things she would do. Losing her virginity to an old man was not one of them.

"You are to be my bed mate. I hear you are still a virgin. Exactly the kind of girl I want," he said and walked to her. She stood her ground, not wanting to show the fear that was rising within her. His sweaty palm slid down her neck, and he cupped her breast.

Bile rose from her stomach, threatening to choke her. She gritted her teeth, clenching her palms at her sides. But as his other hand clamped onto her other breast, she couldn't stop from responding. She pushed his hands away and stepped back. She didn't care if she got punished; she wasn't going to go through with this. A thousand strokes of the whip were much better than having this man touch her.

"You like to play games, do you?" He took his clothes off very quickly for a man his age. Ezinne backed away toward the door, but he lunged at her, grabbing her by the neck. "You are going nowhere. You will feel me inside you today."

He lifted her up, showing an agility and strength she hadn't expected from him. He pinned her down with his weight. She tried to struggle, but it was no use. He held her down with brute force. In no time he'd spread her legs with his knees, his hand shoving at her roughly.

With a grunt he entered her, and pain rocketed through her at his violent invasion of her body. Telling herself to simply bear it until he was done, she let her body go limp hoping he would be quick. She didn't know how long he was inside her. It seemed to go on forever. She was only aware that after a while he was no longer on her body. He stood by the door, giving her one last leering look before leaving.

In a daze, she waited a little while. When she had recovered some strength, she stood up. Her body ached. Still she walked back to her quarters, head held as high as she could. She didn't want anyone to know what had happened. It was only when she got there, when no one was around, that she finally broke down in tears.

Chapter Ten

Emeka held Ezinne's hand as calmly as he could. It was with all the reserves of control he had that he held his body rigid to stop himself from leaping up from the bed and taking decisive action. To demand punishment against the man who had committed such a heinous offense.

For to take a woman without her consent especially outside marriage was to violate her. To make her impure. Untouchable by other men. An accursed woman. In Umunri, such a crime was punishable by banishment of the offender. The woman had to be purified by a cleansing ritual.

By virtue of his marriage to Nonye, he could demand action against the culprit in Umulari. His wife's hometown was essentially an annex of Umunri. If anything happened to their King, their kingdom would fall under the authority of Emeka's father and by default, his command.

He watched Ezinne as she told her story. She seemed to shrink, withdraw back into her mind. The bold, outspoken woman of a few moments ago lost. In its place, a shell of a woman he hardly recognized. She appeared haunted. Tormented. Her eyes glazed over with unshed tears.

When she stopped talking, she turned her head away, pulling at her hand. He held onto her refusing to let go, afraid to lose what was left of her to the nightmare in her mind.

How had she lived with such a thing for so long, in silence? Why didn't she want the offender punished? He needed to understand her reasoning.

"Did you tell Nonye about this?" he asked his tone quiet.

Ezinne looked at him with a blank expression for a moment as if he'd just roused her from her thoughts. "No," she said, shaking her head. He wasn't sure if she was just confirming her words or clearing her head. "I couldn't tell her. I couldn't let anyone else know of my shame."

"What happened after that? I hope the man didn't come back again."

Her gaze snapped up. Desperation swam in her eyes. "It could have been a lot worse. A whole lot worse."

Frowning, he asked. "Why do you say that? Being raped is very bad."

"Yes, but not as bad as being sold off to the same man who raped me in the first place."

"What do you mean?" His tense body tightened even farther, his voice lowered a notch.

"Apparently Ichie Uwaluru wanted to buy me from the king. I found out when Nonye returned and was told that I was being sold. She managed to persuade the king to let me stay with her. The king loves her and would do anything for her. He agreed on the condition that I was bound to her for life. She agreed, and here I am." The melancholy in Ezinne's voice tore at his heart like metal claws shredding it. She still refused to look at him.

"When I found out I was being sold, I swore I would kill Uwaluru if he touched me again. Then kill myself. There was no way I was going to allow him to invade my body for a second time. By binding me to her, Nonye saved my life."

This time she lifted her head. Her eyes sparkled with sadness. Determination. Tears. Despite all that she'd been through, she was a survivor, her spirit and body ready to fight against the odds.

"Now do you understand why I can never go against Nonye's wishes? Why I cannot be disloyal to her? She offered me a lifeline when my life was at its lowest. In spite of appearances, she is the only person who has shown some kindness to me... well, that was before you. You have shown me enormous generosity. But you understand my meaning, don't you?

"I do."

He stared at Ezinne with sadness and admiration. Even after all she'd been through she still had a good word to say about people. In his opinion, Nonye should have protected Ezinne better. But he could see that it wasn't Nonye's fault. At the time Ezinne was raped, Nonye would have been about the same age too, unable to execute sound judgment.

Now his ultimate ire was reserved for his father-in-law, King Agbado who treated his wards in such an appalling way. Offering a child to a man such as Uwaluru with the intention of selling her was cruel.

Emeka wondered at what other atrocities were being committed in Umulari daily. It sickened him to know that Umulari was considered an ally by Umunri. Yet how was it possible that they could partner with a kingdom without regard for its citizens, freeborn or otherwise?

In the morning, he would discuss it with his father. How much of these events did the king know about? Surely he would never condone acts like rape and trading of slaves.

"In my heart I feel the man who violated you should be punished," he said.

Ezinne looked at him before shaking her head and frowning. With his palm, he held her head still so she could look at him directly.

"But I promised you I'll do nothing against him. I'm a man of my word. But if you change your mind, let me know."

"Thank you. I'll go back to my quarters now." She started to get up.

"It is late. You can sleep on my pallet."

For some reason he couldn't bear thinking about her being so far away. After what she had revealed tonight, he wouldn't be making love to her until the offense against her had been mollified. It wasn't because he didn't want her.

Entrenched down he still ached to be with her. But he realized she was a woman in bondage in more ways than one. She would have to be placated and so will the gods before she could be fully healed.

Making love to her would be taking advantage of her and making things even worse. He wanted her free. Free from her past. Free from the yoke of Nonye. Then she could become whatever she wanted to be. If she still didn't want to be his wife, he'd learn to live with it. But at least he'd have done the right thing by her.

"Where are you going to sleep?" Her eyes widened in surprise as she asked him.

"I'll sleep on my lounging chair."

He wanted to know she was safe. And having her sleep next door to him would please him. Though what he'd really like would be to hold her to him all night. But he'd noticed her discomfort since her revelation and didn't want to add to it. She probably didn't want a man lying next to her after she'd just recounted a rape.

"Isn't that going to be uncomfortable?" she queried, eyebrows raised.

"I don't mind the discomfort. I'll get the guards to bring me more bedding to make it comfortable. Do not worry."

Her nod seemed reluctant. "If that is your wish."

"It is." He smiled at her. "Go on. Lie down. I'll be next door if you need me."

He opened a wooden trunk and took out more bedding and walked into the other room. The lamp had already been blown out. It was only the flickering light from his sleeping chamber illuminating his way. He didn't mind the darkness. He made himself as comfortable as he could and settled in for the night.

Sleep didn't come quickly. He spent long moments listening to the sounds from the other room. The creak of the pallet as Ezinne settled onto it. The soft sound of her regular breathing when she fell asleep. For some time, he thought about walking over to the door to watch her sleep but decided against it.

Going there would only be tempting fate. He laid still making plans about what he would do to help Ezinne. He also worked on suggestions he would make to his father about their relationship with the King of Umulari.

Eventually sleep came, and he drifted off, an image of Ezinne in his mind.

***

Something woke Emeka. He opened his eyes, allowing it a moment to adjust to the dimness of the room. His senses attentive, searching his surroundings. There was no light in the room, but a lamp flickered low from the next room. He could hear the sounds of the night life around the palace, the palace guards patrolling. Otherwise everything was silent.

After a while, he heard another sound. It was faint at first. He strained his ears, listening harder. Then he heard it again. The quiet sound of someone crying. Realizing it was coming from the next chamber, he stood up and walked to it.

Ezinne lay on his pallet crying in her sleep. In the dim light he could see the tears streaked down her face. Standing over her, he waited to see if she would stop. She didn't. Instead she trashing about as if she was fighting someone. It looked like she was having a nightmare.

Without hesitation he bent down, picked her up, and placed her on his lap. She struggled for a moment, still in her sleep. He rubbed her back, whispering soothing words in her ear. Gradually she stilled, a soft sigh whispering against his chest as she relaxed into his arms, her arms going around his back.

Holding her, he inhaled the musky scent of her body, her warmth seeping into him, stirring him. Now that she was calm, he would put her down and go back to his lounging chair. Having her in his arms was feeding the hunger within him that wouldn't be sated.

What was the point in torturing himself?

When he tried to lay her back on the padded pallet, her hold on his body tightened. He debated what to do. He couldn't sit up all night. There were important matters to be discussed in the morning. He needed his wits about him.

But he didn't want to leave Ezinne, if she felt more comfortable. Still holding her, he laid down on the pallet, the softness of his skin teasing his body. He was glad for the barrier of his clothes keeping pulsing manhood away from her slick depth.

He would stay with her only for a little while.

Listening to her soft breathing, he soon joined her in sleep.

Chapter Eleven

Ezinne woke up disorientated, unsure of where she was. The gray light filtering through the closed window told her it was early dawn. Yet she knew she wasn't in her own bed. Whatever she was lying on was padded with fur, softer that her sleeping mat.

Glancing around the bed chamber, seeing the artifacts and lion fur hanging on the walls reminded her of her location.

Prince Emeka's chambers!

With a rapid jolt, she sat up, memories of the previous day raced forward in her mind. Emeka getting injured in a spar with Ikem, dinner that never happened, and their luckless attempt at lovemaking.

"Oh," she groaned in horror.

She'd been a walking disaster.

First she'd distracted Emeka causing him to be injured. Then she turned up late to dinner. Finally she'd topped it off my recounting her rape ordeal right in the middle of their height of pleasure.

If her ruinous actions hadn't confirmed to the prince how unsuitable she was for him, revealing that she was 'damaged' ensured he would never touch her again. No man in his right mind would come close to her knowing what had happened to her. She had sealed her own fate by telling him.

She clutched her head as she recalled the ordeal of reliving her nightmare. It had been the best thing to tell Emeka. As much as she'd wanted him, still wanted him, it was much better for him to know the truth about her before they'd made love. She could have kept it from him, allowed him to possess her.

Perhaps he would have realized she wasn't a virgin. But she could have explained that away.

It would have meant telling lies to him. She had already withheld so much from him, especially on matters regarding Nonye. When it came to her own being, her body, she felt she owed him this one truth, as much as it had pained her to see the look of shock and anger in his eyes last night.

She was glad for one thing. There had been no derision in his eyes. At the end, he had looked upon her with compassion. Even when she knew he wanted to get up and do something like find the man who had violated her, he'd still held her, his arms protective around her.

By letting her stay in his bed, he'd allowed her some luxurious comfort. And deprived his body of the same.

Was he still next door? She hadn't heard any sounds from there. She needed to get up and go back to her quarters. Part of her didn't want to move from the bed. It wasn't just because of the luxurious comfort. It held the warmth and scent of Emeka.

She lay back down, closing her eyes, burying her face in the fur, and taking a shuddering breath. Emeka's masculine scent invaded her nostrils, and an innate longing stirred within her.

Then she remembered something else. Last night she'd had a nightmare. It was the rape all over again. The terrifying ordeal had haunted her almost every night. But last night's dream was different.

In this one, Emeka had come to her rescue. He'd pulled Uwaluru off her body and stripped him of his manhood. He'd then picked her up and comforted her, promising that no more harm would come to her. How she wished that the dream was true.

What was the use in yearning for something she couldn't have? She wasn't just a slave. She was a tainted slave. Not fit to be looked upon by a prince. She ached for the man she knew would never be hers.

As soon as Nonye returned, she would plead with her mistress to send her back to Umulari. Anywhere. As long as it was far away from here. She didn't think she could live with seeing Emeka every day, wanting him and knowing she could never have him.

He'd been good to her but it was best if he didn't have anything to do with her any longer. She was no good for him. She'd only bring trouble to him if she stayed. One of these days she would be tempted to go to him and beg him to claim her.

Pushing off the pallet, she stood up and tidied her skirt. She wanted to leave quietly without waking him. When she walked into the adjourning chamber, Emeka was not there. She wondered where he'd gone so early but put it out of her mind as she left his quarters in a hurry. It was probably best that she hadn't seen him. She didn't know if she could have walked away from him.

She went to her chamber, picked up what she needed, and headed to the stream for a bath.

***

Emeka sat in conference with Amobi discussing action required with regard to Umulari. But his mind kept jumping back to Ezinne. He'd returned to his quarters after a brisk early morning walk and swim to find Ezinne gone.

Instantly he'd missed her. A part of him had wanted to see her rise from her sleep to confirm that she was feeling much better this morning. The need to be there for her, to protect her grew every moment within him. Seeing her again this morning would have gone a long way to allaying his concerns about her.

Yet her not being there was a good thing too. It removed her allure from his path. Prevented him from being tempted to make love to her. Even now he could still feel the warmth of her soft body against his and her feminine scent from last night. How he'd managed to fall asleep just holding her he didn't know. He must have used up his last reserve of control.

This morning he'd woken up with her sprawled over him. Her head on his chest, her arms on his shoulder, her thigh and leg across his lap. His manhood had pulsed with the longing to be buried within her.

It had taken sheer will power to extricate his body from her hold instead of turning her over and sinking into her warm core. But he couldn't allow his baser being to take over. She had been used and abused by others. He couldn't do the same to her.

The only viable option for him had been to get out of the bed and go for a vigorous walk through the forest. The cool morning breeze and the wet leaves lashing at his skin was enough to cool his ardor. He'd then swam a few laps in the rock pool before returning to his quarters to find her gone.

"Have you decided what you'll do about your wife in Umulari? Do you still want her brought home immediately?" Amobi's matter-of-fact query drew Emeka out of his reverie.

"Yes," he replied. "In the light of new information, I want her back as soon as it's possible. There are matters I wish for her to attend to."

"I'll inform Ikem at once. He should go to Umulari tonight. Otherwise tomorrow morning."

"Good. There are matters about Umulari that gravely concern me, and the sooner Nonye returns the better."

"The issue of bound slaves is very perturbing considering they are our allies," Amobi replied and scratched his chin, his expression pensive.

"Yes, it doesn't look good that we are allied to a kingdom that still treats people in such a scandalous way. I spoke to my father earlier, and he is in agreement. He'll have talks with King Agbado."

"This is a great relief. I've been concerned about it too after I overheard a few of our citizens discussing the matter too. They are worried that you might reintroduce slavery into Umunri." Amobi paused for a second and stared at Emeka with his forehead creased in a frown. "There is another matter that concerns me though."

Emeka met Amobi's gaze. "Speak your mind."

"You can tell me to mind my own business, but I only raise this since I noticed you seem a bit distracted. In fact, you've been sidetracked for a few days now."

"Amobi, get on with it," Emeka said, his tone impatient. "It's unlike you to waste time getting to the point."

"Well, I only choose to tread carefully here as the rumors may be doubtful."

"What rumors?" Emeka suspected he knew where his adviser was going with his ramblings but he didn't want to make it easy for him. If Amobi had chosen to listen to gossip, he could sit and squirm first.

His embarrassment obvious, Amobi shifted, his chair squeaking in protest. "I heard that you've taken a slave as your concubine. Is this true?"

Emeka took a long breath in before exhaling in frustration. He wasn't angry with Amobi's insinuation. In truth he has glad the man had brought it up.

Speculation would've commenced as soon as Ezinne became a regular visitor to his quarter in Nonye's absence. Nothing stayed hidden in the palace for long. There were always spies everywhere. This was why he always lived his life above reproach. Until now.

Now he'd become a topic for market gossip because of Ezinne. A wry smile curled his lips. He had no regrets about it. Getting to know her has been an exhilarating experience at times. Last night had been excruciating, though.

"Amobi, when did you start hanging around market women and their gossiping?"

Emeka shook his head in disapproval at his adviser who visibly paled at his insinuation. Yet Amobi's gaze didn't flinch. Emeka didn't expect it to. The man's intentions were noble albeit misguided.

"Look at me. You've know me most of my life. Do you think I've taken a slave for a concubine?"

"Ordinarily I would say no." Amobi scratched the goatee on his chin. "But your behavior in the past few days puts doubts in my mind. Yesterday I saw the way you looked at your wife's handmaiden. The look that passed between the two of you indicated there was more to your relationship. And when you got injured, I saw her take a step toward you, though she came no farther."

"Not that it is any of your business what I do in my personal life," Emeka replied. He'd purposefully indicated for Ezinne not to come any closer to him in public to prevent this kind of speculation. He should've known Amobi's observant gaze wouldn't have missed such subtle signals.

Amobi looked up, his frown deepening. "My job involves keeping abreast of everything happening within this kingdom and advising you on the right action. Yes, your personal life is not my responsibility, but if it affects the perception of the people toward you, then you have a problem that I'll need to resolve."

Emeka's irritation rose that Amobi dared to instruct him on matters concerning his personal life. So, he was acting out of character, but he was also a human being.

"Look, I have no intention of arguing about the remits of your job and responsibilities. Firstly, Umunri has no slaves. You know that. So no citizen here can be referred to as one." Emeka paused to emphasis the point, and Amobi nodded in agreement.

"Secondly, the girl's name is Ezinne. Yes, I have a relationship with her but not in the sordid way you are thinking." He let out a concentrated, resigned sigh. He might as well tell Amobi most of it. Sharing it with someone would help to relieve some of the pressure he felt in his chest. "Ezinne is my companion. Nonye assigned her to keep me company during dinner while my wife is away. We have simply gotten close as she's shared some personal things about herself. She is a young girl who has been through a lot. I would not be human if I didn't feel some compassion for her."

Amobi looked at him and raised his brow in a silent query. Emeka knew where his friend's mind had raced to but he had a simple answer for him.

"No, I have not bedded her," Emeka said.

"I'm only asking because I heard she spent the night in your quarters yesterday." Amobi shrugged.

Emeka sat back, shocked. He knew news traveled fast. But Amobi must have an informant close to him. One of my personal guards? He would have to investigate and find out who was leaking information. Although in truth, Amobi was not the enemy. But if one of his staff was that disloyal, who knew where else he sold information to. He had to find the culprit.

"Who told you that?" he asked with a brusque voice.

Amobi had the grace to look chastised and lowered his gaze. "You know I cannot tell you that. The question remains, is it true? If so, then we will have to stop the rumors spreading and come up with a reason why she was there. You are the heir to the throne. Keeping the goodwill of your people is very important."

"I told her to spend the night because she revealed something distressing that happened in her past, and she was distraught. It was late, and I didn't want her going back to the servant quarters. So I asked her to stay. She slept on my bed, and I slept in the adjourning room. Happy now?"

"What was the distressing thing from her past, so I know what information to disseminate?"

"I cannot, or rather will not, tell you that. It's a personal matter to her, and I promised her I would keep it to myself. And don't even think about going to ask her. I know how your mind works. You will have to come up with your own twist to the story."

"Very well. I'll get on with dealing with the matters at hand."

"Yes, you do that. I'll see you later."

Emeka was glad when Amobi left and he had some peace and quiet. He summoned Jide, the head of palace security and informed him that he needed investigations carried out into which of his staff was spreading gossip about the activities in the palace. He wanted everyone questioned and the culprit brought to him immediately. He then dismissed the rest of his personal guards.

He sat alone in his obi, glad for the solitude.

He used the quiet time to mentally prepare for his consultation with the chief priest later that day to discuss Ezinne. It was the one thing that troubled his soul. He needed her at peace.

He was still seated in his chair when an unexpected Nonye glided in with her entourage.

Chapter Twelve

Ezinne was on her way back from the stream for the fourth time that day. Though fetching water was not one of her chores, she had chosen to help out the other servants. She wanted to keep busy so that she didn't have much time to think about Emeka.

Thoughts of him had been swirling around in her head all morning as she sat at the weaving loom. She eventually gave up because her mind wandered so that she made many mistakes.

She had chosen to do something more menial as the physical exertion would quickly wear out her body and mind. She also silently prayed for Nonye's quick return so she didn't have to visit the prince's quarters any longer.

Although she yearned to see him, she knew it was better to avoid him. The less interaction they had between each other the better. Going to the stream and keeping to the servant quarters meant she was less likely to encounter him.

As she walked down the footpath leading from the stream to the palace with her ite balanced on her head, one of the other servant girls approached her.

"Ezinne, you have to hurry. Your mistress is back," the girl named Oma said.

Ezinne stopped, unsure if the girl was joking with her. "Are you serious?"

"I'm serious. You have to hurry back. She doesn't look very pleased at your absence."

"What am I to do?" Ezinne asked, suddenly panicked because she knew how angry Nonye could get. Nonye would not be happy that she had been helping fetch water when she was assigned to other tasks. "Do you mind taking my ite so I can run back quickly?" she beseeched the other girl, hoping she would help her out.

"Of course. Give it to me."

"Thank you so much." She placed the *ite* on the other girl's head before walking in a hurry back to the palace.

Her heart pounded in her chest because she didn't know what to expect. If Nonye was already angry, then perhaps things didn't go too well for her in Umulari.

Or perhaps Nonye found out about Ezinne and Emeka!

She gulped in air into her lungs, telling herself not to panic. There was no reason for Nonye to be angry with her. Her relationship with Emeka was engineered by Nonye.

So Nonye hadn't wanted Ezinne to fall in love with the prince, but that couldn't be helped. No one else knew about it. So Nonye couldn't possibly have found out.

She just had to keep a level head. On arrival at Nonye's quarters, she took another immersed breath to calm her nerves and racing pulse. There was nothing to fear.

Nonye's guard indicated for her to go in.

"Welcome back, my princess." Ezinne curtsied low, keeping her gaze on the floor. Since she wasn't sure what mood Nonye was in, it was best to play it safe.

"Thank you, Ezinne. Rise and come to me," Nonye said, her voice cool and calm. Detecting no anger from her mistress, Ezinne straightened up and looked at Nonye.

The princess looked as regal as ever, composed and sophisticated. Everything that Ezinne would never be.

"I hope you had a pleasant trip to and from Umulari. You look very well. How are the people in Umulari? Did the festival go well?" Ezinne rattled out questions, eager to find out more about Nonye's sojourns and hopefully distract Nonye from asking her questions about her time with Emeka.

Nonye laughter was cheerful. "That's a lot of questions, Ezinne. My trip was pleasant enough. Everyone in the palace is doing well. The festival was great. But my father is a little worried, though he would never admit it about the rumors that there will be a war soon. It is not a good time for war because the crop yield for this year is not as bountiful as it is usually. I doubt if Umulari could sustain a prolonged siege."

"My princess, that is terrible news indeed. I pray to the gods that such a thing as war does not happen in Umulari again." It explained Nonye presence back in Umunri earlier than planned. Ezinne knew Nonye would not have returned so quickly if it wasn't for an important matter.

"I know. I cannot believe it myself. But the atmosphere in Umulari is tense despite the celebrations. My father sent me back to ensure that he has the full support of Umunri in case there is a war."

"Well, I'm sure E—Prince Emeka and the king would not hesitate to support Umulari in their time of trouble," Ezinne spoke, averting her eyes, hoping that Nonye did not notice her slip of tongue. Using the prince's given name was punishable with a few stokes of the whip.

"I have already spoken to Prince Emeka since I returned." Ezinne couldn't miss the deliberate way Nonye had referred to the prince, indicating to her that Nonye was aware she had been about to use his given name. But instead of reprimanding Ezinne, Nonye flashed a quick smile and continued in speech, waving her hand in the air. "He has already assured me that he will do everything within his power to make sure there is no war. Failing a peace negotiation, Umulari has his support. That is good enough for me."

"That is good indeed, my princess." Ezinne sat at Nonye's feet. She racked her mind for other things to talk about but the only thing that came to mind was Dike. "Did you get to see Dike? How is he?" Ezinne asked in a quiet, tentative voice.

For a brief moment, Nonye's lips hardened into a thin line, her hands clenched on the arms of her chair. Then slowly she relaxed. Ezinne sensed that something must have happened between Nonye and Dike.

"Yes, I saw Dike briefly. He looks well and is doing well as far as I know. Anyway, I don't want to discuss Dike right now. I want to find out about you. Where were you just now? For a brief moment, I had a crazy notion that Emeka had done something terrible to you and you had run away." She laughed. "It's crazy isn't it? I should have had more faith and known you would never let me down. So where did you go?"

"Oh, I went to the stream. I was helping out the kitchen servants," Ezinne said, her face heating up with embarrassment. This was the topic she wanted to avoid. But she couldn't ignore Nonye's question. It was odd that

Nonye would think she'd run away because of Emeka. She wondered why she would think that.

"Why would you do that? Your job was to stay close to the prince. To keep him company. Why didn't you do that?"

"But I did. I have been keeping Prince Emeka company every evening during his dinner. He said that was all he needed of me, and that's all I've done."

"You mean you want me to believe he hasn't touched you, hasn't bedded you?" Nonye asked, her tone irritated, her voice rising.

"It's true, he hasn't," Ezinne insisted as the heat of embarrassment crept up her face. The way Nonye asked the question made Ezinne feel as if she was a failure. That she couldn't even get the prince to bed her as her mistress requested.

"Ezinne, don't lie to me." Nonye's eyes flashed with anger, her teeth clenched.

"I'm not lying." Ezinne replied tartly her own temper rising.

"Don't you dare lie to me, Ezinne. I didn't come back here for you to lie to me after the disappointment that was Umulari." Nonye stood and started pacing her chamber. Ezinne was taken aback. Usually when Nonye lost her temper, her first response would be to strike who ever had offended her. That she simply paced the room instead added to the subtle changes Ezinne had noticed in her already. It made Ezinne more curious to find out what had happened in Umulari to bring about the change.

"Ezinne, tell me the truth. I promise you no harm will befall you. I just want to know the truth because I know you spent the night in the prince's chamber last night. But I want you to tell me yourself. Did Prince Emeka bed you last night?"

Frustrated with trying to convince Nonye, Ezinne nearly yelled, "No, he didn't."

Nonye let out a gasp, and Ezinne lowered her head into her hands, frustrated tears banking up behind her eyes.

"I tried, but he doesn't want me in that way. I'm sorry to disappoint you. I'm not beautiful enough for the prince," Ezinne said, her voice low and strangled, her chest contracting in pain, tears clouding her eyes. She was never going to be beautiful enough for the prince, not with her past constantly dogging her footsteps.

Sensing Nonye standing still beside her, Ezinne fought to hold back the tears.

"Ezinne, I know I have never said this to you before. You are a beautiful woman."

Flabbergasted, Ezinne lifted her head not caring if Nonye saw the tears in her eyes. She couldn't believe it. Nonye said she was beautiful. Nonye had never given her a compliment for as long as she could remember. Maybe when they were children but certainly not as adults.

"Shocked, aren't you?" Nonye gave her a weak smile. "Yes, I know. It's not like me. But I've been told I need to be nicer to the people around me. Otherwise I'd grow into a sad, lonely, paranoid person. And seeing my father that way terrified me. So here I'm trying to change. I can't promise I'll be totally different overnight. But I'm willing to try. There is someone I need to do it for too."

Things just got even stranger. How was it possible? Where was the vindictive woman that went to Umulari a few weeks ago? What happened in Umulari?

"I'm really grateful for your kind words, but you're right. I'm shocked. It is not like you at all. Dare I ask who asked you to change because I need to thank them?"

"You may ask, but I reserve the answer for now. All I can say is that it is someone whose opinion matters to me. It does deflate the ego when someone important to you tells you that you are a bad person. I realized the error of my ways. Anyway. Back to the matter at hand." Nonye moved back to her chair and sat down. "Why did Emeka turn you down? What did you do? You are certainly a beautiful woman, and I know he's been watching you in secret for weeks. I only wanted to give him something he already wanted."

"He wanted me? He's been watching me for weeks? That can't be right," Ezinne replied, certain that Nonye was out of her mind. The prince had barely noticed her until the day she'd been presented to him as a companion.

Nonye smiled. "You forget I have experience in these things. I know when a man desires a woman. I have known that Emeka has desired you since we arrived together. It wasn't an overt thing. But I knew. The quick glances he stole at you when you were simply standing there trying to blend into the background. You are a very beautiful woman, Ezinne. Don't look surprised that the prince would desire you."

"But if he felt that way as you say and you knew about it, why were you not angry? Why did you then push me to become his companion?"

"Because I knew he would never go to you himself. He is an honorable man. I have really only come to appreciate that fact lately. I needed him distracted so that I could get on with pursuing my own interests."

"By interests, you mean Dike."

"Well, I have soon come to realize that was a waste of effort. It is a good thing you didn't bed the prince. Because it looks like I'm back in Umunri to stay. So I have to focus on doing my duty as wife regardless of how I feel about it."

"I'm glad to know you have worked out things for yourself. Prince Emeka needs you here," Ezinne said, happy that Nonye had found some resolution for her initial restlessness.

"Yes, indeed he does. This brings me to the other matter at hand. You. I can no longer keep you here. I'm going to send you back to Umulari. My father needs a companion, and I think you'll be very good for him."

Chapter Thirteen

That evening Emeka sat in the lounging chair in his quarters. Nonye sat beside him, regaling him about her trip to Umulari and the success of their recent New Yam Festival. Emeka barely paid attention to her words, nodding and grunting at regular intervals.

For the first time since his marriage to Nonye, she could not keep his attention. His mind roamed and always seemed to settle on Ezinne. He hadn't seen her all day. He had been hoping to pay an impromptu visit to the weaving hut earlier in day, but his plans had changed by the sudden return of Nonye.

It had been a huge surprise, considering he'd been thinking about sending Ikem to go and bring Nonye home. Despite his initial shock, he had to see her arrival as a godsend. It meant he could proceed with resolving the issues surrounding Ezinne as quickly as possible. He could also relax now knowing that Nonye was safe in Umunri and not in Umulari under threat of war.

Nonye's message from her father had been no huge surprise. King Agbado had used Nonye as a bargaining chip and was doing so now to guarantee the future of his reign. Something about the man's tactics didn't sit well with Emeka, though.

It had prompted his visit to the chief priest for consultation about Ezinne. Emeka wanted to be sure there could be a way of releasing her as soon as possible without her having to return to Umulari for the ritual.

Now he waited in expectation for Ezinne. His need to see her had grown despite his decision not to pursue an amorous relationship with her. But the truth was his heart was already lost to her.

While he would do everything to ensure her well-being he couldn't force her to be with him. Anyway, he still had Nonye's feelings to take into account. Despite her faults, he didn't want to hurt his wife in the process too.

"... My prince, ... you have not listened to a word I've said, have you?"

Distracted from his thoughts, he turned and looked upon Nonye. Her lips were pouted, a frown creasing her normally smooth forehead.

"Forgive me, Nonye. My mind was elsewhere," he spoke, hoping to calm her. Guilt washed over him. He shouldn't be thinking of Ezinne when his beautiful wife was seated next to him. But he couldn't help it. It seemed Ezinne had taken possession of his mind as well as his heart.

"I've been sitting here talking all evening, and you haven't paid attention to anything I've said. Did you not miss me? Would you rather do without my company tonight?"

Yes, a voice whispered in his head.

"No," he said instead, hoping to appease his wife. He'd never seen Nonye this upset with him before. Taking her hand in his, he massaged the back the way he knew she liked. "I'm enjoying your company, Nonye. Please don't get offended. I have weighty issues on my mind. I hope you understand."

"Of course I forgive you, my prince."

Two servants walked in carrying plates of food for dinner. They put them down on the table and departed. Still, Ezinne did not come.

"The food is here, my prince. Come, let's eat."

Emeka stood up and walked to the table wondering why Ezinne was taking so long to get there. She was usually in his quarters as soon as dinner arrived and would help to serve it.

He waited for Nonye to sit, before taking his seat.

"Where's Ezinne? Isn't she going to help you serve the food?" he asked, his mind unsettled at the lack of Ezinne's presence. He hadn't realized how much he would miss her if she wasn't around, but not seeing her seated at the table like she'd done the past few weeks or standing at her usual spot in the corner of the room made him restless. He wanted to know she was doing well. It was unlike Nonye not to have someone serve the food.

Nonye didn't look at him but started dishing out the food with a shrug. "I gave her other chores to do this evening. There is no need for anyone else to serve the dinner. I can do it quite well as you can see."

"Sure. I can see. I'm just curious as to why you've suddenly changed a habit I've known you to have since you arrived in Umunri. Not that I'm complaining."

"While I was in my father's kingdom recently, I learned a few new things. One of which is to pay more attention to my husband. I don't want to leave other women to serve your food or provide for your needs when I'm capable of doing so myself. I hope you approve, my prince."

"I very much approve, my princess." Although it's a little too late as I've lost my heart to another woman.

"So it'll just be you and me eating dinner together with no servants under our feet from now on."

"So what will Ezinne do with her time, since you'll no longer need her in the evenings?"

"Don't worry about Ezinne. I'm sending her back to Umulari. My father is getting old and needs someone to keep him company and cheer him up. Since I now live here I need to make sure he is well taken care of. And Ezinne is just the right person for the job."

A finger of cold dread traveled down Emeka's rigid spine as he sat in his chair. What was Nonye thinking?

"What is the matter with you?" Emeka snapped at Nonye, his voice cold and angry. "How can you do such a thing to Ezinne? After all she's been through already?"

Nonye sat up straight, her eyes puzzled, her face furrowed. "My prince, what's the matter? What have I done?" she queried, subdued.

"Are you claiming you don't know what sending Ezinne back to Umulari would do to her? Sending her back to the man who abused her?"

Nonye's eyes widened, and Emeka remembered that Ezinne had said she hadn't told Nonye about the rape. And she didn't want Nonye to know about it.

"What are you talking about?" Nonye asked.

"Didn't your father try to sell Ezinne to Ichie Uwaluru?" he asked, wanting to find out how much Nonye knew. He couldn't believe that she wouldn't have noticed his father's deviancy and cruelty to Ezinne and other slaves all this while.

"Yes, but that was a long time ago, and we resolved that. Ezinne is my sl—servant. My father will never sell her because only I have the right to dispose of her as I wish. She's only going there to keep my father company. I have no need for her here any longer. She will live the life of a special companion in the palace. It is a privileged position."

"Well, she's not going to Umulari," Emeka stated like he was giving an edict.

"Why not? She's mine to command."

"And you're mine to command, Nonye. And I command you to release her from her bonds with you."

"My prince, what has gotten into you? Do you choose to talk to me in that tone because of Ezinne, a servant?"

"She is also a person, a human being who deserves the right to choose what she does with her life. Not bought and sold at your whim."

"But she's already agreed to go to Umulari. Her choice."

"What? I don't believe that."

It could not be true. Ezinne could never choose to go back to a man who had abused her. Why would she do that? He had to see her. He had to see her now. He couldn't stand it anymore.

Scraping his chair back, he stood up.

"I'm going out. I need some fresh air," he said before walking out of his chamber leaving a surprised Nonye.

Chapter Fourteen

"You are summoned to come with me immediately."

Ezinne looked up from where she sat outside her sleeping quarters. One of Prince Emeka's guards stood at ease before her. Assuming it was Princess Nonye summoning her to the prince's quarters, she rushed to put down the skirt she was darning in her chamber before following the guard. Her spirit had been low since the return of Nonye and the news that she would be going back to Umulari. She had accepted it, knowing it was what she had to do under the circumstances.

But when Nonye had broken the news that Ezinne would no longer serve dinner, not even for the last few nights she was in Umunri, her heart had dropped further. She'd realized that Nonye was practically forbidding her from seeing or interacting with Emeka any longer. She would not even get the chance to see him again before she left Umunri.

However it seemed she may yet get a chance to see Emeka since Nonye was having dinner at the moment with him. Maybe the princess had changed her mind after all. Ezinne could only hope and pray. The guard's strides were long, and she had to hurry to keep up. When he walked past the palace, she stopped.

"Are we not going to the palace?" she asked, looking uncertainly toward the prince's quarters, her body longing for one more look at the prince. One more moment in his presence.

The guard shook his head. "No."

Ezinne waited for him to elaborate, but he didn't and simply continued walking away from the palace. She had no choice but to follow him down the path that led to the palace pool. She wondered who had summoned her and where she was supposed to be going. The sun had already set and their way was lit by the bright moon in the cloudless sky.

Before they arrived at the palace pool, Ezinne heard the soothing splash of the waterfall. She loved coming here. She loved the gentle sound of the water. Most of her trips there had been with Nonye when she helped the princess swim. She remembered the night Emeka had kissed her for the first time, a warm passionate kiss that had stolen her breath.

On that night she'd known there was something amazing happening between the two of them. Despite her fears about men, she had yearned for a lot more from him. His touch had only stirred longing buried immersed within her. Craving she'd never known she possessed until that kiss.

Now she knew that kiss would never be repeated. She would not see the prince again. Here at the pool she was probably here to help bathe Nonye again. When they walked into the clearing, the guard stood back. Ezinne was about to ask him why they were there as she couldn't see Princess Nonye.

She turned back to speak to the guard, but he was gone. She walked farther into the clearing and realized someone had left their clothes on the rocks by the pool. At that distance she could not make out whose they were. Fascinated, she walked closer and realized from the design that they belonged to Prince Emeka.

She inhaled a shaky breath, gaze sweeping the shoreline. Heat rose to her cheeks.

Where was he?

She turned around just as there was a splash in the water. Emeka rose from the pool. Rivulets of water running down his perfectly formed body. The moonbeam illuminating his golden skin tone.

"You came," he said as he watched her.

She had no answer but simply nodded. She was a servant. She always did what she was told. Though she hadn't realized it was him who'd summoned her. His dark gaze fixing onto hers. Her feet felt heavy, unable to move. The exact opposite of her heart that raced like an antelope being chased by a lion. She should move. Run. She had no business being here. Not if the prince was naked under the line of water as she suspected he was.

She didn't know how she would react if she saw all of him. Being close to him and not being able to touch him. To taste him. It was torture.

"He didn't tell me who'd summoned me. I simply obey orders."

"I didn't want tongues to wag in the servants' quarters." He walked through the water toward her. Her breathing became shallower as she struggled to take in more air. Managing to move her heavy legs, she turned around. If Nonye found out she was here with the prince alone, she'd never be forgiven. She shouldn't be here.

Yet in her heart she wanted to be here. She wanted to feel his strong arms around her once again. She wanted his lips crushing hers. His embrace making her feel needed and safe.

"Am I so unpleasant to look at that you cannot bear the sight of me?" He sounded so close. His voice, resonant and gravelly, sent her insides into a flutter of emotions. She closed her eyes briefly and inhaled deeply before turning to face him.

He stood in front of her, magnificent even in the moonlight. Surely a god among men. A short cloth was wrapped around his waist, but the rest of him bare to her view. He was a powerfully physical man, a prince known for his hands-on approaching to leadership. His body bore all the signs of a man who had worked hard.

For a moment she didn't breathe, just stared at him open-mouthed. His eyes sparkled, but there was no amusement there. It was a sheer, dark, intense gaze. Full of destiny, determination, and desire.

"You are the most wonderful and good-looking man I know."

"And yet you are so quick to depart from me." He raised his eyebrow as if he didn't believe her words. "I hear you agreed to return to Umulari."

A sinking feeling invaded her mind. "I did."

"Then why feed me that entire story about the cruelty of King Agbado and the rape by Ichie Uwaluru when you are so quick to return to them. Were you simply seeking my attention? I would have given it to you without the need for lies."

"I... I did not lie to you." She gasped at his hurtful words and lifted her gaze to look at his face. His lips were set in a firm, thin line. His hands clenched by his side. His eyes blazing with anger and pain.

"Then tell me why you would choose to go back there when I have offered you a place in my home as my wife. When I offer you a kingdom."

He stood there still not making any move toward her though she felt the heat radiating from his body. She so wanted him to hold her right now.

Why can't he understand?

"Because it's the best thing to do," she managed to gasp out of her clogged throat.

"For whom?" he snapped.

"For everyone," she retorted. "Can you not see that? I cannot stay here and watch you and Nonye play happy family while my heart breaks a piece at a time." She turned away.

In a flash, he held her, his warm body encasing hers, her back pressed next to his chest. The air was fragrant with his spice. He leaned his chin against her head. She heard him inhale a long breath before he spoke.

"But you can be a part of that family." He leaned back and turned her around to face him. She kept her head down, but he lifted her chin. His eyes glittered with fiery craving. "Why will you not be with me?"

"Because I'll not be your wife against Nonye's wishes. I can't hurt her that w—"

He cut off her words as he kissed her with a single-mindedness she'd never seen in him before. Her soft lips were crushed beneath his punishing ones. She didn't want to fight him. She wanted him. But if she didn't, the kiss would have overpowered her anyway. She had no option but to submit to it.

She opened up, surrendering to his demanding tongue. It swept into her mouth, razing everything in its path, all knowing. All conquering. Any resistance vanished. Any thoughts of doing the right thing by Nonye dissolved.

She wanted this. Emeka. Here and now. She heard thunderous drum beats and realized it was the sound of her heartbeat loud in her ears. She moved her hands up his chest and clung on to his shoulder, holding on for dear life as her knees buckled. It was a good thing he held onto her waist. She would have slipped on to the ground in a mushy pool like runny pap.

A wave of heat swept her body, threatening to burn her up. When Emeka tilted her head to get more of her, she moved with it, wanting more of him. He lifted her up. She wrapped her legs around his waist as he walked forward. She didn't realize where he was going until she felt the coolness of a rock against her back.

Emeka raised his head; his chest lifted and fell as he sucked in air. His expression was dark and tormented.

"Ezinne, I want to make love to you. My mind has ceased to make coherent decisions. All I want right now is you. You are the only one able to end this. Tell me to stop and I will."

She couldn't believe that this man, this prince was leaving the decision to her. Not that she could say no to him. He could take her, and she would offer no resistance. Yet he was giving her the choice. In that moment, she knew he loved her and would do anything for her.

No one had ever offered her anything like he'd offered her. He had given her so much. Tonight she could give the gift she'd wanted to give him for so long. Herself. Even if it was for the last time. Tomorrow she would pay the price and return to Umulari.

***

Emeka stood still, waiting for Ezinne to say something. It was true he'd delegated the decision to her. Finding out she was serious about returning to Umulari had broke down his reserves. His principles had dissolved into the air. He could no longer stop himself from wanting her. Only her words would stop him.

The fire in his blood was lit and raging out of control. It was because of his love for her that he stood still when he wanted to sink buried within her. He needed to connect with her on every level. He would go mad otherwise. There was too much anger and pain in his body.

He wasn't even sure that he could be gentle with her if she agreed.

"Make love to me," she whispered in a hoarse voice before leaning in to place tentative, soft kisses on his chest.

The feel of her warm lips on his cool skin broke down his restraint. Letting out a loud groan, he pulled her head up and kissed her. It was fierce. Passionate. He parted her legs and stood between them as he let his cloth fall from his hips. His painfully swollen manhood nudged her wet core.

"I'm sorry," he groaned against her lips as he pushed into her tight warmth. "I'll be slower next time."

Her inner wall wrapped around him, slick and hot. He paused to let her adjust to his girth before setting a rhythm that was slow at first but soon picked up speed as he lost himself to the feeling of being inside her. He knew that this time would not be long.

The fever of his release built nearing it crescendo. He'd wanted Ezinne since her arrival. And now to finally have her softness against his rigidity, her moist depth stoking the fires within his body.

She writhed beneath him, his hands holding her to absorb some of the impact from his thrusts. Her soft moans grew louder; her brown eyes now the color of the red earth. The love and admiration in her eyes pushed him on. Nothing else—no one else—was more beautiful. No one else made him feel this heat, this frenzy. He moved to get her to her peak, knowing that only then could he allow his own release.

Gripping her with one hand across her back, he found her hooded gem and rubbed it. She erupted around him, clenching him tight, her lava overflowing. Her scream rent the quiet night air. He couldn't hold on any longer. He joined her in his release, clinging onto her body for anchor in a floating world.

Chapter Fifteen

The next time he made love to Ezinne, he took his time as he promised. He spread his shoulder wrappers on the sandy shore, laid her down, and worshiped her body like she was a goddess.

In those moments, there were no thoughts of his duty to the kingdom or his wife. It was simply him and Ezinne under the moonlight sky. Exhausted they lay together, clinging to each other. The air was warm, their hot sweat-slicked bodies cooling in a light breeze.

After a while of lying still without saying anything and just listening to Ezinne's slow breathing, she stirred.

"What is the matter?" He lifted his head to stare into her brown eyes. She bit her lower lip.

"I'm worried someone will come and find us here." She grimaced.

"Do not worry. No one will come. I've instructed my most trusted guard to stand watch. No one else is permitted at the pool tonight."

When she didn't look convinced, he kissed her, enjoying the taste of her for a brief moment.

"Tonight is for the two of us. Tomorrow's worries shall come soon enough." He didn't want to think about the next day or all the troubles that were sure to abound. He just wanted his time with Ezinne. Just the two of them and no interruptions.

He stood, extending his hand to her. "Come," he said to her when she just laid there staring at him in awe. He was used to people looking at him with admiration. Yet somehow when Ezinne looked at him, it felt different. As if he was the most important person in her world.

This was why he couldn't understand why she didn't want to marry him. Why she would put Nonye's needs before hers or his.

She took his hand without question, and he pulled her up. He walked to the pool still holding her hand. He loved the feel of her. Loved having her beside him. In his heart he knew it was the right place for her.

How could he reconcile it with the fact that he'd sworn to live a monogamous life. His father had taken only one wife against advice from his council of elders who had multiple wives.

It was seen as abnormal that the king did not have more than one wife. It was a sign of status and power. However, his father hadn't caved in. When he had become of age, Emeka had sworn he would follow in his father's footprints, yet here he was going back on that promise.

What was he to do?

He turned to gaze at Ezinne. She stared up at him her face lit in a wary smile. "Now, who looks worried?" she queried, her brow arched in a mocking fashion.

He forced a smile on his face. He should take heed of his own advice.

"You dare to question your prince?" he joked before lifting her and throwing her into the water.

She yelped. When she stood in the pool, she splashed water at him in retaliation. Laughing, he dived in and joined in the play-fight as they both laughed and she squealed. After a while, she disappeared under the water. In the moonlit night, he couldn't see her beneath the surface. When she didn't rise after a few moments, he got worried and called out her name turning around on the spot.

Then he felt a hand drag his leg. He lost his balance and fell into the water. She stood up laughing at him. "I got you there."

Trying to look serious, he stalked toward her as she backed away. "You're going to pay for that."

"I'm not afraid of you," she teased and ran out of the water.

The sight of her wet, dark body in the moonlight stirred his libido. With heart pumping overtime, he chased after her, quickly catching up to her, and lifting her against his body.

In no time they were back on the makeshift mat, this time her body covering his. Watching her silhouette aligned with the moon with the rippling pool behind her, she looked like a goddess rising out of the water, her braided hair cascading down her back, her eyes blazing with her desire, her body rocking with her motion.

Afterward, they both dozed off on the mat; he covered their bodies with his spare wrap. He didn't want to leave her. He didn't want to go back to the palace and face the consequences of his actions. Not yet.

One thing was sure; he would not let Ezinne go back to Umulari. There had to be a way. He would find it. When sleep claimed him the last thought on his mind was of Ezinne as his wife.

***

"Ezinne, wake up."

She stirred, her brain still unable to process the words. Her mind still in her dream. She dreamed that she was sleeping under the stars with Emeka. That they'd made love most of the night. She liked the dream and wanted to stay there. But someone was shaking her.

"Mmmh." She stretched with languid movements before opening her eyes.

Prince Emeka stood over her, the sky above him gray with dawn's early light. She jerked upwards and she looked around her. They were at the palace pool. They'd slept there all night. It wasn't a dream.

Then it dawned on her. If Emeka didn't sleep at the palace last night, which meant Nonye would be looking for him. And Ezinne!

What have I done?

Panicked, she rushed up, grabbing her clothing. "I have to get back to the palace. Why did you let me sleep here?" She shook her head as she put her clothes on avoiding Emeka's watchful gaze. "This is wrong. This is so wrong."

"Don't you dare say that!" He grabbed her shoulders. "What we shared was the most beautiful thing a man and a woman can share. I'll not have you reduce it to something to be ashamed of."

"Can't you see Nonye will be looking for you? And when she realizes I've been gone all night too, she'll figure it out. I can't let that happen. I have to get back now before she wakes."

He shook his head in frustration. "There is nothing hidden, Ezinne. Can't you see that? This thing between us didn't just happen last night. It's been happening since you stepped foot on Umunri soil. It was destined to happen. You belong to me as much as I belong to you."

"Well now it has to end. Because I cannot let it go on. As much as I want to be here with you, I know it will never happen. Nonye will not allow it. The gods will not allow it. Let me go."

"I won't let you go, Ezinne. You may be set in your view, but so am I. I'll tell Nonye myself."

Her eyes widened in disbelief. "You'll tell her and put Umunri in danger. Do you realize what will happen when she goes to her father and complains? He could break all ties and declare war on Umunri."

"Ezinne, I really don't care about that anymore. Don't you see? I'm willing to risk it all for you. Moreover, there are other things at stake now." He reached low and rubbed her belly, his palm warm against her body. Her skin tingled with sensation. "You are probably carrying my child."

She gasped, her face heating up. She hadn't paid much mind to that fact during their lovemaking. But in the cold light of day, it was a strong possibility. He had spilled his seed inside her several times during the night without precaution.

Fear spiked through her mind, icing her blood. She couldn't fall pregnant. That would make things even worse. Oh gods! What had she done? What had they done?

She clenched her fists and looked up at Emeka. He had the shielded, stern look on his face again. She couldn't read his thoughts. He might be calling her bluff anyway. After all Nonye wasn't pregnant, and she'd been married to Emeka for two months already. There was a strong possibility that Ezinne wasn't either.

"I don't think I am. Well, it doesn't matter anyway."

"It does matter. You cannot take my child out of Umunri. I'll never allow it. Regardless, it is against our laws to abduct a citizen of Umunri."

"What? Abduct? There is no baby yet to abduct," she shouted at him.

"Well, you have to stay the required period so we can be certain."

"You cannot do this. You cannot make me stay," she said, anger making her shout as she moved away from him.

"Ezinne, if you push me, I'll forcibly detain you here," he said with vigor. There was no mistaking the seriousness in his voice. Ezinne couldn't believe the man she loved was saying this to her. The man who had spent all night making love to her was suddenly turning into the kind of man she despised. He was going to compel her to do something she didn't want to.

It didn't matter that in her heart she wanted to stay. It was the notion that he would constrain her that annoyed and saddened her at the same time.

She shook her head, walking backward. "You do not mean that." She looked at him as if he was a stranger.

"Do not put me to the test." He stepped toward her. "Tell me why you would put Nonye's needs above mine when every time you body and heart declares undying devotion to me?"

He grabbed her shoulders and held her firm. She shook her head. "I cannot tell you," she sobbed, tears clouding her eyes.

"Tell me now. Or by the gods, I'll find out the truth for myself even if it means going to Umulari and talking to the king myself. Tell me," he shouted as he shook her body.

"I cannot go against her wish because we are bound by blood." Tears cascaded down her face.

"You mean the oath you took?"

She shook her head as her tears blinded her. "Not that."

"What then?"

"She is my sister!"

Shocked by her words, Emeka's grip on her shoulders slackened, and he staggered backward as if she'd delivered a physical blow to his body. Finally free of his grip, she did the one thing she should have done last night when she first arrived at the palace pool. She ran.

Chapter Sixteen

She is my sister!

Emeka paced his obi, his mind in turmoil. Ezinne's words ricocheting within his head. How was that possible? Ezinne was a slave. Nonye was a princess of Umulari. They were both separated by status. One instructed. The other served. How could a servant girl and a princess be blood sisters? He was nearly going mad trying to figure it out in his head.

It didn't help that Ezinne had run off when she'd told him such abominable news. Was that a sign that she'd told him a lie? That she'd made it up. Was this staged for him? Was there another purpose to it all? What was really going on? Who were Nonye and Ezinne? Because he certainly didn't know either of them as well as he'd thought he did.

He'd returned to the palace and sent his guards to summon Ezinne and Nonye. He would get to the truth of the matter today. He also summoned Ezemmuo. The chief priest was the one person he could trust to tell him the truth. He no longer trusted either woman.

Like the smell of a decaying corpse, the rank arrangement between Ezinne and her mistress could no longer be avoided. Nonye's obsession with keeping Ezinne bound to her, and Ezinne's refusal to do anything to displease Nonye.

He should have noticed it before. Now he couldn't miss it. Their relationship was unhealthy and had always been. He should have noticed it when Nonye presented Ezinne to him. Yet his lust for Ezinne had blinded him to the facts.

Well, no more!

He'd had enough of being fooled. And if he found out King Agbado had a hand in this whole sinister arrangement, he would convince his father to call off the peace treaty with Umulari.

He whirled around as Nonye came into his receiving chamber. She didn't look pleased. He didn't care right now as he scowled at her.

She curtsied. "Good morning, my prince. You summoned me?"

"I did." He turned away from her to Jide, the head guard who'd come in behind Nonye. "Where is Ezinne?"

"We haven't found her yet, my prince," Jide replied.

"Keep searching. I want her found and brought here immediately."

"Yes, my prince." The guard bowed, turned, and walked out.

"What's happened, my prince?" Nonye asked.

"You tell me."

"How do I know what's happened? You stalked out last night. I waited for you, but you didn't return, and I went to bed. I only woke up this morning to note that Ezinne hadn't shown up to help me dress. Where is she? Why are you looking for her?" She glared at him, her expression suspicious.

"I was with Ezinne last night."

"What do you mean?" Nonye's eyes narrowed into a slit, and her frown deepened.

"Ezinne and I are lovers. We spent the night together."

Her eyes widened like a round dish, and she shook her head. "No, you didn't." She turned away from him.

"We did, and this morning she told me something I cannot begin to comprehend. How could you have hidden something like that from me, Nonye?" He glared at her.

Nonye whirled around her mouth agape. Now she looked frightened. "You cannot believe whatever she told you. Yes, I admit I was wrong in seeking Dike out, but nothing happened. I promise you." She took a step toward him, her hand lifted in a placating manner.

It was as if she'd physically hit his face. Emeka's blood turned to ice. What was going on here? "Wait." He lifted his hand stopping her from coming closer. "Who is Dike and what has he got to do with this?"

Nonye froze, her features pained. She lifted her hand and clutched her head.

"Answer me!" he snapped.

Nonye's head jolted upright, her eyes shone with unshed tears. "Dike was the man I wanted to marry before my father arranged for me to wed you."

"He is your lover?"

The tears dropped from her eyes. "No, not anymore. I have not been with him in that way since my betrothal to you. On my last trip to Umulari, we finally called everything off, and I vowed to focus my devotion to you and our marriage."

Emeka stood still. He couldn't make out what emotion he was feeling. Yes there was anger. After all, his wife had a fondness for another man. It was a blow to his ego. That's for sure. To think that all the while they were together, she was possibly thinking of another man.

But then again hadn't he being doing the same thing, all the time he'd been thinking about Ezinne? Did that make him a better person than Nonye? Could he really stand in judgment of her deeds? He was no longer without reproach. He'd changed all that last night.

So yes, it hurt him to know his wife was interested in someone else. But he would have to live with it.

"Do you love this man? This Dike?" he asked as calmly as he could muster.

"No, my prince." She lifted her head, her features shame-faced.

"Tell me the truth or I'll not be held responsible for my actions." He was tired of all the lies.

She nodded her head. "I did once. But I have put him aside. I promise you. We cannot be together. My father forbade it."

What kind of man went about controlling and destroying lives at their whim? What was wrong with King Agbado? He appeared to be a mad man the more Emeka found out about him.

"So you didn't want to marry me."

"It doesn't matter what I want. My duty is to be a good princess and do my father's bidding." She knelt in front of him. "Please, my prince, forgive my indiscretion. I promise I'll do as you bid. I'll release Ezinne from her bonds immediately."

"Get up," he said. He needed to think. There was so much information rattling in his brain. He needed time to process them all and make the right decision.

Nonye stood and went over to her chair beside his and sat.

"Yes, about Ezinne. How can you be so cruel to your own blood?"

"What do you mean? I treat her better than the other servants. I take care of her like she is my own sister sometimes."

"But she claims she is your sister."

He couldn't miss the shock on Nonye's face. Her mouth agape, her eyes wide. "That's a lie." She looked as shocked as he'd felt when Ezinne had told him. So if she didn't know then how possible was it?

"Ezinne wouldn't lie to me."

"What? You would believe that nonsense. I'm a princess. My father is the king of Umulari. My mother was the queen. Ezinne's mother was a slave. How can you reconcile all those facts with her being my sister? It's impossible, and I refuse to believe it."

"Do you know Ezinne to tell lies? To be untrustworthy?"

"No. But this is outrageous. Impossible."

"Who is Ezinne's father?"

"I don't know him. I never met him. He was one of the slaves, I guess. Not much was said of him excerpt that he died before Ezinne was born."

"But you and Ezinne grew up together, played together."

"Yes, her mother was my mother's handmaiden. So she was often in the palace as a girl. Since we were about the same age we played together."

"But after a while you stopped playing with her. Why?"

"My father forbade it. He threatened to have her sold off. I cared for her and didn't want her gone. She was my best friend. The only thing I was allowed to do was to take her in as my handmaiden. I couldn't oppose my father. If he had sold Ezinne, things could have been a lot worse for her."

"As soon as she is found and brought here, you will release her. Do you understand?"

"Yes, my prince." Nonye paused, shifting in her seat as if nervous. "But why would she tell you she is my sister?"

That he couldn't answer. "I don't know."

His guard stepped into the obi. "My prince, Ezemmuo is here."

"Good. Send him in," he said to the guard who nodded, bowed, and stepped out. At last someone who could shed some light on these dark matters.

Ezemmuo stepped in, his metal staff rattling as he walked, the stringed shells on his ankles jingling. His face and body were painted in red, black, and white markings. Around his neck he had an amulet which was said to ward off evil spirits. There was a leather satchel hanging on his shoulder.

"It is well with this household," Ezemmuo said when he stopped in the middle of the chamber.

Nonye stood, then curtsied. Emeka bowed. "Ezemmuo, nno." He welcomed the chief priest.

"Nonye, please bring the okwa oji for Ezemmuo."

"Yes, my prince." Nonye departed to bring the kola nut and pepper dip refreshment for their guest.

"Welcome," Emeka said again to Ezemmuo. "Please take a seat."

Ezemmuo moved to the seat closest to Emeka's on the right-hand side. Emeka also sat down. Now that Ezemmuo was here, he could afford to relax a little. Matters would soon be resolved.

Nonye returned with the wooden bowl of kola nut and pepper dip and presented it to Ezemmuo. The chief priest took one on the nuts in his hand, lifted it up, and said incantations blessing the household. When he was done, he split the nut and presented it to Emeka who nodded and passed it back to him. Ezemmuo took a piece and chewed. Nonye presented the remaining to Emeka who took another piece.

"Keep the other piece for your wife," Ezemmuo said when Nonye went to put aside the bowl.

"Nonye, take a piece," Emeka said. Usually a woman didn't share in the kola nut except on special occasions.

"I don't mean her. The other one."

Flabbergasted, Emeka turned to Ezemmuo wondering if the man had lost his senses. "I only have one wife, and she stands before you."

"Not according to the gods. The woman in front of me was never meant to be your wife. Why do you think the gods have not blessed your union? Even as I speak your heir grows in the womb of another. Or do I not speak the truth?"

Nonye slumped into her chair, looking pained. Emeka froze in shock. How was it possible? He'd only made love with Ezinne last night. It was true that Ezemmuo was in conference with the spirits of their ancestors. But this?

"Ezemmuo, what are you saying? Nonye and I were married in the traditional way. We performed all the rites. Why would the gods not acknowledge that marriage?"

"There are untold evils perpetuated in Umulari. The gods are not happy about that, and it is time to reverse the fortunes of evildoers. Great offenses have been committed against innocent people. You are a tool in righting those wrongs. The gods say that you married the wrong sister."

Nonye gasped out loud, and Emeka groaned in silence. So it was true.

Just then, there was a scuffle outside the entrance, and Ezinne walked in looking harassed. His guard stood behind her. Ezemmuo turned to her and pointed.

"She is the wife chosen for you by the gods. She is your princess."

Chapter Seventeen

She is your princess.

Ezinne stood by the door, her posture rigid, unsure of what she'd heard. Her eyes moved from Nonye who was slumped in her chair looking like her world had ended to Emeka who looked at Ezinne as if he'd seen a ghost. The only one who appeared composed was Ezemmuo. But he was the one pointing to Ezinne while he'd uttered those unbelievable words.

Had the man gone senile? Nonye was the princess. Not Ezinne. Never her. She was the one that primped and catered to the princess. Ezinne was the servant. As she was ordained to be from birth.

"This is madness. Ezinne is a slave, sired and birthed by a slave!" Nonye was now sitting up, shifting in her seat, obviously agitated. Ezinne couldn't help feeling pity for the other woman. This news must have come as a big shock to her. It had shocked Ezinne when she'd found out the truth of her birth. At least she'd had years to get used to it. Nonye had only been told moments ago.

"If she is a slave, then so are you," Ezemmuo interjected, his tone relaxed and matter-of-fact. "You were both sired and birthed on the same day by the same parents."

Ezinne heaved a sigh of relief. At last someone else had validated what she'd known most of her adult life. She knew no one would have ever believed her if she'd said it herself. Emeka had not believed her this morning.

The enraged expression on his usually friendly face had sent her running into the forest, wanting for the earth to open up and swallow her. If he didn't believe her, no one else would.

Ezinne glance over at Emeka, but his eyes were on Nonye who made a gurgling sound as if choking. Nonye's eyes rolled back in her head, and she slumped into her chair. Emeka moved and picked Nonye up as Ezinne raced to his side.

"Get me some water," Emeka instructed the guards. One of them rushed to get the drink while the other waved the large feathered fan. Ezinne knelt beside him holding on to Nonye's cold hand. She bit her bottom lip with worry.

Nonye had always been the weaker of the two of them. When they were children Nonye was the one who got ill more often. Despite her airs, she was the fragile one. This was one of the reasons Ezinne had always fought to protect her.

"Don't worry. She has only fainted. The news has come as a shock to her. She will awaken soon," Ezemmuo said when he approached and placed his hand on Nonye's head.

The guard came back with a wooden tray containing a bowl of water, a gourd and a bronze chalice. Ezinne took one of the cloths she kept on her waist beads, sprinkled water on it, and placed it on Nonye's forehead.

Emeka looked at Ezinne, wearing a sad smile before turning to the chief priest with a frown on his face. "Ezemmuo, I'm even more confused. How can one be a princess and another a servant if they were both sired from the same parents?"

"My son, I'll explain everything in a little while. Let the girl awaken first and I'll tell you how it all came to be." Ezemmuo went back to his chair. Ezinne tried to quell her own concern and restlessness about Nonye. Regardless of what had happened in the past, she didn't want any harm to come to Nonye. She was still her sister.

Nonye stirred in Emeka's arms. He took the bronze chalice from the guard and gave Nonye some water. She gulped it down with her eyes closed. Then she opened them and stared up at Emeka in confusion.

"What happened?" she asked before turning around to see Ezinne and Ezemmuo. "Oh no." She gasped, taking her head in her hands again.

"Stay calm," Emeka said to his wife before turning to their guest. "Ezemmuo, please explain to us so that we can understand what happened."

"Very well." Ezemmuo made himself comfortable in the chair and began. "As a young man, King Agbado was very ambitious. He was not happy to have a delegated council that made decisions for the kingdom. He wanted sovereign power all to himself. So he went to an unscrupulous dibia to help him gain power. He was told he was going to make a great sacrifice in order to achieve his aim. He agreed. Power was more important to him than anything else he owned."

Ezemmuo paused as if to ensure everyone was paying attention to his words.

"There was a power struggle between Agbado and other members of the council. He got rid of his enemies with the help of the dibia. To attain the throne, he had to sacrifice his heirs. His wife never bore him any children."

Nonye gasped again, her face losing its color, and Emeka glance at her. Ezinne squeezed Nonye's hand, hoping to reassure her.

"But Nonye's mother was the queen, wasn't she?" Emeka asked.

"No. Agbado had several affairs with different other women including the woman who gave birth to Nonye and Ezinne. At the time she served the queen. In the queen's desperation to bear children and produce heirs, she had offered Nonye to the king. She wanted to bring up any child that was born as her own. The woman fell pregnant but unbeknown to them she was carrying twins."

Eyes wide, Nonye turned to look at Ezinne, a silent query in her gaze. Ezinne smiled and nodded. She'd known they'd been born on the same day.

"You mean Nonye and Ezinne are twins?" Emeka looked shocked as well.

"Yes, they are fraternal twins. Nonye was born first. The queen took her and presented her to everyone as her own. Several hours later, Ezinne was born. The king, who knew the consequences of having heirs meant he would lose his power, consulted the dibia again. The dibia told him the only way things would work for him was if one of his children served the other. He could only name one as his. The other he had to reject and abandon."

"Ezemmuo, you are certain of this?"

"Our ancestors do not tell lies," Ezemmuo replied in a stern tone. "The two girls have been aggrieved. The gods have been offended and waited for the right time to strike. This is the right time."

Emeka watched both women. Ezinne could read the concern in his eyes. It must not be easy for him to take in all this news at once. It was unfortunate there had been so many secrets buried in their family. Ezinne was grateful it was now all out in the open. Maybe a solution could be found at last.

"What do we do to set things right?" Emeka asked.

"Agbado has to start by acknowledging both of his children. Otherwise the consequences on his head will be great."

"What about Ezinne and the bond she has with Nonye?"

"Those bonds have already been dissolved. Otherwise, you would never have noticed Ezinne. Why do you think your first wife offered her to you in the first place? When the path of destiny is set by the gods, you might detour from it, but eventually you get back on it. The gods have designed it so that we arrive at this day and the truth is bared for all to see."

"Does that mean I'm to have two wives?" There was a frown on Emeka's face. Ezinne wondered if the idea was suddenly unpalatable to him as her heart sank. He had asked her again to marry him this morning. Had she changed his mind by revealing her true relationship with Nonye?

Ezemmuo shook his head. "As I said before, Nonye was never meant to be your wife. Her life path lies elsewhere. Your future is with Ezinne. I have said it all. He who has ears let him hear. Now, I'm ready to leave." Ezemmuo stood.

"Thank you for coming, Ezemmuo. I'll walk you to the door." Emeka arose and followed Ezemmuo outside.

Nonye's grip on Ezinne's hand tightened. "You knew this all along." Her voice barely above a whisper. Ezinne had to strain to hear the words. Nonye's face still looked pale and distressed.

Ezinne nodded, her stomach feeling heavy. "I did."

"Why did you never tell me?" Nonye asked, her agitation apparent.

"Would you have believed me?" Ezinne asked.

Nonye broke the gaze and looked away shame-faced, her lips turned down, her eyes lowered. It was the first time she'd seen Nonye back away from a confrontation.

"I promised our mother that I would not tell anyone," Ezinne added. "The king threatened to kill us all if it ever came out I was his daughter as well. I couldn't take that chance. I had no choice but to keep quiet. I didn't want anything bad to happen to you. I already knew how mean the man could be. I've experienced it firsthand."

Nonye lifted her sad eyes and held Ezinne's gaze again. "I know. I was shocked when I found out he wanted to sell you to that leery old man, Ichie Uwaluru. But tell me, something else happened, didn't it? I can see it in your eyes."

"I cannot say." Ezinne shook her head, tears clogging her eyes. She was the one to look away this time.

"Please. You've kept so much from me, and I'm just finding out that we're sisters. Blood sisters. I'm still in shock. Now I understand why we used to be so close. We were always more than best friends." Nonye pulled on Ezinne's hand tighter, pleading with her eyes, tears glittering in their depths. "Please. I promise to be the best sister you ever had. Just tell me."

"Ok. You have to promise to not tell a soul."

"I promise."

Ezinne paused. "I was raped... by Ichie Uwaluru, and the king knew about it."

The tears fell from Nonye's eyes. "I'm so sorry for all the pain you've suffered especially the ones I've caused. Please forgive me."

"I forgave you already. Most of the things you did because you didn't know who I was. It was not your fault."

Nonye reached across and pulled Ezinne up before hugging her. Tears stung Ezinne's eyes. She lowered her eyelids. For the first time in a long time, she felt as if she really belonged. She'd reconnected with her sister. Things were going to be all right after all. Even if she didn't have Emeka, knowing that Nonye wanted to stay her sister gave her comfort.

Emeka returned to his obi, and Nonye stood back, wiping her face with her hand.

"I'll leave the two of you to talk," Nonye said before moving to the door.

"Nonye, wait. We all need to talk. Your place is here." Emeka held her arm stopping her.

"Don't go," Ezinne said worried about what Nonye would do now that she knew Ezinne had been with Emeka last night. "I'm sorry about what I did last night with Emeka. I have wronged you."

Nonye looked from Emeka to Ezinne and shook her head. "Didn't you hear what Ezemmuo said? I'm the impostor in another woman's home. I have no place here." She walked back and took Ezinne's hand putting it on top of Emeka's hand. "I forgive the two of you. You were meant for each other. I kind of knew that from the way you looked at each other for months. I was just blinded by my selfishness to see things for what they were." Her voice sounded choked, and she paused, coughing briefly. "My prince, you better take care of Ezinne or I'll have the warriors of Umulari here in a flash. She is my sister and a princess. You'd better treat her as such."

Nonye turned to Ezinne and smiled. "You take care of Emeka. He is an honorable man. The best husband you could ever have. Take care of each other. And don't worry about the peace treaty. I'll make sure my father keeps to his side of the bargain." Determination and tears shone in her eyes. Nonye nodded once, withdrew her hands, and walked out the door.

Ezinne stood there in silence, not knowing what to do, her hand falling to her sides. It was a shock to her that Nonye had so relinquished Emeka and actually given her blessing to the two of them. She looked up at Emeka who also stood watching her in return with such a look of intensity. Her stomach tightened, her heart pounding, heat rose in her body. Was he going to send her away?

Then with a growl he lifted her into his arms, holding her in a tight hug as if he'd never let her go.

"Don't ever scare me again like you did today. I couldn't bear it if anything happened to you," Emeka spoke, his voice gruff with emotion as he leaned his head against hers.

"I won't. I've realized that no matter what happens my place is by your side, if you still want me as your wife." Ezinne's voice filled with emotion. She couldn't bear to think of a life without Emeka.

"Of course I do. Didn't you hear Ezemmuo? You are my wife, divinely chosen by the gods," he said, lifting her chin. The intensity of his feelings shone in his eyes.

"Then who am I to argue with the gods. I'm yours, here to stay, my prince."

"Welcome home, my heart. My princess," he said before kissing her with fervor.

THE END

Author's Note

Thank you to everyone who purchased and read Men of Valor, Books 1 – 3. I hope you enjoyed reading the stories about three courageous women who defied convention in a time when tradition dictated the lives of all, and of the men who loved them regardless.

If their stories have left you panting for more, don't despair. There are more Men of Valor stories coming soon. We'll get to see Nonye walk the path to redemption in her own story as well as the story for Jide, the palace guard. You can read the prequel to his story in Her Protector, which is free to download.

Be sure to add me on social media for up-to-date information on upcoming releases. I look forward to connecting with you.

If you enjoyed this story or any of the others, please tell your friends and followers by leaving a review on the site of purchase or sharing a recommendation on Goodreads. Thank you for your support.

You can reach me on my blog, Facebook, Twitter, Google+ or Pinterest

For latest news and giveaways: http://kirutayewrites.blogspot.com

Read book excerpts and free short stories: http://www.kirutaye.com

Made in the USA
Coppell, TX
15 April 2021